SPECIAL MESSAGE TO READERS

This book is published under the auspices of

THE ULVERSCROFT FOUNDATION

(registered charity No. 264873 UK)

Established in 1972 to provide funds for research, diagnosis and treatment of eye diseases. Examples of contributions made are: —

A Children's Assessment Unit at Moorfield's Hospital, London.

•

Twin operating theatres at the Western Ophthalmic Hospital, London.

•

A Chair of Ophthalmology at the Royal Australian College of Ophthalmologists.

•

The Ulverscroft Children's Eye Unit at the Great Ormond Street Hospital For Sick Children, London.

You can help further the work of the Foundation by making a donation or leaving a legacy. Every contribution, no matter how small, is received with gratitude. Please write for details to:

THE ULVERSCROFT FOUNDATION,
The Green, Bradgate Road, Anstey,
Leicester LE7 7FU, England.
Telephone: (0116) 236 4325

In Australia write to:
THE ULVERSCROFT FOUNDATION,
c/o The Royal Australian College of Ophthalmologists,
27, Commonwealth Street, Sydney,
N.S.W. 2010.

Molly Good is a teacher who combines a full-time teaching job with writing, whenever she can wangle the opportunity. She has written several novels, novellas, children's plays and stories. She also enjoys writing spoof poetry. She lives in Sussex with her husband and grown-up sons, and when not teaching or writing, loves to walk on moors or cliffs, beside the sea.

AN OLD WIVES' TALE

When the Reverend Nicholas Nesbith and family move to sleepy Pomery-upon-Axle, they think that life will meander along uneventfully, with little to contend with other than harvest festivals, summer fetes and other such village activities. They could not have been more wrong. The arrival of the formidable Matilda Golightly and sinister Albert Noonday coincide with the first murder in Pomery within living memory. The village is thrown into a whirl of panic, suspicion and amateur dramatics — and then the second murder occurs . . .

MOLLY GOOD

AN OLD WIVES' TALE

Complete and Unabridged

ULVERSCROFT
Leicester

First published in Great Britain in 1998 by
Citron Press
London

First Large Print Edition
published 2000
by arrangement with
Citron Press
Connors Corp. Limited
London

British Library CIP Data

Good, Molly
An old wives' tale.—Large print ed.—
Ulverscroft large print series: mystery
1. Detective and mystery stories
2. Large type books
I. Title
823.9′14 [F]

ISBN 0-7089-4241-5

Published by
F. A. Thorpe (Publishing)
Anstey, Leicestershire

Set by Words & Graphics Ltd.
Anstey, Leicestershire
Printed and bound in Great Britain by
T. J. International Ltd., Padstow, Cornwall

This book is printed on acid-free paper

This book is for my wonderful family.

Author's Note

Geoffrey Chaucer wrote *The Canterbury Tales* in the late fourteenth century. In the *Prologue*, he describes a group of pilgrims travelling from Southwark to Canterbury Cathedral, where Thomas à Becket was murdered. The quotations are taken from his description of the Wife of Bath.

Prologue

And thries hadde she been at Jerusalem;
She hadde passed many a straunge
streem

Geoffrey Chaucer,
The Canterbury Tales

September

Matilda stood looking out of her drawing room window in an attitude of uncharacteristic stillness. She had no feeling of foreboding. Rain, soft as a baby's skin, was falling silently, trickling over the parched ground, but there was a chill in the air and she was only too aware that autumn waited just around the corner, with the cold dankness of an English winter queuing up behind. Matilda liked the sunshine and longed for her next journey to warmer climes. Even had she known then what the future held in store for her, it would have made no difference to this pleasant anticipation of her travels. Matilda was never one to let another's inconvenience interfere with her pleasures. She had repeatedly told her five husbands this.

Her travels abroad had begun after her first marriage, at eighteen, to Gerald, the anxious elder son of a merchant banker. His death — on their honeymoon in Egypt — had come as rather a blow at the time, although she comforted herself with the knowledge that claustrophobia is seldom fatal, and that it is unusual for anyone to be locked in a pyramid accidentally. It was a pity that she had not missed him until she returned to the hotel. The Egyptian police had been at pains to tell her that they might have got to him in time if she had. She checked a sigh. One couldn't think of everything, and all that unpleasantness had been a long time ago. Anyway, she had had four more husbands to mourn since then.

Up until last year, she had travelled alone or with a husband; after Geoffrey's death, she had the idea of forming a company of like-minded people to travel together. Their first journey had been such a success that she was now planning to repeat the experience. This thought brought her back to the present and, turning from the window, she walked over to her little rosewood table where the final list for next year's journey lay. She cast her eyes over the column of names. They were a diverse company, and it was surprising that they had gelled together as a group. She had not thought it possible, when they began their first pilgrimage, but everyone had entered into the spirit of the quest and each had contributed something of themselves.

It had been good to hear from them all again. She could picture the group exactly, although it was five months since they had parted company. Would they still be the same when they next set out together? she wondered. In such a close-knit company, a change of mood can make a big difference. She hoped that they would have plenty of stories to tell. She enjoyed a good yarn.

There was no need for her to have worried. As she returned to her place by the window to look out at the garden, growing misty in the September rain, she was blissfully unaware that, while she mused about her fellow travellers, the hand of fate was approaching her unhurriedly with murder coiled secretly in its palm. When it came to telling stories, she would be the one with the most interesting story to tell.

Part One

In al the parissh wif ne was ther noon
That to the offring bifore hire sholde
goon

Geoffrey Chaucer,
The Canterbury Tales

1

Noonday lay in the darkness watching the luminous minute hand move closer and closer to the hour, until the two hands were as one. Midnight at last. Three more weeks and ten hours exactly. Twenty-one days. Five hundred and fourteen hours. Then he would be free: this time, permanently. There was no way he was ever going back.

Albert hadn't thought much about where to go. With no ties and no one waiting for him, he could settle anywhere he chose, and that suited him fine. Might just check on the money first, though. You never know. Can't trust anyone nowadays.

His suspicious mind and Matilda's hand of fate ensured that, in three weeks' time, with all the country to choose from, they both found temporary refuge in the same small village, and got to know each other in rather unusual and dangerous circumstances.

* * *

Matilda Golightly stood in the shrubbery and watched her house burn to the ground. She was very annoyed. Matilda rarely felt out of sorts, but Geoffrey ought to have paid to have the whole house rewired. She'd told him so, often enough: indeed, she had just thrust her head out of the window to tell him again when he lost his grip on the ladder he had climbed to rescue her kitten from the attic gable. She wished now that she had had him cremated. It would have served him right.

* * *

Leonora Babbington-Banbury tapped the thick vellum letter with her pince-nez and summoned her husband, who shambled back into the breakfast room from whence he had just made good his escape.

'Henry?'

'Yes dear?' Henry hovered just inside the door, hoping for an early reprieve.

'Matilda's coming.'

'Right-oh.' He relaxed a little. Couldn't see a problem.

'She's had a fire. Place gutted.'

Henry's uncluttered face clouded over. He was fond of Matilda. 'Much damage, then?'

'Yes indeed, Henry. Considerable damage. She will be with us for quite some time.' Leonora was becoming testy. Her relationship with her sister was somewhat ambivalent and it irked her to lose control.

Henry decided it was better to hide behind silence, having learnt at his nanny's knee that least said, soonest mended. He knew from experience that it was the best course when dealing with Leonora.

'Then she's off again to Africa in April.'

'Africa?'

'Yes, Henry, Africa. Another of her art pilgrimages.'

'Right-ho.' It didn't seem that he was to be taxed by any of this. Leonora was in sole charge of domestic arrangements at the Manor, but he knew his wife well enough to know that she had called him back for a reason.

'Henry?'

'Yes, dear?' Here came the reason.

'I will be first at the communion rail on Sunday. You will see to it.'

A frown of unaccustomed thought creased his habitually vacant expression. It amounted to an obsession on Matilda's part that hers would be the first lips on the chalice and she loved to annoy her sister. Both sisters liked to have their own way and flew into rages when thwarted. Henry's bright morning was spoilt by this chill cloud of promised discord. 'As usual, dear?' Dutifully.

'As usual.'

His frown deepened. They both knew that there was precious little anyone could do, once Matilda had made up her mind, but Leonora would never admit it. 'Yes, dear.' Unhappily.

'That will be all, Henry.'

'Right-ho, dear.' He was through the door in a blink, before she could change her mind, pottering unsteadily into the cool of the conservatory, intent upon a stroll through his woodland. As he shut the door behind him and stepped outside, the frown of concentration gradually disappeared and he pushed her instructions to the back of his mind. Today was Thursday. Sunday was a long way off.

He whistled for the dogs and ambled away in the direction of Banbury woods, that had belonged to his family since the Conquest. By the time he had reached the comfort of the soughing trees, he was pretending to himself that he had no recollection of having been spoken to by his wife at all.

* * *

The siren of a departing ambulance somewhere in the village drowned out the rumbles of the removal van. Empty of its load, it rocked off into the last glowing rays of evening sunshine, leaving the Nesbiths alone in the echoing vicarage and more than a little afraid of this new undertaking.

The significance of the siren would not become plain until the day after tomorrow. For now, there were far more pressing problems to think about.

The late Victorian house was twice as large as their previous semi-detached, and their meagre possessions looked unable to fill more than a tiny corner. Sally moved into the dining room, where little Joe was happily absorbed in unwrapping his toys and alternately shredding and chewing the newspaper wrappings. He looked up as she came in and grinned with delight, toddler-wobbly on chubby legs, with black newsprint and dribble on his chin giving him a premature five o'clock shadow. Sally returned the smile and felt cheered at the sight of the children's paraphernalia. That would fill a room or two.

Amy was fast asleep in her pram, oblivious to any change in her life, and that was how it should be, thought Sally. Adults always complicated things. What could be more straightforward? A move to a larger house, essential for their growing family; Nicholas's first parish after three years of being a curate; and, most exciting of all, swapping a busy, polluted industrial town for the idyllic life of the countryside. Clean, fresh air and old-fashioned country values. Peace and quiet at the pace of a slothful snail.

Sally stepped into the garden, overgrown and neglected after the previous incumbent's lack of mobility had prevented its proper upkeep. She took a deep breath, filling her lungs with clean air and enjoyed her moment while at the bottom of the garden, something hidden sighed and stirred from its post-prandial slumber, eventually making its way lazily across the grass toward her.

⋆ ⋆ ⋆

Pomery-upon-Axle, five hundred inhabitants and mentioned in the Domesday book, was a manorial village clustered round a broad oval green where flowing willows dipped gracefully into a well stocked duck-pond. Half a mile away was the manor house, from whence successive lords and ladies had looked out at the poor man tenanted at their gate. At one end of the main street, a narrow lane led to the twelfth-century church of St Wilfrid's, with the vicarage standing obediently at its side. A tall, rose-brick wall separated the churchyard from the vicarage garden. This wall was viewed with relief by the modern wives of recent vicars who, unlike their

Victorian counterparts, did not care to live in such close visual proximity to the eternal reminder of their mortal state.

There was a tiny cluster of three shops and a Post Office at the north end of the village. Finding it difficult to survive in the face of the giant superstores, those that did were meccas for spreading gossip, and their staunch supporters willingly paid over the odds for a friendly face and the latest scandal.

The ivy-clad pub called — puzzlingly, in this land-locked corner of England — the Pieces of Eight, flourished at the end of the lane leading to the church and proved each Sunday that religion was a sociable and thirsty activity.

At the other end of the street stood the school, its tarmac playground edged by wire netting fixed onto a brick wall. Built in the same year as the vicarage, the large rooms were designed for the old solid fuel fires where farm children could hang their clothes and dry their boots round the guard after a three-mile trek across muddy fields. Now they were taxied in from the outlying villages, but the day would come when someone did their sums and decided that it would be more economical for these country children to swell the classes of the town schools in Chadbury or Silminster.

The modern heating system was expensive and inadequate for the high-ceilinged rooms, that were made dark by narrow windows set up high. Paint and plaster crumbled like thick porridge from the damp walls and the sagging wooden floors nurtured splinters of graded sizes, storing them up to enter limbs secretly on every unsuspecting occasion. A cramped gymnastic lesson was a good time, or the entrance of bare-footed infant angels for the Nativity play in front of parents and governors. No amount of pacifying will quieten splintered angels. Unheavenly noises off-stage had long been an accepted addition to the remaining angelic winged hosts, as they sidled in to catch the shepherds unawares.

Enlarged concentrically with two modern crescents and a small estate behind the cottage, the village had become desirable to commuters and unaffordable to the sons of the soil. The incomers, anxious to belong, had added their money to the general village fund, that had been slowly amassing over the years for the building of a new village hall with suitable amenities. Three years ago, the target had been reached and a year before Sally and Nicholas moved in, Pomery-upon-Axle had become the proud possessor of a new hall — with a matching new committee, unable to agree even the time of day.

Most of the picturesque cottages which hugged the green and bristled with newly trimmed thatch and whitewashed walls belonged to incomers. It was easy to spot those that did not. They were the ones with straggly grey-tops, streaky yellowing walls and well-established gardens. No one would ever see the curtains twitch in these houses, but nothing went unobserved. Newcomers needed to practise this skill — usually for about thirty years — before they were on a par with their more experienced neighbours.

Anyone who thought they were anyone in the village of Pomery-upon-Axle lived in the narrow no-through road, Squires Lane, which led to the iron gates of the manor house. There were four substantial family houses set back from the road, an airy sixties-style bungalow with indoor swimming pool and, close to the village, two modest semi-detached houses that some who lived in the larger dwellings liked to consider not part of the lane.

Mrs Agatha Kingsway was one such person. She lived in the house nearest to the manor with her husband, who worked away from home as much as he could.

At the time that Sally Nesbith's unexpected visitor was making its way through the long grass to effect an introduction, Agatha

Kingsway was on the phone to Mary Stringer, who had only lived in the village for two years and was struggling to make her way in the village hierarchy. The reason Agatha bothered with her was that Mary always appeared so eager to help and didn't seem to mind what she did. Mary lived in one of the older closes of bungalows to the south of the village, but aspired to a house in Squires Lane. It was her closely guarded secret that her house was rented, but she had expectations. With any luck, she would be able to buy the house she wanted soon without anyone knowing her true current position.

Agatha wanted to finalise the details for the vicar's welcome party to be held in the village hall on Saturday night.

'You have understood what I've been saying, haven't you? You are to pick up the baby-sitter from Number Three, Laurel Close and take her to the vicarage. Then you pick up the vicar and his wife and bring them to the hall. Bring them straight to me, and I will do the rest.'

'What about Mrs Babbington-Banbury? Won't she expect to meet them first?' asked Mary Stringer, bristling in spite of herself at the way in which she was being ordered about.

'I will introduce them to Leonora myself,'

said Agatha huffily, with the subtly intimate emphasis on the Christian name. 'Now, shall we go over it again?' she continued, irritating Mary.

'No, no, I understand what to do.' Mary repeated her instructions parrot-fashion and managed to bring the conversation to a close, holding the receiver meditatively before replacing it gently in its cradle. She was glad that she had got rid of the crinolined doll she'd won at the fair — and that used to disguise the phone — before Agatha came to visit last week. Only yesterday, Mary had heard her too-loud voice refer disparagingly to the one owned by Agatha's daily help as a vulgarity. Lucky to escape that one.

Agatha was a useful friend to cultivate. She was well bred and *au fait* with the ways of the type of people whom Mary craved to emulate. She couldn't deny that the friendship was a strain, though. Mary was always worried that one day she might commit a *faux pas* of such magnitude that she would be tossed to the bottom of the heap. This thought made the butterflies hover under her new, expensively made dress that she had bought from the shop recommended by Agatha: and then she knew what she would do. She would phone Pauline and tell her what she should be doing on Saturday. She was just in the mood to do that.

Leaning across, she picked up the receiver and dialled Pauline's number. A cautious voice answered and Mary got her own back on Agatha by bullying scraggy Pauline until she apologised for being as stupid as Mary made her feel.

* * *

The arrival of the new man of God excited no interest at the Manor. Henry Babbington-Banbury had always found it simpler to let other people organise his opinions for him and had married a woman well able to fulfil this task. It was far from arduous, as Henry could remember but one opinion at a time and didn't mind how long he was expected to keep it. Not that he was a slacker. He had been known to become quite animated with his borrowed views, in company. Leonora would feed him another one every now and then, when she thought about it, unless he was being schooled to agree with her on a particular subject at a designated time. On those occasions, it was hard work and uphill all the way.

Henry and Leonora ran all the local committees by virtue of their position and, as chairman, Henry would have the casting vote and the opinion that carried the most weight. Schooling him to give the right answer could take several days if the problem was complex. Even then, he had been known to get it wrong until alerted by the excruciating pain of a brogue across the instep. Fortunately, by the time he had recovered, the enigmatic expression on his wife's face would indicate that he had said the right thing after all and he was able to relax until the next time.

Leonora Babbington-Banbury, daughter of Colonel Lancet-Brickway — patriarch of the west country Lancet-Brickways, who had been mentioned in dispatches since the first dispatch had been mentioned — had no need to concern herself about the new man at the vicarage, for she would direct him in all his decisions, just as she had directed the previous incumbent for the last twenty-five years. She would see him about the new headmaster on Saturday night and arrange immediate action.

The five Babbington-Banbury children were largely indifferent to the new arrival, with the possible exception of Charlotte, aged seventeen, who had spent all her life so far struggling in the embrace of a good cause. At present, she was grappling with the philosophy behind organic farming, and hoped that the new vicar would support her views and preach on them as he visited his rural flock.

Emma — at eight, the youngest of the brood — was too wrapped up in her menagerie to consider anything else but the arrangements for her imminently hibernating animals, while the twins — Georgina and Thomas, thirteen come November — thought only about themselves and their secret world that distanced them from everyone else. The oldest, another Henry, thought it enough to be handsome and amiable, making it his policy never to worry about anything at all.

Each Babbington-Banbury was sufficient unto himself and — with the exception of the twins, and the need for Henry to be instructed — they rarely conversed with each other but adopted the unnerving habit of talking together at the same time on totally different subjects, without appearing to wait for answers. Visitors would pray that they encountered only one at a time, for every stranger was viewed as a potential sounding-box, required to listen to the aired premise with wholehearted enthusiasm. An injudicious nod or shake of the head by a visitor confused by the variety of subjects with which he was expected to agree or disagree, could incur righteous indignation and an insistence that he endure another patient explanation of the finer points of the argument in order to change his opinion. If both parties did this, then the visitor was doomed to an action replay at half speed, but double the fervour. Indeed, not many people made a return visit after such a test of endurance, leaving the field open for more innocents to sample the traditional Babbington-Banbury welcome and baptismal fire. The new vicar would be treated no differently.

* * *

Matilda Golightly enjoyed a leisurely breakfast before settling the bill incurred by her enforced stay at the Royal. She was philosophical now about her plight. It was a nuisance to see one's house and belongings go up in flames, of course, but they were only things. She had always been far more interested in people.

A woman of forceful character tempered by great charm, she had the countrywoman's ruddy complexion and sturdy body with wide hips that should never have worn trousers. All five of her husbands had sought to tell her this — but they were dead now and she was very much alive, so, she reasoned, she was in the best position to choose for herself. The colour she most favoured was brick-red.

Pausing to chat to the chambermaid and advise her to make it up with her boyfriend, she swept into the lift and arrived in the lobby where all eyes were drawn to her larger-than-life figure and ringing laughter as she shared a joke with the liftman. A taxi was ordered for her while she paid and a chain of bell-boys transferred her luggage into the boot, allowing Matilda time to ask after the manager's wife and warn Tracey from reception that Ned, the barman, had a bit on the side.

The taxi took her to the station, where help to move herself and her belongings to the train appeared as if by magic. She settled back into the inadequately padded seat and chatted to her fellow passengers with some animation, her gap-toothed smile embracing and infecting the whole carriage with bonhomie. Being rather deaf, she usually shouted her observations and was still shouting when she alighted at Chadbury to find Leonora and Henry waiting for her with the Rolls. Leonora, never quite sure if she was fond of her sister or not, bore the noise with fortitude; but, by the time they reached the manor, Leonora had the beginnings of a severe headache.

* * *

Sally Nesbith was turning to go in when her eye was caught by a movement in the long grass, accompanied by a snorting and snuffling sort of noise. The grass was knee-high and the colour of straw, a legacy of the dry spell that had only just come to an end. As Sally watched, apprehensive but fascinated, a large snout parted the brittle grass and sniffed the air. Apparently satisfied, the nostrils moved toward Sally, bringing with them two enormous ears curled over a face visited by becoming coyness. A huge pink and grey body with bulging abdomen indicated that she was not alone in her travels. Peering myopically at the new tenant, the animal trundled forward, uttered a few throaty grunts and collapsed at her feet with a contented sigh.

2

Arrangements for the party had gone as smoothly as these things ever do. There were far too many sausage rolls and not enough sandwiches, despite the list drawn up and distributed by Agatha Kingsway, this being her only practical contribution to the evening. Old Enid Brandon had spilt a jug of milk all over Pauline Jones's mince-pies, to her chagrin but everyone else's secret relief. How to dispose of Pauline's cooking without her realising it was the recurring problem at every gathering to which she made a contribution. Even Mary Stringer could not manage to tell her the truth. It was a joy to throw the soggy, moth eaten-looking remains into the bin openly, without having to keep a furtive lookout over the shoulder, in case Pauline should see and be quietly upset.

The rest of the milk was found to be off, twenty minutes before the party was due to start but a whip-round from everyone's fridges produced enough for those who craved tea or coffee rather than the vinegary boxed wine, that represented the height of decadent sophistication to the native Pomeranians.

Mary Stringer set off to collect the baby sitter and bring the vicar and his wife to the evening arranged in their honour, while the jockeying for position began. Agatha Kingsway won hands down. She contrived to be six paces from the door, directly in the line of sight of anyone coming in and near enough to consolidate her position by six quick steps before the pounce. Smiling smugly, she waited, confident of her coup, while lesser beings shrugged or tutted or muttered darkly about come-uppances before remembering that they were Christian people and loved all their neighbours. The more practical among them decided that that sentiment should be qualified by the addition of a scale of one to ten to allow them a more achievable success rate.

All heads turned as the Nesbiths entered but Agatha's quick start forward was stopped short by the realisation that they were not alone. Leonora Babbington-Banbury had ensnared the quarry, and swept them across the room, her husband and Charlotte trailing inconsequentially behind. The sudden realisation that eyes were staring and lips were still caused a general shuffling of feet and outbursts of simultaneous conversations

— carefully gauged to be of short duration, in case the opportunity should arise to be introduced to the newcomers.

Nicholas Nesbith looked his captor firmly in the eye and recognised that, for the moment, escape was impossible and he would have to hear her out. He had met plenty of Leonora Babbington-Banburys in his time as a curate and in the village of his own childhood, and had developed a successful strategy for dealing with them: namely, hear them out, concur with their views and then follow one's own conscience. It never failed. He nodded attentively as she instructed him to visit the local school in all haste and admonish the headmaster for allowing the teaching of heathen religions, to ban old Frank Whittle from whistling as he dug the graves, and to support her in her views that the Harvest Supper should be a beacon of sobriety.

Satisfied that she had delivered her instructions to compliant ears, Leonora Babbington-Banbury moved away regally to dispense her expertise to Nanette French, chief organiser and arranger of church flowers.

Nicholas Nesbith turned away thankfully, only to find Agatha ready and waiting, blue rinse quivering, with a captive Sally pinioned like a butterfly on a card. Grateful as she was to meet the lynch-pin of the village, without whom everything would grind to a standstill, Sally really wanted to ask someone about the pig at the bottom of her garden.

* * *

After effecting her own introduction, Penelope — as Sally had decided to call her, for no better reason than that it began with the same letter as 'pig' and the animal was female — had fallen asleep at her feet, uttering a gurgling stream of well-satisfied grunts. No amount of cajoling could persuade the pig to move, despite the discovery that she had her own makeshift shed hidden among the stunted apple trees at the bottom of the garden, well equipped for the comfort and well-being of her kind, with enough fresh food to tempt and satisfy an anorexic alligator.

Nick scoured the correspondence dealing with the move and nowhere did it mention animals of any sort. Old Stoneygate had left a week ago for a pre-retirement holiday with relatives in the Bahamas, and Nicholas did not feel that phone calls to such far-flung outposts were within his pocket, even if he knew exactly where Stoneygate had gone.

They would have to ask the neighbours but, faced with this unexpected problem after the trauma of a moving day, they both conceded with mutual exhaustion that tomorrow was indeed another day and that troubles often disappeared overnight if left alone. Feeling slightly guilty, they shut the door on their sleeping beauty, noisily abandoned in her slumberous posture, and hoped that, by the morning, the problem would be solved, or gone. Preferably both.

Amy woke them at dawn and a furtive look out of the dining room window revealed no Penelope; they hoped that their prayers had been answered. Joe's incredulous shrieks of delight, as he explored the garden later on, proved their hope to be in vain. Penelope was sauntering around the trees at the end of the garden, snuffling lazily into the grass when the mood took her. Seeing Sally coming to see what Joe had found, Penelope broke into agitated snorts and approached her with the light of adoration in her little piggy eyes.

Sally had spent two trying days keeping Joe away from the pig in case she decided to sit on him, keeping the pig away from herself, looking after Amy and unpacking boxes, only to find that they were not the ones for which she was looking. Nick had gone to the church this morning to familiarise himself with everything he would need on Sunday morning and, in the afternoon, he had locked himself away with his sermon — for there would be no time to do it, that evening, with the welcome party that had been arranged for them. Sally had seen no one to ask about their problem and then they had been dropped by Mary Stringer and pounced upon by Mrs Babbington-Banbury — neither of whom, Sally felt instinctively, would know anything at all about pigs. Anyway, it seemed such a strange question to ask a perfect stranger. Her normally untroubled countenance clouded a little as she scanned the room, looking for a soul in whom she could confide.

Outside, the clear, dark sky was studded with diamond stars. A warm Indian summer breeze stirred the treetops, impatient for the questing movements of autumn when it would scurry through the leaves and claim its dead.

Sadie Strangelove stood back from her bedroom mirror and admired the result of her labours. Clever girl. Understated elegance. Black with the slash of scarlet silk at her throat. Hair dark and glossy, falling in gentle waves that framed her face. Rubies on her fingers and pinned to her breast. Sheer stockings and patent shoes, with heels high enough for femininity but not so high as to be vulgar. She consulted her slim gold watch, discreet opulence on satin skin the colour of pale biscuit. Nine o'clock. Just right for a late arrival who wants to be noticed. Smiling secretly to herself, she swayed her hips toward the door and let herself out into the balmy night, a chiffon scarf round her head to keep each hair in place.

* * *

The tension had gone out of the evening now that the predators had caught the prey and established the pecking order. Charlotte Babbington-Banbury had been the last in line to make her earnest request that the vicar preach organic Christianity, appearing satisfied with his well-judged response. As she lumbered over to inspect the food table, her dipping skirt and unwise choice of blouse singling her out as a girl of unfrivolous nature, Nicholas turned away thankfully to look for his wife. Sally was deep in conversation with a stooping ancient, his cheerful face lit up by bright blue twinkling eyes in a wrinkled leathery skin. Seeing Nicholas free at last, she beckoned him across.

'Nick, this is Mr Whittle. Frank. And he

thinks he might know something about our pig — only it's a secret, I think.'

Nicholas looked as confused as he felt.

Sally lowered her voice. 'You remember the ambulance that was leaving at the same time as our furniture van? Well, it had the owner of our pig in it. Only he's not supposed to own it. He had to give up his farm and sell everything to repay rent that he owed, but he wouldn't part with Penelope, so he put her in our garden, with Stoneygate's approval.'

Frank Whittle stage-whispered. 'Old Bart was supposed to sell everything, but he reckoned that when she'd farrowed he could keep the little 'uns as rightfully his and start again. There's no room for her at his sister's, where he's gone, so he asked the old vicar and Stoneygate said Bart could keep her in his garden. Bart put a few pieces of wood together to make her a shelter and went out there to look after her every day — but then he collapsed, the day you arrived.'

Sally looked worried. 'So there's been no one to look after her since Thursday?'

Frank looked studiously at his sturdy brown shoes. 'Not exactly.'

Sally and Nick looked questioningly at him. 'Not exactly?' they chorused.

Frank shuffled his polished brown boots. 'I've been doing it. Coming in through the gate in your wall. I would have asked permission,' he added hastily, 'but if you'd wanted her out of your garden straight away, I'd have been stuck as to where to put her.'

'So you've got somewhere now, have you?' asked Nicholas mildly.

'Not exactly.'

Sally and Nicholas were beginning to realise what 'not exactly' meant. And that it could cause them trouble in more ways than one.

Feeling absurdly foolish at this piggy conspiracy, Sally lowered her voice to ask ungrammatically, 'Who does he owe money to? Is it anyone here?'

Frank Whittle nodded sagely. 'That's right.' His blue beacon eyes swivelled in a semi-circle until they rested on the tweed-encased back of Henry Babbington-Banbury.

Sally looked troubled. This could make things difficult for Nicholas. 'What about explaining to Mr Babbington-Banbury? Now that — er — Bart is in hospital? Perhaps he'll be sympathetic.'

Frank frowned darkly. 'Happen he might. But *she* won't.' His gaze moved casually to take in Leonora Babbington-Banbury as she menaced poor Pippa Brown over the abandoned display of wild flowers, that Pippa had arranged in the lady chapel for last

Sunday. '*She* sees to everything up at the manor; and if she claps eyes on that sow, she'll have her in Chadbury market before you can say 'bacon'.'

Sally had formed her own opinions of Leonora already, and could not but agree.

At that moment, Nicholas felt a tug at his sleeve and turned to look into the face of Enid Brandon, the spiller of milk onto other people's mince-pies. Little did he know that there was much more that he needed to know about Enid Brandon before agreeing that she should decorate the pulpit for the Harvest Festival. Or at any time at all. Unfortunately, a distraction occurred and an, 'I'm not sure how these things are arranged,' became a 'Hm,' that she translated as a resounding 'Yes!' and ran off to tell Nanette French, chief flower organiser, of her triumph.

Nanette's instinctive reply was fortunately doomed to oblivion: for, at that moment, she too saw what the vicar had seen and what had caused him to utter his unwise, 'Hm.'

Sadie Strangelove had arrived in a cloud of Chanel and was making a seductive bee-line for the new vicar, watched open-mouthed by both sexes for very different reasons.

* * *

Matilda Golightly had intended to join the party that evening: but Emma and the twins wanted to hear all about her visit to Africa to see the gilded temples of the Cameroons and, in the end, she was enjoying herself too much to make a move. She rather liked Leonora's children and regretted that after five husbands she should have none of her own.

3

Briony Brightside crept into the back of the church, mousy but dignified. They were in the middle of the first hymn, and she hated being late, but at least the singing masked her entrance. Sometimes, Hugo made her so late that she had to wait outside in an agony of frustration, trying to listen for the right moment to come in between the epistle and prayers, when she would attract the least amount of attention. But today was not so bad. Quite by accident, this morning, Briony had discovered upon leaving that the bedside clock by that Hugo had judged his performance was fast, hence her arriving almost on time. She wondered if Hugo had found out yet.

He was like a child throwing a tantrum to get attention but, once obtained, he was still not satisfied. This morning, he had thought himself ill, a good standby. She knew that he would probably not be there when she returned, or would go out soon afterward. His miraculous recoveries were legendary. But why did he do it? She wished that she had the answer, because she was almost at the stage where she couldn't take any more.

They sat for the reading of the epistle and Briony looked at the full church, populous in honour of the new vicar. Henry and Leonora Babbington-Banbury sat in the family pew in the front on the left, their younger children fidgeting and scuffling well-shod feet on the hassocks. Briony had heard that Matilda Golightly was staying with her sister at the moment, but she was not there this morning. Agatha Kingsway sat stiff-backed on the right side of the aisle, with Mary Stringer looking strangely out of place at her side. Mary was an attractive redhead with milky white skin, but was sharp-featured and always on edge. Briony smiled ruefully, consciously stopping herself from wringing her hands together. She could talk.

The vicar's wife sat near the back on the left with her little boy and the baby. Briony thought that she looked approachable and wondered what she thought of them all and how difficult it must be to integrate into an old village such as Pomery.

One row of scrubbed cubs and two of brownies swelled the ranks, with two superior pews full of scouts and guides behind. Frank Whittle sat in his church warden's seat with Edgar Bryan opposite. Edgar's slight, effeminate figure was gracefully composed as he perused the new man with interest. Nicholas was younger than Edgar had thought he would be. He'd have to work hard to live up to Stoneygate's reputation — but then, Stoneygate had been a one-off. Edgar had never met a kinder man. Things could be different, now, with this new one in charge. No reason as yet not to give him a chance, but Edgar was enough of a cynic to doubt if things could ever be quite the same.

Pauline Jones sat in front of her with Enid Brandon. Briony hoped that what she heard was not true. Old Enid decorating the pulpit. Surely Nanette French would not allow it? Her eyes slid across to where Nanette sat with her husband. A lovely couple, Briony had always thought. With Nanette's artistic talent and her husband's flair for making anything out of wood, their house had the look of those photographed in the glossy magazines but the feel of a real home. To let Enid help at all with the flowers was a demonstration of her generous nature. But the pulpit? Briony found it impossible to believe.

Hugo had been out last night and so Briony had gone along to the village hall to join the welcoming party. She had witnessed Sadie's arrival and heard Enid's excited declaration to Nanette, but she had been so surprised to see Sadie there that she missed

Nanette's reply. Briony had been surprised to see Sadie because she had thought that Sadie was with Hugo. That begged the question. If he had not been with Sadie, then with whom had he spent the evening?

Briony didn't relish her husband's infidelities, but she did like to know who they were. Not knowing made her nervous. She knew that they could not go on like this for much longer, but shrank from making the first move to eject him from her life. After all, she had loved him once, and her legacy had been a complete surprise to them both, so he hadn't married her for money. Neither of them had had money when they got married. Perhaps they were just wrong for each other and it was no one's fault. The money — her money — got in the way, now, and made it difficult to see clearly.

She seated herself ready for the sermon and tried to keep her mind from wandering, missing Matilda's entrance as she crept in during the offertory hymn, and slid hugely into the rear pew on the opposite side, a benign expression on her over-large ruddy face and a twinkle in her china-blue eyes.

Nicholas looked down at the sea of faces and was grateful for Sally's smile of encouragement. For a split second, he felt a cold breath of fear cover his mouth, preventing him from speaking at all. Resolutely fixing his eyes at the back of the church, he tried to begin by glancing at his notes, lost his place, babbled from memory and ended abruptly five minutes later when he happened to find himself at the end of a sentence.

Briony's wandering thoughts missed all but the very beginning, but Leonora and Agatha saw and heard all, satisfied that they could assess his character from this performance.

It was time for the communion. Leonora rose unhurriedly, confident that her self-given right to be first in line would not be challenged this morning. Briony felt a whisper of a breeze go past her and, suddenly, there was Matilda striding up the aisle, and linking arms with her sister as they advanced upon the altar. When they knelt, it was Matilda who was on the right and who received the wafer first, her upturned eyes full of piety.

Leonora took hers through thin lips and vowed to have a serious word with Henry after the service.

The congregation spilt out into the sunshine to the strains of the Pastoral symphony, played by Dawn Evans on a damp organ with two sticky stops. Nicholas shook hands with his congregation and Leonora and

Agatha had the chance to be gracious, secure in the knowledge that their new vicar was as putty in their hands.

Matilda's genial smile embraced all the assembled company. She was pleased with her morning, so far. It was good to get one's own way, especially if it meant irritating Leonora. She had loved to annoy her, ever since they had been children, and Matilda had never forgone her childish pleasures.

When all was done, the Nesbiths entered the vicarage garden with their children, Nicholas aware that his first service at St Wilfrid's had been — if he could be permitted the old joke — a curate's egg, and Sally still worrying over Penelope, the purloined pig. Weren't they accessories after the fact, now?

She made up her mind that she would visit Bart in hospital, that afternoon, and explain that the pig would have to go. She was prevented from doing this because Frank arrived, as she was getting ready to leave, with the news that Bart had died that morning.

'So is the pig his sister's responsibility now?' Sally asked hopefully.

'Not exactly,' said Frank.

⋆ ⋆ ⋆

Albert stared morosely at the four walls that he was forced to call home. Not much better than the four walls he had lived in for the last three years, except that he could walk out of these any time he felt like it. High above his sagging bed with its stained mattress, a fat black spider was swinging itself along into a festoon of web where it crouched, waiting. Albert shut his eyes.

An all-pervasive smell of cooked cabbage and dirty dustbins wafted up from the basement. How that old bag had the cheek to charge rent for this slum, he didn't know. Cracked sink, peeling paint, torn lino. He thought lino had had its day, years ago. This stuff must have been here for twenty years. Didn't look as if it had been washed in that time, either. There were lumps of accumulated dirt piled up underneath the rips, so that to walk anywhere was like walking on sticky pebbles.

The only window was stuck shut, although its cracked panes looked as if they wouldn't stand the strain if moved, anyway. They rattled ominously with every lorry that passed. The noise from the traffic was a constant annoyance, a droning that got inside his head and disturbed his dreams. Often, he lay awake unable to sleep at all, imprisoned by the noise that was outside and the secrets locked within himself. He began to pace up and down. This was worse than prison, because he had a choice and was not doing anything about it. He didn't have to be here. There must be better places, better towns. In the morning, he would move on and find one. Somewhere nearer the money.

Unbeknownst to him, he was moving closer and closer to Matilda, where their paths would cross and entwine, bringing danger and excitement to the village of Pomery-upon-Axle and not just a little to themselves.

* * *

The two marrows made an unseemly gesture, that sent ripples of barely hidden mirth along the rows of Cubs and Brownies, blasé at their second outing to church that month. Nicholas had seen the problem too late, and cursed his inattention as he mounted the pulpit. Only when in sermon position did he realise that he had to stand between these plump green beacons that, he noticed with increasing incredulity, were embedded at forty-five degrees in huge flowerpots filled with what looked like plaster of Paris. Unsecured apples stood along the rest of the ledge, just waiting for an involuntary movement to send them winging into the congregation.

With a sinking heart, he took in the noisome strings of onions and garlic cascading down the outside of the pulpit, secretly suspended by some sort of dirty grey elastic, and the strands of corn woven through the delicate sixteenth-century carving depicting the twelve apostles.

Too late to cut his losses and run, so he began to speak, bolstered by the thought that, despite one or two setbacks and an inauspicious beginning, the Harvest Supper on Friday had gone really quite well, there was hope for him yet — if he found the courage to stay. He leant forward incautiously and a wizened Bramley skidded toward the edge, but stayed balanced until he was able to pull it back. Shutting his mind to all extraneous things, he began his Harvest sermon.

* * *

No one who had elected themselves as organisers of the Harvest Supper had been able to agree on anything, but Leonora was in the habit of winning and the organisation proceeded more or less to her plan. Her insistence that it be a 'dry' evening, after an 'incident' that had apparently occurred last year, caused many low mutterings, but she got her own way.

Eventually, a collation of cold meats, salad and cheese was decided upon, with trifle, fruit juice to drink, and cups of tea or coffee for afterwards. Things appeared to be going smoothly at this point, until the actual night when Sadie Strangelove, recently interesting herself in the social life of the church, came along just as all the tables had been laid and Agatha, who had taken no part in the laying of the tables, was left in charge.

Sadie had made her request to the vicar, on the evening of his party, that the supper be candlelit. He had had the presence of mind to defer this major decision and thought that it had died a quiet death. Sadie had had other ideas, walking into the hall on Friday with enough candles and holders for each table.

If it had been anyone else, Agatha would have been able to chill them away by a look, but she knew that she commanded no respect from Sadie and that Leonora's orders were going to be flouted in front of her eyes. Smiling dreamily to herself, Sadie placed two candles on each table, stood back to admire her handiwork and then disappeared to complete her toilet.

Sighing thankfully, Agatha whipped round

and took them all off the tables again, hiding them behind the urn in the kitchen. Sadie could think what she liked. It would be too late when she came back.

Agatha had only just finished when the first people started to arrive and so quickly seated herself at the table at the far end, traditionally reserved for those who considered themselves important. She left room for the Babbington-Banburys, who would sit beside the vicar and his wife, but made sure that she was next in line. Seeing the Nesbiths arrive with Frank Whittle, Agatha half-rose to beckon them over but, before she could stop them, they had sat down at a centre table, deep in conversation with the old man, oblivious to their surroundings.

Exasperated at this departure from tradition, Agatha was making her way across to them when a whole wave of people arrived, among them the Babbington-Banburys. The room was filling up. She must move the Nesbiths now, before it became embarrassing.

Her pale blue rinse glided swiftly across the room, anxiety creasing the powdered skin of her forehead. Leonora raised her eyebrows at Agatha as she made her way to the top table. Matilda had elected to sit with the ladies from the sewing circle to discuss her own tapestry work, which was surprisingly fine, and there were soon unseemly chuckles of laughter from their corner of the room. Matilda was in full flow.

Hardly a spare seat anywhere, now. Resisting the impulse to grab them both by the arm, Agatha was leaning over to murmur that their seats were over there, when the room was plunged into darkness.

Light was restored just as suddenly and all eyes were drawn to Sadie, who stood bemusedly by the light switches. Opening her eyes wide, she exclaimed in surprise, a slight lisp completing the desired effect, 'I'm so sorry! I thought that the candles would have been lit by now!' Her gaze bathed the room until it rested upon Agatha, caught like a rabbit during lamping.

After the candles had been found and lit by every available man who could walk, Agatha turned to regain her seat, only to find Sadie sitting in it and Leonora scowling with equally venomous impartiality at her and Henry, who was drooling over Sadie like a Doberman at dinner time.

Nicholas said a prayer and the supper began.

4

They were getting nowhere with Frank Whittle. The pig had been left to old Stoneygate who had, apparently, grown attached to her during her temporary sojourn with him after her cruel eviction. On his return from his flighty visit to the Bahamas, he was to settle down in rural retirement — ten miles away, in a cottage bought years ago for the purpose — and would have room for her there. Nicholas and Sally had been trying to explain that she was now the property of Bart's creditors, no matter to whom she had been willed, but Frank would not be convinced.

At the time that Sadie doused the lights, his standard rejoinder of 'It's written in black and white. Seen it myself when I was a witness' was beginning to get them down.

Sadie's theatrical gesture caused the Nesbiths to look up and it was then that they noticed the bottles of wine, along with suitable glasses, which had appeared on the tables during the last few minutes. Nicholas was surprised, but assumed that Mrs Babbington-Banbury must have changed her mind. After their abortive attempts to explain the points of elementary law concerning inheritance and creditors to Frank Whittle, a drink was just what he needed. Thankfully, he proffered their glasses, and became more optimistic as each satisfying glug left the bottle.

Under Leonora's icy gaze, Sadie Strangelove admitted with coy smugness and covert glances at Henry, that she had provided the cost of the wine and the hire of the glasses out of her own pocket as her 'contribution' to the evening. Leonora retaliated by taking Henry's glass away and changing places with him so that it was she who sat next to Sadie instead. Henry sat next to Charlotte and ate his supper, which flickered enticingly in the candlelight, while Charlotte kept up a monologue on green matters as she shovelled her cheap inorganic pork into a mouth already full of salad with pesticide dressing.

Sally put Penelope firmly out of her mind and began to enjoy herself. Beside Frank, they were sitting with Nanette and her husband Harry, young Pippa Brown, who supported herself by selling her delicate water-colours and collages on hessian for the local tourists in Chadbury, and Harriet Needham and her husband Robert. Harriet was another flower lady who, Sally learnt, worked part-time in Chadbury, fitting in the hours to enable her to fetch the children from school. Robert and Harry worked in Silminster, Robert as a draughtsman and Harry as the manager of a do-it-yourself shop, always yearning to be at home doing what he advised on all day.

The candlelight softened the faces of the diners and the wine their temperament. For Sadie, the evening was a triumph.

Dawn Evans was seated at the piano — of the sort that belonged in a theatre showing silent films and was best suited to those who sang out of tune. The first chord of 'Come, ye thankful people' brought the talking down to a murmur and Leonora swept to the front of the little crowd gathered at the piano, pulling Henry with her. She had a fine contralto voice, if a little penetrating, and liked to show it off. She started and Dawn caught her up, the rest of the singers arriving breathless in the fourth bar. They entered God's garner at about the same time, but were pipped at the post by an extra deep breath that allowed Leonora's 'Harvest Home' to outstay them all.

The evening drew to a close with 'Jerusalem', a virtual solo by Leonora, and it is to be feared that the closing prayer for many was one of thankfulness that they had

had the foresight to move away before Leonora's feet moved upon the mountains.

Sally and Nicholas stayed to help clear up and walked home closely in the moonlight, full of contentment with their lot. If only they could do something about Penelope, their cup would be full to overflowing.

* * *

Nicholas held on to the memory of Friday night and delivered his sermon without a hitch. He finished with a well-chosen Biblical punchline and swung round to face the altar for the Creed. This was his undoing. The sleeve of his surplice caught a wrinkled apple on the polished surface of the pulpit's edge and, in attempting to catch it, he swept its two neighbours through the air in a wide arc. A further unwise lunge to restore his fruit caused a teetering flowerpot to lose the battle with gravity and shatter onto the stone-flagged floor. The marrow bounced twice and lay exhausted beside the pottery fragments and its erstwhile casing of grey plaster of Paris, poorly mixed.

A pew-full of Cubs started to fight over the unlovely apples, admonished in hissing whispers by Akela and her auntie, while Brown Owl looked disapprovingly from across the aisle. Nanette French rubbed her hand across her forehead and Sally was torn between helpless sympathy and the desire to collapse in a heap of giggles.

Somehow, the rest of the service was got through, but Nicholas vowed that in the future, he would listen carefully to everything that Enid Brandon said to him and enunciate his answers as if he were in elocution class and she were his critical tutor.

* * *

So it was Maureen. Briony should have guessed when she saw her in the Post Office and wouldn't meet her eye. How long, she wondered? With a sigh, she realised that it didn't matter. It was always going to be someone. Someone else and not her. The only surprising thing was that he should attempt to cover his tracks at all. Or perhaps he cared so little that this half-heartedness at concealment was part of his contempt for her. She wasn't worth the bother.

Sadie must have tired of him quickly. She was out of his league, really. Amusing herself until something much better came along. Funny that she'd started coming to church now and then, and her turning up at the Harvest Supper had set a few tongues wagging. She wasn't usually popular among the women — they resented the effect she had on their husbands — but she had made a few friends that night. Not many people ever managed to get the better of Leonora and Agatha, and Sadie had done it twice.

Briony smiled, in spite of herself. Leonora's face had been a picture of genteel fury and Agatha had sulked all evening, squashed up between the fire-extinguisher and little Edgar Bryan. Briony's smile faded. And all the time, Hugo had been with Maureen.

Maureen was the wife of Simon Wintergreen, their local G.P. They lived in Squires Lane, although his practice extended to include Tidworth, Mole and all stations between and around. He had the reputation of being a ladies' man and was the subject of much gossip in the villages, but Briony had always thought that it was just his good looks which gave others the assumption that he was playing the field. Although, if that was the case, why had Maureen strayed? Hugo was no catch, Heaven knows, but there was no denying that women found him attractive. Briony's eyes filled with tears. She must make a decision. Decide what to do about Hugo and do it. There had been enough dithering about already.

* * *

Albert Noonday moved into old Bart's bungalow on the day of the Harvest Supper. He made himself unpopular very quickly, and many people believed ill of him, but a murder in Pomery was the last thing anyone expected.

* * *

There was something the matter with Penelope. Despite herself, Sally paid frequent visits to her illegal lodgeress and was always rewarded by a series of pleased grunts and a lop-sided grin. Sally was an educated woman and not prone to anthropomorphism, but Penelope's devotion to Sally and the pig's orphan state, when left pregnant by an unknown father, had made it impossible for Sally to turn her in. If the police arrived, she would acknowledge a fair cop, but plead extenuating circumstances. One look at Penelope's vast quivering belly — and her patient Madonna expression when in repose — should be enough to tip the balance and convince them that they were not dealing with an animal but a victim of society.

Sally leant over the pig's vast body, prone among the fresh straw. No private look between them, no acknowledgement of her presence. Either Penelope pined for another, or she was ill. Sally hurried back indoors and phoned for Frank Whittle.

* * *

Nanette finished her arrangement of autumn leaves and carried them to the dining room table. She set them on the polished surface, protected by a crocheted mat and stood back to admire her work. Reds, golds and yellows glowed in a copper bowl, reflected in the table's polished light.

Nanette lived in one of the semi-detached houses at the bottom of Squires Lane. Harriet Needham lived in the other and they had been friends from the moment they met. Harriet and Robert had two children, both girls, who attended the primary school in the village. Nanette and Harry were childless, despite years of hoping, but it was a disappointment that they kept to themselves. Only Harriet thought that she knew that Nanette grieved daily in silence.

Sometimes, if Harriet had to work late, Nanette would pick the girls up from school and look after them until their mother returned. For Nanette, it was a sweet sorrow, but she never shrank from the task. She was fetching them today and she checked her watch to make sure that she would be on time.

By now, she was inured to the pain of waiting at the school gate with all the mothers, some of whom did not seem to be pleased to see their children. Nanette used to think, if he or she were mine, how I would love to see them after a day without their company. But she had got used to this, as she had to everything else in her life. She was strong. She had much to be thankful for really.

Gillian and Hattie ran to her, pleased to be out of school, delighted to be going home with Auntie Nanette who spoiled them. They walked along the green, stopping to feed the ducks, a treat that Mum hardly ever had time to allow, before racing each other into the house to be the first to open the chocolate biscuits that were their special Auntie Nanette treat. Nanette took a deep breath and joined them in the kitchen, exuding calm contentment.

Sally leant over the babies plugged into the row of bulging teats, fascinated by their pinkness and rapt expressions. Eight healthy ones and one little runt that had done no more than draw a single breath. Penelope looked exhausted.

'Who wouldn't be, after nine births assisted by Sally the well-meaning but clueless midwife and Frank, the cheerful amateur?' she muttered.

She had been on the point of calling the vet when the runt had popped out and Frank had pronounced it to be the last. He had spent the time whistling tunelessly while he scratched the sow's head, uttering occasional words of encouragement while Penelope had proved herself a stoic. Even if pethedine had been on offer, Sally knew that the pig would have refused it on principle. Penelope was the earth-mother of all piglets, doing her brave bit for the preservation of porcine sisterhood.

There were just two clouds on the horizon. How could Sally bear to part with Penelope now? And, where was she going to hide eight vociferous piglets in the vicarage garden? The vicar's wife had fallen from grace, guilty of being an accessory to deception and hanging onto stolen property. She could only hope that her previous good character would be taken into consideration.

* * *

The doorbell chimed and Nanette went to answer it, knowing that only one person's finger could make that imperious sound.

Agatha stood on the doorstep, bright of smile and determined in eye. There was going to be another onslaught. Agatha was going to cajole her again into helping to start Pomery's own Amateur Dramatic Society, an enticing possibility for some since the building of the village hall. Suppressing a sigh, Nanette bade her come in and went to warn the children.

Later, in her mind, she blamed the distraction of children in the house for her eventual acquiescence to the scheme — for, on that early November afternoon, the two who were joined together formed the embryo PADS, that was to grow into a monstrous cuckoo, biting the hands of those who would gently rear it.

5

Burnt Oak farm belonged to the Babbington-Banburys and they never had any trouble leasing it to advocates of the good life, who felt that they could make a go of it on the land. It was worth the inconvenience of effecting the occasional eviction.

Albert Noonday began to reorganise the farm to his liking, spurning advice and practical help alike. Tall, dark and spare, his cadaveric face housed eyes sunk deep into the sockets. To look into his eyes was to gaze into a bottomless well. There were many areas of his life that he would prefer to keep hidden and he did not encourage confidences.

It was amazing how easy it had been to forge his references. That's one thing prison had taught him. How to make a good job of forgery. He'd seen the advertisement for the living in the local paper while passing through Chadbury and thought straight away how it would suit him to lie low for a while. The money was in safe hands, he hoped, not far from here. Nice and handy. Hangdog was due out in a month and, when he was free, he would come looking for Albert — but he wouldn't dream of looking for Albert on a farm. Albert knew about farming. Worked on one for three years, hadn't he? Seemed like the chance was sent.

Snotty woman had given him the once-over, but she'd hardly looked at the references. Just goes to show. He'd got enough money for three months and then he'd have to take what was his. The others wouldn't like it, but he'd got to live, hadn't he? In the small hours of the chilly mornings, he thought what might happen if Hangdog found him. He was half-Neanderthal, that one. No reasoning with him at all. If Fraser said they weren't to touch it, then they weren't to touch it. It was all right for Fraser. He wasn't out for another three years. It was hard on the outside. Hangdog would do job after job and end up back inside, because he was stupid, but Albert Noonday wasn't doing any more time. Not for anyone.

As the weeks went by, he began to relax and believe that he was safe. He was seen about the village more and started spending some evenings in the Pieces of Eight, sitting by the hearth and making one pint last the evening. People could be useful sometimes and biding his time here he could watch them all go by. He was soon on nodding terms with the regulars but rarely entered into a conversation, preferring to listen and keep his own counsel. The eyes soaked it all up, though, and the Pomeranians began to be wary of their secrets.

It had just been decided that he was very much a cold fish, when he struck up the most unlikely acquaintance with Pauline Jones. If the truth be told, Albert was as surprised as everyone else.

It had been a ladies' darts night and darts were the one thing that Pauline was good at. Albert watched with mounting interest as she inched her team ahead, and fell into conversation with her as she sipped her victory port and lemon. The following evening, she just happened to be there again, although this was most unusual for her, and so did he. Eventually, the pint became two halves and pork scratchings to be shared between them, and Albert's gaunt face began to take on a softer, more meditative look.

Pauline went to Burnt Oak, some afternoons, to clear up for him while he was in the field and, if he was not back in time to stop her, she would cook them a meal, that he prayed would not include pastry. Even if it did, he found himself missing her when she did not come.

* * *

Nanette was to be in charge of costumes and Harry the making of the scenery for Pippa to paint. This much was decided after an hour of the meeting held in the back room of the Pieces of Eight.

Agatha had done her job well, delegating Mary, who had lumbered Pauline with the task of advertising this preliminary meeting. Notices had appeared in the Post Office and general stores, the bus shelter, church porch and village hall notice-board. Two rather crooked advertisements had been covered in polythene and fixed hopefully to the oak trees on either end of the green. One lasted five days, the other was sabotaged in five minutes, by a capricious wind due to Pauline's timidity with the hammer. Another time, she would get Albert to do it for her. The thought of having someone to ask, someone who would help her because they wanted to, gave her a glow that she felt sure must be obvious to all who saw her.

At a quarter past eight, twenty-nine Pomeranians of mixed ages and abilities were gathered together in the small room that soon became stuffy and Agatha was very pleased with the turnout. Outside, the dank November fog hung like heavy cobwebs and spread unwelcome chill whenever a window was opened to seek fresh air.

The pub was seventeenth-century, solidly built, with thick oaken doors that allowed only the faintest noise from the rest of the building to penetrate. Every now and then, someone would leave the room, letting in a gust of pub laughter and clinking glasses with the bitter-sweet smell of beer and acrid smoke on the expelled breath.

Gradually, Agatha realised that not all who left returned, having insinuated themselves out of the back room and into the bar by a kind of unconscious osmosis. Why could no one agree on anything? she wailed inwardly. No one could agree on what to perform or when. Some people assumed that Agatha was going to produce, while others were vying among themselves for the job, quoting previous experiences and, in some cases, tedious reminiscences. They hadn't even settled on a name for the group.

Agatha had thought that Pomery Amateur Dramatic Society (PADS) was the obvious choice, and had already tentatively approached Pippa with the view to a logo using paw prints. But no. Some people wanted to put more emphasis on the singing side in the title, and suggested Pomery Amateur Operatic and Dramatic society (PAODS) that lacked the punch of her simple acronym and was unpronounceable anyway. POADS was not much better and PODS (Pomery Operatic and Dramatic Society) sounded positively disgusting.

Suppressing her alarm at the depleting company, as she glanced at her watch to find that it was five past nine, Agatha realised that if something wasn't decided soon, the whole venture would be doomed before it even began. Wild-eyed, she sought an ally and found it from the most unlikely quarter.

* * *

Georgina and Thomas Babbington-Banbury had sneaked outside again after their mother's brusque goodnight. She never checked on them twice. Or she never had done whenever they had escaped for one of their evening jaunts before. Emma was already asleep, having locked herself in so that her pet rat, Lancelot, could have the freedom of her room at night. Charlotte was reading her pamphlets designed to change the world. She had recently left organic farming in the lurch and was now married to unleaded petrol, and anyway would no more have concerned herself about her siblings than would their father.

Henry junior had gone to this meeting about acting. Not that he was bothered about what they did, but he had been known to drop them in it by an incautious remark in the presence of their mother. What they did not know was that Aunt Matilda had seen them go, and was at that moment following them, the lightness of her feet belying her bulk.

They knew just where they were going and made their journey in silence, walking with their dark heads close together in twin communion. The little cottage was on the outskirts of Pomery, set back from the road. As they approached it, the glow from the front room window shone fuzzily through the mist and the night air felt smoky in the back of their throats. The paved path leading up to the door was smooth and well kept. In the spring and summer, densely packed circles of colour swirled across the gardens on either side of the path. Impossible to see what was growing now in mid-November but, summer or winter, it made no difference — for, when the children came here, it was always dark. They tapped on the door and it swung open, swallowing them into the light as the door shut between them and the murky darkness of the forbidden night.

Matilda lost them at the cross-roads, her hearing not acute enough to pick out the direction they had taken. She resolved to do some more exploring tomorrow to see where they had gone and walked back slowly to the manor, deep in thought.

* * *

Sadie Strangelove somehow made her voice heard over the pockets of argument that rippled all over the room. Another husband, brought along against his will by his wife of ten months who thought that togetherness in marriage meant being together all the time, was edging toward the door and the muffled noise of unshackled enjoyment. Sadie's soft voice halted his progress: a fact not unnoticed by his wife, who spent the rest of the evening smouldering at Sadie while she stored up the beginnings of the row that they would have, the minute they got home. He slept in the spare room, that night; at the next meeting, they were at the cinema in Silminster.

Other wives were made of sterner stuff and reluctantly admitted that what Sadie said made a lot of sense.

'Why don't we pool all our ideas and have votes? What doesn't get chosen this time can be given priority the next,' she began reasonably, her soft voice stilling the storms. 'We can leave choosing the name for another time. Now, when do you think that we could have a show ready and what shall we do?'

The women's first reaction was to bristle, for not all had been at the Harvest Supper to see Sadie's triumph and Agatha had been at the brunt of it. Over the faces of the men swept a look of rapt attention full of suppressed eagerness to do whatever was bid them, as long as it was what Sadie wanted. She waited, a serenely confident smile on her lovely face, while the women weighed up what to do.

Sadie's suggestion was so sensible that Agatha was annoyed with herself for not being the one to put it forward. This made her want to reject the idea out of hand but, although often unwise, Agatha was never foolish. A third of her prospective cast, the men, were willing to make a decision. A third was better than none at all, which had been the situation before Sadie had spoken. Agatha decided to throw in her lot with Sadie and the men.

It took a further half an hour to reach an agreement that an agreement must be reached, and ten minutes for the suggestions to be made, pooled and voted upon. At ten past ten, it had been decided to put on a variety programme on the Friday and Saturday of the first May bank holiday weekend. Funds raised would be used to buy more equipment and facilities for the regular users of the hall.

For the moment, the thorny question of who should produce and what they were going to call themselves was shelved. A further meeting was arranged for the following week, while all the men bar one, seeing that Sadie was fully occupied, inched toward the door to 'get them in' before the evening's drinking was over.

For the last half-hour of the meeting, Sadie had been making sure that Henry felt the chemistry working between them. He was an easy catch — she preferred more of a challenge — but she had decided that it was time. She had not missed his look of admiration as she brought the meeting to order and it was no trouble to telegraph an intimate moment.

She sat next to him as if by chance, during the voting, and was in no hurry to move. Gradually, the room emptied, but still they sat until they were the last ones left. For Henry, the interest in Sadie was as deep as his casual nature could allow. No one was ever sure of what lay behind the glowing chocolate-drop eyes of Sadie Strangelove.

They left together as the landlord was calling time and Henry did not return home until twelve the next day. Georgina and

Thomas saw them in the lights that blazed from Sadie's house in Squires Lane, the modern one with indoor pool. They were moving crablike through the doorway, locked in each other's arms. The twins shared a look of grown-up understanding and notched up the sight as fuel to use at a later date, should it be necessary. Mother did not approve of Sadie and, when irritated with Henry, she often mentioned the fact that if she did not support him, he would have to find a job. Hugging each other with glee, his brother and sister let themselves in through a side door and crept off to bed. Matilda heard them come in and resolved that, next time, she would be quicker off the mark.

* * *

The affair with Maureen had been of short duration. Not that his peccadilloes had ever been a subject of discussion between them, but Briony always knew. In some ways, she was better off when he was straying. He would be out of the house most of the time, and there was less opportunity for her to say the wrong thing, that was all she seemed to be able to do nowadays. Sunday mornings, the only time when Briony was anxious to leave the house on time, he stayed in. As far as she could work out, all his lovers — with the exception of Sadie — had been married women, and Sunday morning seemed to be the time when all married women were expected to be at home with their husbands.

All last week, he had been home by seven and not gone out again. At the weekend, he had brooded until the evening on Saturday, when he popped into the Pieces of Eight for an hour or two, returning home gloomily before last orders had been called. Sunday, he had left to play golf at one, just as Briony was serving up their lunch, and had not returned until after Briony was in bed. She assumed that he had found someone else, and was almost glad, except for the niggle of hurt that never went away. It wasn't as if he enjoyed his infidelities, for pity's sake. If anything, they made him more miserable.

She was surprised when he stayed in on Monday and Tuesday but felt that she knew where she was again when he went out on Wednesday, until she found out that he had been at the meeting about the dramatic society which Agatha was trying to start. There must have been a reason. Someone there whom he wanted to see. Hugo had no interest in amateur dramatics. Surprisingly, in this assumption, she was proved to be quite wrong.

* * *

Of all the bad luck, he had been spotted in Silminster picking up a part for the tractor. They charged to deliver and, needing every penny, he'd said that he would collect it. Hangdog must have come this way to check on the money and seen him on the way to the yard. Albert would have noticed someone following him on the quiet lanes that led to the farm, so Hangdog must have got his address from the tractor place before turning up on the doorstep to shout the odds. Simple. Now Hangdog could visit any time he liked and the chances of Albert being able to dip into the money had fallen to minus a hundred. Albert had to find a way of making more money that wouldn't land him back inside. Later that week, the opportunity was to come to him — but he didn't recognise this gift horse, at first. It took an innocent remark from Pauline to put him on the right track.

6

Looking back over the years, Sally always counted the beginning of their new life in Pomery from the day they finally said goodbye to Penelope and her brood. The strain of keeping the existence of a sow and eight piglets at the bottom of the garden secret was distracting, and the memory of the final debacle was wont to kindle the fire in her cheeks and judder her heart into irregular rhythms.

It was all right, at first. The little pink creatures stayed close to their mother all the time, determined not to miss a drop of the rich piggy milk that Penelope produced with optimum casualness. She proved to be an excellent mother, never rolling onto or attempting to eat her offspring as other sows of more heathen turn of mind were known to do. Bursting with milk, she patiently suckled her young, lying on her side with a beatific expression on her face; Sally knew that her faith in Penelope had been justified.

Unfortunately, this honeymoon period did not last for long.

The sheltered housing for the snouted

refugees was at the farthest end of the garden. The eight-foot wall surrounding the vicarage garden and separating it from the churchyard at the bottom was tall enough to hide the illegal immigrants from view. The problem was the noise.

Sally had not realised before just how noisy one tiny piglet could be, and there were eight of them. In a very short time, there were rumours in the village of strange noises at the bottom of the churchyard where no one ever went, the last living relations of those resting there having died fifty years before. The whole area was overgrown with brambles and no excuses were needed not to go and investigate. Sally crossed her fingers and thought that they might still get away with it.

Then came the day when the piglets started to explore their surroundings. They embarked on sorties into the flower beds, snuffling along the rows of late vegetables, their tiny hoofs dibbling into the newly turned earth until it resembled a dimpled wasteland. For extra fun, they would suddenly appear at the French window, only to run away again, startled by their own reflection, leaving behind cunningly pungent evidence of their visits.

In vain, Sally and Nicholas tried to curtail the piglets's worst excesses, but they found that they were dealing with real troupers who planned their most ambitious safari, their Oscar-winning performance, for the day when Leonora Babbington-Banbury dropped into tea.

Leonora was at her most gracious, not allowing the Nesbiths's enforced frugality to affect her for one minute. She sat elegantly on the frayed sofa, drinking her tea, while Joe played on the floor with his bricks and Amy executed her newly learnt crawl so that she could be nearer to everything that was forbidden her. Sally felt fairly sure that Leonora would not want to venture outside. There was a fine drizzle blown about by a biting wind: a day for keeping indoors, and Leonora had already braved it once to come here at all.

Leonora wanted to speak to Nicholas, and he was at the bottom of the garden with Frank, improving the shelter and rigging up some kind of barrier that would stop the piglets from straying. Sally left her with the children, firmly shutting the door as she murmured something about going to find him. Out of sight, she pelted down to the shelter, in a panic in case Leonora should become restless in her absence. Luckily, Joe's vocabulary was not up to explaining where his daddy was.

Nicholas left his task unwillingly, leaving Frank to cope cheerfully with the temporary fencing and the unfriendly elements. Come to think of it, he had never seen Frank anything but cheerful. Later that afternoon was to be the first time Nicholas would ever see him otherwise.

There were two matters upon which Leonora wanted to instruct him. Firstly, the arrangements for the Christmas services — to which Nicholas simply nodded, having already discussed and fixed the times of the services with Dawn, his organist. The music was in her hands and the rest his responsibility. Sally sat back amused, impressed with the way in which Nicholas gave Leonora the idea that he would do everything she said, while obviously intending to do nothing of the sort.

Secondly, Leonora wanted to warn him against Edgar Bryan. Sally was to get the content of this conversation from Nicholas later, for, happening to look round to see where Amy had crawled to, she was horrified to see a small pink shape looking in through the French windows. It was one of the piglets; as she gazed at it with a sinking heart, it was joined by two of its siblings.

In the good weather, Sally and Nicholas had arranged the large old settee and chairs near the windows, so that they could look out at the garden with the windows open. They planned to build a patio here, if they could obtain permission and save up enough money. Once the weather became wintry, they had turned the furniture round to face the fireplace where a wood-burning stove crackled cheerfully, throwing its heat into the room. A sturdy childproof guard protected their children and dried the occasional nappy.

Leonora was seated on the settee facing the fire, while Sally and Nicholas sat in the chair's on either side. This was how Sally had been able to see the escapees while Leonora remained blissfully unaware of the three soft snouts pressed inquisitively against the misty glass. If Sally did not move fast, Leonora would not remain in ignorance for much longer. Praying that Joe and Amy would not notice before she reached them, Sally flashed Nicholas a significant look — the significance of which, not surprisingly, he did not understand — mumbled an excuse and fled. Joe looked up from his bricks as she shut the door while Amy dribbled into her educational toy.

Seconds later Nicholas, sitting in the chair to the right of the hearth, caught a glimpse of his wife as she crouched down outside the window, moving slowly out of sight, her progress hampered by something just out of view. With an effort, he drew his attention back to what Leonora was trying to say.

It appeared that she had taken a dislike to Edgar Bryan. He lived on his own, had no visible means of support and had been seen by her coming out of Banbury copse late at night on more than one occasion. When challenged, he had replied that it was a right of way and that it was his right to use it.

Banbury copse ran along the back of the manor, reached by a footpath running down the outside of the Babbington-Banbury land from the middle of the village. The wood, which extended a good mile further, belonged to the Babbington-Banburys too, but there were two footpaths, both public rights of way. One completed a circle from the village; the other led down the middle of the wood, joining the road which led to Mole. Leonora liked to discourage anyone from using them and Nicholas wondered if her complaints about Edgar were out of pique, at being thwarted by this small man with the courage of his convictions.

Four damp snouts were pressed against the glass and Frank Whittle was armed with a garden spade. Nicholas watched nervously as Sally whizzed past, eyes wild and staring, cradling a pink baby while Frank used the spade like a broom to sweep the rest away. Three gone, one returned, one more to go. Sally's action replay cleared the field and received a standing ovation from a delighted Joe, thankfully drowning out the muffled squeaks and curses that were making their way down toward the bottom of the garden.

Leonora turned round to look at Joe, who was pointing to the window shouting, 'Piggy, piggy,' a phrase which Nicholas found difficult to explain and so did not try.

Shrugging his shoulders casually, as if Joe spent all day shouting, 'Piggy, piggy,' for no reason, he reopened the subject of Edgar Bryan, thus bringing Leonora's attention away from Joe and the window.

This was fortunate for, at that moment, Penelope came into view, snuffling along amiably outside the window, pausing to peer short-sightedly at Joe, of whom she was rather fond, and making soft grunting noises in her throat as she stared through the glass.

Nicholas moved with the speed of an ant-eater's tongue. Using only four strides, he leapt out of his chair, pulled the curtains together with a flourish, flicked down the light switch and regained his chair before Leonora could turn her head. He heard Frank Whittle's growl, Sally's 'Sshh!' and Penelope's grunt fading away into the distance as he remarked, with studied nonchalance, 'Such a miserable day outside, isn't it?'

Leonora left very soon afterward. As Nicholas guided her through the hall to the front door, she thought that she caught sight of Sally creeping upstairs covered in mud, clasping the remains of a torn shirt around her. But Nicholas didn't mention it, so Leonora thought that she must have been mistaken.

Stoneygate returned from his holiday soon afterward and settled down to his well-earnt retirement with Penelope et al. He didn't have any trouble with his conscience until it was time for the pigs to go to market, which caused him to reflect seriously on the meaning of life. Penelope ended her days childless, while Sally decided that, after the uncertainties and exhaustion of clandestine pig-keeping, amateur dramatics would be a pleasant diversion. She resolved that she would turn up at the next meeting.

* * *

Matilda sat in the drawing room at the manor with her wool and canvas and reflected on her enforced stay, deciding that she had settled into the routine of the Manor and Pomery very comfortably. There was enough to occupy her fertile mind with the children, the gossip, and time to work at her tapestries, which gave occupation to her busy fingers. She had thought to make a brace of kneelers for St Wilfrid's. If she finished them before her next journey, then they could be dedicated at a special service. Leonora wouldn't like her getting all the attention, she thought with satisfaction, not at all ashamed of this ungodly thought.

Matilda loved people, warts and all. In fact, if she saw no obvious imperfections, she became bored with their company. There was something funny about Leonora's new tenant — and she still had to find out where the twins went on their forays into the dark, when they should have been in bed. As for Sadie Strangelove: there was a woman with a past, if ever there was one. Takes one to know one, so they say. She gave a shout of laughter, startling Wing, the ancient butler as he came in to draw the curtains. She wasn't just comfortable, she was really beginning to enjoy herself.

7

A cold November shivered out with a sprinkling of snow on its last day. December fought back with a fortnight of mild weather, and Christmas Day dawned disappointingly warm and wet. The village had enjoyed or endured a flurry of carol services, parties, carol singing and ebullient goodwill. Merry Midnight Mass revellers swelled St Wilfrid's like marrow-fat peas jostling for place in a ripening pod. Year's end drew near, dying quietly at last with a whimper and fizz. Newly made resolutions faltered among grey January skies and Pomery Amateur Dramatic Society started rehearsals for their first production.

The company had evened out to about twenty members plus a singing chorus, with a core of fifteen regular actors and dancers, not including Nanette and Harry. Agatha got the job of producer by default. Only four people turned up at the first proper meeting and three of them voted for her. While she was on a winning ticket, Agatha suggested that the name should be confirmed as PADS and the motion was passed unanimously. The main contenders had found better things to do anyway and having stirred up dissent, never again returned to the society.

Pippa and Sally could dance and had been persuaded to lead the troupe of eight May maidens in the opening sequence as they frolicked on the green to a wide-smile and fixed-expression rendering of 'Spring, Spring, Spring' with Dawn on the gap-toothed piano. A wet winter had further disabled the dampers, which made the tune difficult to follow and a sense of rhythm vital. Seven of the maidens had this last commodity and one did not.

Robin Hunter, husband of Pat Hunter, dedicated May maiden, had elected to perform a comic song and monologue. The Hunters were incomers who lived in Southey Close. In their early thirties and childless as yet, their enthusiasm was to prove an asset to the company, although Robin's habit of forgetting his lines tried patiences to the extremes of controlled good manners.

It had been decided that the centrepiece of the show would be a short farce written in the thirties, entitled 'No Spring Chicken,' with predictable characters and plot involving husbands and wives, misunderstandings, dropped trousers, hiding in cupboards and mystified visitors. Hugo, Harriet, Henry and Sadie were to play in this, with Becky and

Robert Franklin from Harringay Crescent and Robin Hunter.

Pippa and Sally were to do a tap dance to 'Singing in the Rain', followed by Robin's monologue, 'Hast tha' seen our Mary Jane?', delivered in a Yorkshire accent with Welsh overtones. Finally, the whole company would sing a medley of choruses from popular songs. Deep bows to rapturous applause, and PADS would be on the map.

Then came the rehearsals.

* * *

Albert had satisfactorily reorganised his finances by Christmas. It had taken a few weeks but, with a bit of determination, you can do what you set out to do. His appearance helped. Not to put too fine a point on it, he scared people. One look into those eyes and they were like putty in his hands. He'd had more than his share of luck, of course. Give Lady Luck her due. Although how the postman could have confused Noonday with Nonsuch was a mystery to him.

Opening that package had been his first coup. That fool of a postman had left the post outside the back door while Albert was out in the top field. If he'd been there, Albert might have returned it, knowing that he had ordered nothing of this kind. He hardly had any post, anyway. Just circulars and the like.

He'd opened it carefully, in case it was something he might want to keep — and when he saw the video in its lurid box, he almost threw it away. He hadn't got a video machine and that sort of thing wasn't in his line. Useless. Then he thought that he might sell it, next time he was in Silminster, so he put it in the dresser drawer and forgot about it until a few days later, when he looked more closely at the address and thought that he could just be on to a good thing.

Pauline was his fount of all local knowledge and, that evening, he asked her who this Nonsuch was. When she told him, he could barely conceal his smile in his glass. Gold dust! A bigwig who lived in one of those fancy houses in Squires Lane. Married with a prissy wife and two children at private school. Company director and, best of all, running in the local elections with a good spiel about family values and decency.

Albert choked into his beer when Pauline got to that bit and she had to buy him another. All it took was one phone-call and, after a bit of bluster, Nonsuch came running. One meeting was enough to convince him that Albert meant business. Albert didn't ask for much, but ensured that it was regular. Bank account under another different name, checked monthly. He had the doctor pay him in the same way.

Albert had noticed the car parked several times and could not miss what it was parked there for, but had not realised who it was and how useful the information could be. It wasn't until the same car passed him and Pauline one Sunday, as they were returning to her house after she had treated him to the pictures in Chadbury, that he began to formulate a plan. Pauline had told him whose car it was. You didn't take your wife to a deserted farm track every lunch hour. Not unless there was something wrong with you.

They always parked over the far side of the farm, in an area not cultivated at the moment. Albert had been thinking what he could make of the acreage that would bring him extra money but needed a low outlay, and consequently had visited it quite a few times to look at it and think. The couple in the car were far too busy to notice him, but he remembered the car. In his ex-line of business, that was part of the job. Know your wheels.

The woman had been more difficult to track down. Village gossip was rife concerning the doctor and his wife in their 'open' marriage, so threats to tell his wife were a non-starter: but if she was one of his patients . . . Albert made it his job to find out. First thing to do was to get a good look at her.

On the first of December, he put his plan into action. Having checked that they were there, he slewed his car across the track where it joined onto the road and waited, sheltering behind an oak that had seen its share of country behaviour. As soon as he heard them coming, he opened up the bonnet and stared lugubriously into the engine. The doctor was reluctant to get out and the woman put her hand across her eyes, as if she had a headache. She probably had now, cooped up in that steamy car.

Albert sauntered over to explain that he had broken down and, if they wanted to get out, they would have to help him push her out of the way. The doctor was jovial, brazening it out, and between them they pushed Albert's car to the side of the track. Albert insisted on walking back to the car with him and, in doing so, managed to get a good look at his companion.

Next thing was to get her identified. Easier said than done.

For a fortnight, he looked for her in vain. She didn't necessarily live in the village, of course. The doctor's practice spread out to

Mole and Tidworth. She could be from there and she might not be his patient after all. It was all very frustrating.

A fortnight to the day of his pretended trouble with his car, he waited for them again, but this time in secret; when they turned into the road, he followed them. The doctor drove out of Pomery and dropped her on a deserted stretch of road halfway between Mole and Tidworth. Albert could see no houses here and was beginning to wonder what was going on. He had to go past her, or she would notice him slowing down and wonder what he was doing there.

When he looked into his mirror, he understood. She was getting into another car tucked into a lay-by. He might have guessed that they would not risk being seen together near her house, wherever that might be. She was getting into her own car and preparing to drive away. Automatically noting the registration number, he drove on, hoping that she would be coming this way, and not turning round to go back the way they had come.

He came to a T-junction and had to make a choice. He chose left, drawing into the side of the road and waiting for her to pass him. After five minutes, he realised that he had chosen wrongly and cursed loudly. Still. He had the registration number and for the next week, whenever he had the time, he would drive around looking at parked cars in roads and driveways. And at last he found it in the drive of a small close on the outskirts of Mole.

He called on his professional training. Watch and wait. Check that she's with the doctor on his land. Drive to her house. Ring the doorbell. Act put out. Ring neighbour's doorbell, ask for a Mrs Hickton next door.

'There's no Mrs Hickton here. Sorry. I'm Ms Cook and next door is Mrs Rodway.'

Look crestfallen and leave. Piece of cake. Ring the surgery, ask to check the time of Mrs Rodway's appointment. Worried husband speaking. 'She is on Doctor Wintergreen's list, isn't she?'

Helpful girl. 'No appointment for today. I'll just check in her file. No. There's no record of an appointment for her this week at all. Shall I make one?'

'No, thank you. Better check with her first. Goodbye.'

Bingo! Easy to fix up a meeting.

He'd paid up straight away. Couldn't do much else, could he? And now he would have almost enough money. He could milk them for as long as he liked. They weren't going to say anything. It might not be necessary to start on what was salted away, after all, if he could pull off just one more of these — and he thought he knew where to direct his attention.

Albert smiled into his beer while he waited for Pauline to arrive. Looked like his affairs were all sorted.

8

March

What erring spirit guided Robin to choose to sing 'A modern Major General', no one was ever quite sure. The possessor of dark good looks and an authoritative air, enhanced by the suspicion of embonpoint, was more than enough to make him look the part, and that is the best that can be said on the subject. His erratic memory produced memorable variations of the words which, of course, had to be repeated by the bemused chorus, who soon took on a distracted air as they strained their ears to hear and remember what they should sing next.

Robin remained blissfully unperturbed until soundly carpeted by Agatha and forced to change his choice of song if he could not find a way to memorise the words. At the next rehearsal, he was word-perfect although a little inclined toward extravagant gestures with his arms. It was unfortunate that only his wife knew that this was because the words were written in cue form on his cuffs. She did not think to mention it to Nanette, who was in charge of the wardrobe.

The May maidens were a merry group, due to be dressed in flowery frocks with festive circlets in their hair, but they practised in sweatshirts and leggings with slouch socks and trainers. Privately, Agatha thought them too substantial-looking for the wispy, ethereal creatures she had imagined, but forbore to comment. At least they were reasonably competent.

Joining Pippa and Sally in fairy dalliance on the green were Pat Hunter, wife of forgetful Robin, Becky Franklin, Barbara King from the greengrocer's, Hilary Young from the church flower circle and two teenagers, Frances and Lola, from Fullers' cottages on the road to Mole. Lola had an expression on her face that could turn milk sour but danced like a sylphide; Frances had a smile of pure sunshine and two left feet with a life of their own. She also had an unfortunate effect on inanimate objects and all things electrical. For the sake of her smile and sweet nature, Pippa and Sally rearranged the choreography and thought that they were safe.

Rehearsals were organised in two parts. The dancers and Robin would arrive at half past seven, to be put through their paces, with the actors following on at about quarter past eight. Harry had made the single set with three opening doors leading to a passage along the back, so that entrances and exits could be swift. There was also a walk-in cupboard to accommodate up to three people and a lit window giving onto the passage, so that it could appear that people were arriving from the outside and also be used as an additional comic device.

Pippa transformed the shell into an oak-panelled drawing room with 3-D furniture painted onto the wood and framed portraits hanging on the walls. An appeal to the village provided them with actual furniture to sit on or use. Fortunately, no one else wanted to use the stage and the dancers were to dance in front of the curtain and so they were able to leave the furniture in situ and devote all their time to rehearsing, which was just as well.

The surprise of the whole company was Hugo Brightside. Privately, Agatha had always disliked him for his womanising and the way he treated his wife, but it could not be denied that he was becoming their star actor. She had feared that he would let them down, by not turning up or not bothering to learn his lines, but he did not miss a single rehearsal and was word-perfect by the third week. Most importantly, he showed a gift for comedy that served as a help and encouragement to the rest of the cast. This was sorely needed.

Sadie and Henry had gone off the boil, and it was Henry who had cooled down first, to Sadie's deep annoyance. Sadie was playing Hugo's wife, who had to spend most of the play passing across the stage just after Hugo had hidden another woman in the cupboard. She would then have to wait in the passage until it was time for her to do it again. The woman hidden in the cupboard was usually Harriet, but occasionally it was Becky and sometimes both together. Harriet and Becky were good friends and had been admonished several times for missing their entrances, because they had settled down to a good gossip.

Henry played Harriet's jealous husband and Robert played Becky's, while Robin played a benign caricature of a vicar who had to call often because he had forgotten that he had called before. In his character, Henry was supposed to spend much of the time creeping about in the garden and arriving suddenly, to catch his wife unawares. In practical terms, this meant that he spent much of the time in the passage with Sadie, engaged in icy exchanges, arriving on the stage distracted, his lines lost in the frost of Sadie's retorts. In exasperation, Agatha decreed that a third person should always be present when those two were in the passage. This kept them apart but caused a bottleneck behind scenes and uncomfortable silences on stage while waiting for arrivals delayed by bodies getting entangled in the rush for the door.

After Henry's enforced entrance through the fireplace, due to overcrowding, Agatha gave an ultimatum. Either Sadie and Henry stop this nonsense, or they were both out of the production. An uneasy truce manifested itself, just enough for the show to go on. But, unknown to the merry players, a far more serious upset was waiting in the wings to appear in Pomery, which would make a lovers' tiff and PADS problems seem like a mere bagatelle.

* * *

Things were ticking along nicely. No hurry to tackle the other one, yet, but it might be useful if any unexpected expenses cropped up. Albert thought he must be dreaming when he saw the man in Pomery. Rumour had it that he'd got plenty of money and gossip from Pauline put it at the million mark. He looked as if he was living the life of Riley and wouldn't miss a pound or two.

He didn't know that Albert knew him. That was the beauty of it. Albert had all the time in the world to drop his bombshell. Funny how people never look at drivers. He hadn't given Albert a second glance when his services were called upon to ferry the man to the airport as a favour to Fraser's fence. But Albert knew all about him. That had been just before the job that caused him to be sent down — but he never forgot a face.

Things were definitely looking up. He might even marry Pauline and settle down. Try anything once. Other people had gone respectable: why not him? But a lot can change between Wednesday and Friday, as Albert was to find out and, by late Friday evening, he wasn't feeling so cocky. He had the beginnings of a suspicion that he had might have made a big mistake.

* * *

Hangdog came to visit Albert again on Thursday evening. Checking up on him. Making sure Albert did not forget that Hangdog knew where he was. Fraser sent his regards with a reminder of how much money he expected to be waiting for him when he got out. Just so that there would be no mistake.

Albert kept his face calm but pounded the packet of cigarettes in his pocket until they rolled into a tight ball. Thinking of Fraser always had that effect on him.

When he opened the door on Friday evening, he was surprised to see who it was but not too alarmed. The mountain had come to Mohammed, but it made no difference. It was unnerving to find that he had been recognised, after all, but it still didn't change anything. He still held all the cards. All the same, when his visitor had gone, he began to have second thoughts about his expanding business interests, as he liked to call them. For the first time since he'd started, he began to see that they could be seriously dangerous to his well-being, but a week passed with no more incident and he began to relax.

There was a darts match on the following Friday night and Albert went with Pauline. Strange how, for the first time in his life, he was beginning to feel that he belonged. He wasn't sure if it was for him, yet, but it seemed to be better than anything he'd ever had before. If he could only get rid of the cloud of annoyance generated from behind bars and manifested in the shape of Hangdog, he might almost be happy. He could even move in with Pauline quite soon, perhaps. No need for the sideline, then. He could be completely legit for the first time since he was seventeen.

This thought buoyed him along as he watched Pauline's team win their match and, when they left together as a couple, his head was full of plans that tentatively included the two of them.

Pauline was quietly pleased with herself for helping her team to win the match and enjoyed walking in silence with Albert at her side. Albert said little, still wondering if what he planned was possible. They went back to Pauline's cottage, where she put the kettle on and rummaged in the kitchen to see what she could find for them to eat. She found a plate of sausage rolls that had been left over from the W.I. on Tuesday and, because he could see that they were not Pauline's offerings, he ate several before she could find some of her own cooking for him to try.

After he had gone, she ate two herself and then went to bed. Waking up at three, she was violently sick and blamed the sausage rolls. When they found the body, the next day, she blamed them again at first, but couldn't have been more wrong.

⋆ ⋆ ⋆

It was Tom Denton, the postman, who made the discovery. There was a parcel to sign for and he was blowed if he was coming all this way again. He'd got into trouble about another parcel that was supposed to have been sent to Pomery and not arrived, so he was being extra careful, this time.

Past eight o'clock, and all the curtains still drawn. Farmers didn't lie in. Tom knocked loudly on the door and peered through the window, shouting Albert's name. He'd better hurry up. It looked like rain again.

Tom walked round to the back and found that a window had been forced open. The splintered frame was twisted outward and little flakes of green paint were sprinkled on the windowsill. Worried, he went back to the front door and called again, this time trying the handle. To his uneasy surprise, it opened, and he listened for a moment before putting his bag down and going in. As he was to tell afterward, there was a silence of the sort that makes your spine tingle and he felt like running away, but couldn't.

He stood where he was and shouted, straining his ears for an answer before beginning to look in the rooms. It was much neater and tidier than he had expected and he supposed that it was due to Pauline's influence. No good at cooking, but she could clean, all right.

The bungalow was arranged in the form of a T, with three bedrooms and a bathroom forming the upright stroke, and a sitting room and kitchen the horizontal. There was only one door, which opened into a small hall.

Tom hesitated, unnerved by the silence, and then walked toward the sitting room. From the doorway, he noticed an empty bottle of whisky on the table with two glasses beside it, and thought he might understand — although if the other person was Pauline, it wasn't like her. Reluctant to search further now, in case he should embarrass the two of them together, he called out again, stubbornly determined not to go away without an answer or explanation. He had just shouted for the second time when he heard a noise behind him and turned round sharply to see Pauline coming in the front door.

She gave him a fright, appearing like that, but when he told her how long he had been trying to make someone hear, it was Pauline who was frightened. She kept thinking about those sausage rolls. They decided to go into his bedroom together and found the body straight away.

They saw the still mound on the bed and held their breaths, willing their ears to pick up the sound of breathing in the room, but they were to be disappointed. Tom glanced at Pauline and saw that, in a matter of seconds, the colour had drained from her face.

Cautiously, unused to the unexpected in their lives, they approached the bed and forced themselves to look at a flour-white face with eyes that stared vacantly at the ceiling. There was no doubt that the man was dead. And that wasn't all. There was a sound in the passage. Someone else was in the house, coming closer and closer with shuffling footsteps. They turned to see a shadow emerge into the light. Standing swaying in the doorway was Albert Noonday, looking almost as pale as the man in the bed — who was a total stranger to Tom and Pauline.

* * *

News came via the Post Office, where Winnie Tomkin presided over the Pomery gossip with the expertise of a seasoned chairperson. Tom had come back from Burnt Oak with a policeman in tow, parked his bag and then gone off again to the station to give his statement. Not before she'd got it out of him, though. Fancy! A murder, here in Pomery. She'd always said there was something fishy about that Noonday! Those who couldn't crowd into the Post Office got their news second hand from those who spilt out onto the pavement and then took it into the general stores for a third hand airing. By midday, the man had been strangled, poisoned, shot, stabbed, or frightened to death.

At last, the knots of excited whisperers dispersed and the village seemed to get back to normal, but the atmosphere was electric with anticipation. A murder and a murderer in the same house in Pomery. Who would have thought it? No one doubted from the beginning that it was Albert who was responsible.

* * *

Inspector Peter Datchett, a long thin sort of policeman with thinning mousy hair, and Sergeant Barbara Treeve, a blonde, slim, elegant sort of policewoman, were interviewing Albert Noonday, a.k.a. Newington, in connection with the death of one Lee Ringmer, known in the criminal fraternity as Hangdog because of his expression and hound-like devotion to Fraser Roberts, resident psychopath of Brigtown jail.

The stuffy interview room in Chadbury police station was made more uncomfortable by the long silences that punctuated each question asked by Datchett. Albert exercised his right to remain silent, after declaring himself to be innocent of this crime that had occurred in his own bed. He hadn't been in his bed at the time, he said.

Albert's record had been studied and, as far as they were aware, he had never been involved in crimes of violence. Or else he had never been caught before. That and not running away were the two anomalies in what should have been an open and shut case. A falling out of thieves culminating in murder.

Datchett was not happy. It didn't feel right. But they had enough to hold him for forty-eight hours. Forensic might come up with something by then.

Tom and a tearful Pauline were allowed to return to Pomery, once their statements had been taken. Apart from an obsession about sausage rolls on the woman's part, what they had to say was straightforward. The forced window was being checked by the SOCO, but Datchett thought that Noonday could have done it to divert suspicion. Not his style, though. He was a worried man. He had the feeling that this was one of those cases that would produce the least amount of satisfaction and the maximum amount of aggravation.

His long nose was proved to be unerringly

right. As if the murder wasn't enough to puzzle over, when they searched the bungalow, they opened the parcel which the postman had been trying to deliver. Inside, exquisitely wrapped in silver paper with a blue bow, was a rat which had been dead for several days and kept somewhere warm.

9

April

Matilda Golightly looked around at the assembled company and smiled complacently. She had triumphed again with her faultless organisation. They had enjoyed a splendid dinner and were now relaxing in the state room especially adapted for this luxurious cruise. Discreet service ensured that glasses were never empty — that was not a good idea, in one or two cases — but the stewards were very experienced at helping any of their passengers to bed, should the need arise.

They were a varied bunch, brought together by an interest in art, although the nature of this interest differed sharply from one to the other. Among the group, the academics and the innocent search for what is good and true vied with commercialism, while some simply wanted a convenient reason for indulging their zest for travel.

Matilda fell into this category. A naturally gregarious lady, she had devised the first tour after the death of her fifth husband, recruiting by means of advertisement in the Lady. Given this way of making contact, she was astonished and delighted to find that her motley crew came from all walks of life.

She had begun the saga of Pomery-upon-Axle during the main course and, as her voice was louder than everyone else's, she continued without interruption until coffee was served in this sumptuous room. By now, she had reached the part where she became actively involved and the mention of murder kept her audience listening — although not all were in thrall.

'I had not been inactive during my stay at my sister's house and already knew much more about the village and its habits than my sister, who has lived there since her marriage. She never listens, you see.'

This statement caused one or two amused looks to be exchanged, but the story was becoming too interesting to risk interruption. There was a general settling down into soft furniture as all heads turned expectantly toward Matilda Golightly, five times widow of Bath, founder member of this merry band of pilgrims.

As she had said, Matilda had not been idle during her enforced stay at the Manor. Her days were divided between her tapestry — which she had set herself to finish before the end of May — and getting to know the village and its inhabitants. Leonora introduced her to all those whom she thought she ought to know, but Matilda preferred to make her own judgements in these matters and had soon formed her own opinions.

Her fieldwork in this area stood her in good stead when Albert Noonday became prime suspect for the murder of Lee Ringmer: although when Matilda read about his nickname, she always thought of him as Hangdog. Leonora had been outraged that she should have been duped by Noonday, whose real name was revealed to be Newington, and who had spent ten years of his adult life behind bars. When he took over the tenancy of Burnt Oak farm, he had not long been out of prison after serving three of five years for his part in a daring robbery on a bank in Birmingham, where the gang had tunnelled through from the fashionable boutique next door.

They were only caught because a member of the gang had a fetish for women's clothing and wore a designer outfit to a disco, where he was spotted by an off-duty policeman who recognised the garment from the description sent out after the raid. He was sent to a different prison from the others for fear that his wish to appear as a woman might be part-way granted if he came into contact with Fraser Roberts and his faithful hound.

The money was never recovered and, although carrots of reduced sentences were dangled in front of all the members of the gang, none of them would tell where it was. The police theory was that Hangdog and Noonday had teamed up to dip into the money before Fraser and the others got out, and that Noonday got greedy. It didn't quite equate with what they knew about Fraser Roberts. Conning him was a dangerous thing to do, but maybe the two of them had a plan. Peter Datchett's maxim was never to be surprised at the optimism of the criminal fraternity, when it came to putting one over on each other or the constabulary.

Matilda was interested in the case from the start. She wanted to help poor Pauline and, besides that, she had been watching Albert Noonday ever since he arrived and she had formed her own ideas about what he got up to in his spare time.

Her active part in the solving of the mystery began on the afternoon of the murder. Leonora had arranged a committee meeting for the fete and nothing short of a sick horse would have caused it to be cancelled. Lowering clouds, which had threatened all day, finally gave up the uneven contest and capitulated, just as most people were setting out for the Manor. The sudden heavy rain shower, incorporating sharp pieces of hail, caught them all; they arrived very wet and in need of hot tea.

Leonora invited her guests into the drawing room, where Mrs Routledge, the housekeeper, brought them their tea and lit the fire. Matilda arrived last, and was immediately commandeered to help run the white elephant with Sally and Pauline. After that, there seemed to be no other topic of conversation than the murder.

'Poor Pauline,' Sally sighed. 'She's been so happy, these last few weeks.' A thought struck her. 'Where is she now? Is there anyone with her? Nick is at home with the children, but he ought to be visiting her, to see if he can help.'

'Enid went back to wait for her, this morning. She'll probably stay the night, as well, so Pauline's all right for the moment,' said Mary Stringer, looking up lazily. She resumed gazing thoughtfully into her teacup but missed nothing, watching the proceedings from under her sweeping brown lashes.

'I suppose we should be grateful that he killed that man and didn't butcher poor Pauline,' added Agatha, waxing self-conscious concern.

'Are they saying that Noonday killed him?' asked Matilda innocently.

'Really, Matilda. Who else could it have been?' Contempt and sisterly oneupmanship from Leonora.

'Funny that he didn't run away. Mrs Tomkin was telling me that Tom told her that Noonday came into the room when he and Pauline were there. Looked as if he'd just woken up. And he overheard one of the policemen saying that the man had been dead a good few hours. If he'd killed him that long time ago, why didn't he run away?'

Matilda covertly studied the reactions. Puzzlement with a dollop of unease. They all wanted it to be Noonday. Because, if it wasn't, the murderer could be at large and strike again. Closer to home, maybe.

The door opened onto preoccupied silence as each one present thought about their safety and that of their families. Quentin Weatherby stood for a second, framed in the doorway, before catching Leonora's eye and seating himself on the edge of the gathering. He was a retired head of an accountancy firm and had volunteered his services as fete treasurer. As the previous owner of this title wanted to stand down, his offer had been accepted. He had moved into 'Foxholes' in Squires Lane just before Christmas, and had soon made himself a part of the village.

Leonora did her hostess bit.

'Quentin! Do come in and make yourself comfortable. Agatha, will you find Quentin some tea?'

Agatha looked as if she would rather find him poison, but had no alternative but to pour the tea herself. She hoped that it was cold.

Matilda played a favourite private game with herself. It only worked with men, of which species she possessed unlimited knowledge. She viewed the new arrival with detachment, as if she had never met him before. Tall, silver-haired, elegant. Strong features. No moustache.

Matilda wasn't fond of moustaches. William had had a moustache, when she'd first met him, and she made him shave it off. It was maintained that his death from blood poisoning, soon after they were married, was due to a cut sustained while making sure that his face was smooth enough to pass muster. Total rubbish, of course. Newspapers will say anything, nowadays.

Where was she? Oh yes. Thickening round the waist but a firm body still. A fine figure of a man, although he was stooping a little today, as if he had had a disappointment. Watchful eyes. She wondered again why there was no wife in tow. Definitely a man with a past. She really must get to know him better.

He accepted his cup and sat down carefully. Agatha recovered herself enough to sit near him and engage him in conversation.

'We were talking about the murder. It's put rather a dampener on the day, I'm afraid.'

Clear blue eyes ranged round the assembled company before he answered, in a voice smooth as honey, 'Does anyone know who the victim is?'

Leonora took charge and snapped briskly, 'A stranger. A friend of Mr Noonday, as far as we can gather. I think we've exhausted the subject, don't you? Let's talk of more pleasant matters.'

For the next hour, the organisation of the fete was the sole topic of conversation. Leonora was in command — as she had been, for the last twenty-six years — and, to the annoyance of others, she did it very well. They had just decided to pause for more tea when Wing entered the room with the news that there was a telephone call for Mrs Golightly and would she like to take it in the study?

It took a minute or two for the caller to understand that she had to shout, but eventually Matilda found out that it was Enid Brandon on behalf of Pauline, asking if Mrs

Golightly could spare a few minutes to come and talk to her. Matilda said that she would come straight away.

She had spoken to Pauline before. Pauline had been rather in awe of her, but Matilda was used to that. Most people were. Matilda had had her doubts about Noonday's suitability as suitor, but could see no ulterior motive for his interest in her. Pauline had no money and her cottage was rented. She earnt her living by charring for others and helped out in the Post Office on two afternoons a week.

A tingle of apprehension ran down her spine. Could that be it? Had he been planning to rob the Post Office by using Pauline's innocent information to help him? She did hope not. She really hoped not.

Enid Brandon opened the door and Matilda stepped through quickly from under the dripping grey thatch. Pauline was in her overstuffed armchair, with red-rimmed eyes, pale and haunted. Enid went to put the kettle on.

Matilda reflected on the general inconvenience of deafness and especially now, when dealing with someone who was in shock. She knew that she shouted, but she couldn't help it. And, unless Pauline spoke up, Matilda would never be able to help her. Pauline didn't look capable of raising her voice to a mouse.

Sighing inwardly, she produced from her capacious handbag her *bête noir*, the hated devil's device that only saw the light of day in extreme circumstances. She attached herself to it and switched on. With her hearing aid in, she was able to hear Pauline tell her what had happened this morning when she went to call on Albert Noonday.

* * *

The party at the Manor broke up after Matilda left and, as by now the rain had a sullen, set-in look about it, not many people stirred out of their houses once reaching home.

Agatha's husband had returned during the day, but had not bothered to seek out his wife. He was well into his stamp album by the time Agatha returned, and stayed in his study all evening. Agatha settled down to read some plays that had been suggested for the next PADS production — in an effort to take her mind off the current one, which was heading for disaster — and hoped that the murderer had indeed been Albert Noonday. For the first time in their marriage, she wished that Gerald did not have to work away so much.

The Frenches and the Needhams had supper together in the Frenches's house. Gillian and Hattie had the run of the sitting room for their games and then afterward they were allowed to watch a video while their parents talked. Nanette listened to them playing and tried not to think about what was uppermost in her mind.

* * *

Simon Wintergreen was on call and edgy. Maureen studied him from behind her book and wondered what was wrong. He was trying to read, too, but he had not turned a page in ten minutes. Twice, he had jumped up when the phone rang and had seemed almost disappointed when the calls were of the selling double glazing variety. She supposed that it was the current girlfriend causing trouble. Sometimes she wondered why she stayed with him. He was so transparent. It was a relief when a call from a patient came and he left the house with barely a goodbye.

* * *

Hugo stayed in, as he had done every night recently, and Briony knew it was the right time to follow Matilda's advice, but she doubted that she could.

Matilda had come across her doing the church flowers after Christmas, when all she could find had been evergreen leaves and branches. Somehow, they seemed to echo her own life. Bare and uninspired. She had been indulging in a rare bout of selfpity when she found that she was not alone.

Matilda's greeting had made her jump but she appreciated the companionship as they set about the vases together. Why she had confided in her, she still didn't know. Matilda, of all people. She'd had to shout it out. Broadcast her unhappiness and Hugo's infidelity. She told Matilda how they rattled around, barely speaking to each other, in their over-large house she longed to fill with children. Strange how much better she had felt, just by doing that.

And then Matilda's cheerful advice. Give as good as you get. Don't let him tread on you. Put him in the wrong for a change.

Common sense told her that Matilda was right. But knowing and doing are two different things. He would begin to look around for someone else to amuse him, soon. Bound to, but in the meantime, tomorrow was Sunday, which seemed to be the day that brought out the worst in both of them. If she was going to do it, that was the time. Tomorrow morning, when he started to make her late for church.

The rain began to drip out of the waste pipe onto some flowerpots she'd left underneath and the steady rhythm got into her brain, tormenting her until she had to go outside and move them. It was late by then and the lane very dark and still. Through the trees, she could see the soft lights of Sadie Strangelove's house shining muzzily, made mysterious by the curtain of drizzle. A movement from the lane caught her attention and she peered into the night.

She had felt rather than heard someone there, walking past her up the lane. Whoever it was moved softly and it was too dark to see properly, but she was sure that she recognised them. Surely it was Georgina and Thomas Babbington-Banbury hurrying toward the manor. Where had they been, all by themselves, so late?

Shaking her head, Briony went back indoors and turned the key. She supposed that the murderer had to be Albert Noonday. Matilda hadn't seemed convinced, this afternoon. She locked the back door and all the windows and went to bed.

* * *

The murderer slept badly that night. How to be quite sure? There was nothing that could be done about it at the moment. It would have to be the waiting game, again: but, one thing for certain, it was not all over yet.

* * *

Matilda promised that she would help Pauline and to this end made out a plan of campaign. First engage a good lawyer for the hapless Noonday, so that she could find out from him what he had told the police and ask a few questions of her own. Then there were several residents of Pomery-upon-Axle who had a lot of explaining to do, starting with the man who was a friend of her own niece and nephew. She resolved to attend to this straight away.

Matilda liked nothing better than a tramp through the woods and, straight after breakfast every morning and after tea in the afternoon, she would take the circular route from the manor and back again. If Henry was not about, she took the dogs. They did not need supervision, because they knew the route blindfold, and so it was a good time for her to think about Pomery and those who lived there.

It was surprising whom she met under the trees. There were the regular walkers alone or with dogs, the occasional pair of lovers, moody adolescents or someone with the world on their shoulders gone to the woods to think it all out.

Edgar Bryan was one of the occasionals. Leonora claimed that he walked there at unsociable hours and that he was up to something. The vicar had been unable to discover that he was doing anything wrong, but Leonora remained unconvinced. She instructed Matilda to keep an eye on him. Leonora would have been surprised to know that Matilda was already doing this very thing: because when she at last succeeded in following the twins, one moonlit night, it was to Edgar Bryan's cottage that they went.

Alarmed, she had waited in the darkness, unsure of how to proceed. She knew that she couldn't take chances with their safety, but she had heard them returning from one of these jaunts before and they had seemed in high spirits. They didn't seem to be throwing money about, and they did not behave oddly. At least, no more oddly than was usual for a Babbington-Banbury. She was willing to swear that whatever happened in there was completely innocent, but why wait until dark if this was so?

She had stood, irresolute, for a few minutes and then taken action. She crept up the path and peered through the windows at the front of the house.

The curtains were drawn, but there was a chink of light through which she could see someone moving. She recognised Edgar Bryan, but could not see what he was doing. He was standing up and appeared to be looking at something on the floor. Every now and then, he darted forward, but Matilda could not see what he did before he moved back again. She could hear the twins talking excitedly on the other side of the room. One thing was clear. They were in no danger and, if they found out that she had been spying on them, all trust would be gone. Matilda had gone home, making up her mind to speak to Edgar Bryan at the earliest opportunity.

She watched for him all the next day and, when she spotted his small figure entering the wood, she followed, her brogued feet scuffling heavily among the dead leaves. She caught up with him in a clearing where an old iron horse trough was rusting into the leaf layer and hailed him before he could disappear into the beech coppice.

He did not look surprised. After all, he must have heard her, but he looked wary. Never one to beat about the bush, she had asked him straight away why the twins visited him and he had told her. As far as Matilda was concerned, that was that.

After this first meeting, they often caught up with each other and Matilda found in him a kindred spirit. Both were amateur students of psychology and both were made curious by strange behaviour in their fellow man. Edgar Bryan had detected something odd about Albert Noonday before all this business had begun, too.

Matilda trudged along in the rain with her yellow sou'wester pulled down over her ears. Her head still rang from using that dratted instrument. A trickle of cold rain made its own chute and filled her collar down one side; her efforts to march along to a rousing chorus from *Carmen* were temporarily halted while she hunched up her shoulders to get rid of the rest.

Edgar's cottage glowed dimly through a grey pattern of raindrops. She was hurried in out of the wet and sat down in front of a bright and sweet-smelling apple-log fire. Her host rattled about in the kitchen and produced a cup of steaming grog, which hit the spot at the first sip.

'When you're ready,' he encouraged, leaning back in his chair.

Matilda enjoyed the quiet warmth a little

longer before beginning, 'First thing that strikes me is what was he doing in Albert's bed?' She held her hands round the chunky glass and let the steam warm her nose.

Edgar shifted uncomfortably, picking up his own drink as if the glass were too hot to hold. 'There could be an explanation for that.' He looked at her candidly.

Matilda knew about the world and did not need this delicacy. But she lowered her eyes modestly as seemed to be expected. 'But if that's the case, why was Albert sleeping somewhere else?'

'Single bed, was it?'

'I don't know. I can ask Pauline.'

'Albert could have been uncomfortable. Spent the rest of the night . . . Where did he spend the night?'

'On the sofa, Pauline thinks. Although he came from the bathroom when he heard their voices.'

'Funny sort of an arrangement. The man been dead several hours, did you say? Any idea how he was killed? And is it certain that it was murder?'

'No, on both counts. Pauline was very unsure. She thinks that there was blood on the carpet by the bed, but the carpet itself is dark and so are the sheets and blankets. She was too confused to take it all in. All she knows is that Albert thought it murder straight away and she heard the policeman in charge say so, too. Of course, it was all round the village in an hour, thanks to Winnie Tomkin: and so that is what everyone in Pomery thinks now.'

Matilda said what was uppermost in her mind, knowing that Edgar would treat it with detachment, and keep it in confidence. 'Edgar, if it wasn't Albert and it was murder, how did the murderer know that this man was in Albert's bed?'

'No way of knowing, before. Must have had a good look round first.'

'And how did he know that the man was there in the house in the first place? Pauline didn't know anything about him. He must have turned up out of the blue, so how did anyone know he was there?'

'What are you getting at?' But Edgar already knew. If Albert was innocent, the murderer had not intended to kill the stranger but Albert himself. He had expected to find one man in bed and, when he did, coming upon him in the dark, he killed him, thinking that his victim was Albert. That could mean that the murderer was someone whom Albert had got to know since moving to the village, someone who lived in Pomery itself.

Inspector Datchett passed the bank statements found in Albert's dresser drawer over to Sergeant Treeve. 'What do you make of these?'

Barbara Treeve wrinkled her pretty nose as she read carefully through the entries. At length, she passed it back to the Inspector. 'Regular deposits. Small amounts. Could it be blackmail? Has he done this before?'

'Not on record, he hasn't.'

'If he was all right for money, why should he need to kill Hangdog? He could afford to wait until Fraser gets out. They'll go for the money then, won't they?'

'Do you know what I think?'

'What?'

'I think we've got the wrong man.'

'Sir?'

'But we'll give him a run for his money, eh?' Peter Datchett grinned wolfishly. It was not often that he permitted himself to smile. He didn't like villains who disturbed his peace — and Albert Noonday was a villain, in his book. He didn't believe the new leaf business. Once a villain, *et cetera, et cetera*. Albert Noonday didn't know it, yet, but he was in for a bad time.

10

Matilda engaged young Fortesque of Gibbs, Gibbs and Truebody to represent Albert. She did so for Pauline's sake and because she had always championed the underdog and did not believe Albert Noonday to be guilty. Her particular request to engage the youngest member of the firm had surprised Gibbs *père* and the urbane Truebody, but Matilda was rich enough to call her own tune and they readily complied.

Matilda wanted someone inexperienced whom she could bully. She needed to be privy to any confidential conversation he might have with his client and to keep tabs on any new developments, for she had decided in her wisdom to solve this case herself. Matilda was no stranger to sudden death.

On Monday morning, she borrowed the Rolls without asking if she might, and drove into Chadbury to wait outside the police station until Fortesque emerged. It was a pleasant sunny day and she watched the street become alive with people intent on living their day. She especially liked to watch the young couples arm in arm, engrossed in each other's company. An old hand at love, she could have taught them a thing or two. Smiling with her reminiscences, she almost missed him as he hurried importantly down the steps.

Jeremy Fortesque was puzzled as to why he had been chosen for this job and more than a little daunted. His pale face was creased with worry as he ran down the steps, his fair hair flapping in his eyes and his bulging briefcase threatening to burst its white papers like a head of cotton. He had no experience in dealing with murder and had been holding on to the hope that Albert would plead guilty, changing his own responsibility to damage limitation. But Albert had been adamant. He was innocent, and Fortesque would have to prove it.

Matilda's shriek pierced through his anxious catalogue of all the things that could go wrong and the ways in that his career could be blighted and, before he knew it, he had been yanked into the Rolls and was facing the third degree, himself. It didn't take Matilda long to find out all she needed to know.

* * *

Monday morning in Pomery saw everyone going about their business as usual, but there was a different atmosphere. Murder had left its shadow. There was a watchfulness, a carefulness of speech when all most people wanted to do was to shout it from the church tower. Murder in your own backyard is sensational. And frightening.

Nanette was taking the girls to school this morning because Harriet had to be in early for stocktaking. She held their hands tightly, one either side and they jumped up and down as they walked, chattering all the while. She couldn't listen to half of what they were saying because her mind was full to bursting with her own thoughts. On the way home, she would go into the church to sit for a while. If she went home straight away, she would find some housework or gardening to do and the time — her time — would be gone.

She waited outside the gates until the whistle went and with a final wave to the little girls headed for St Wilfrid's, cool but welcoming in the early morning sunshine.

* * *

Henry junior was on cloud nine. The visit to her studio had gone well and now she had agreed to have a meal with him in Chadbury, tomorrow night. This anticipation sustained him as he strolled through the lower meadow, swishing the grass with a hazel wand, while fancying himself as a young Constable on the look out for suitable hay wains. Lord of all he surveyed.

It was a well-guarded secret that Henry himself was no mean artist. Well guarded by Henry, that is. It was always a worry that someone would find out and suggest that he painted for a living. Having reached the age of twenty-five without ever having earnt so much as a penny, it would be a great inconvenience for him to have to do so now. However, he did not want to appear to be spineless in Pippa's eyes. Not that she had said anything. She was too kind to do that. But his lack of employment was beginning to make him feel uncomfortable whenever he was in Pippa's company.

He had brought his sketch book with him again today. Had been carrying it around for a month or so now. Wouldn't do any harm to make a few more rough drawings. Might even work one of them up into a whole canvas. Henry wandered on, happily ignorant that, tucked away on a page of his sketch book under his arm, were a few lines of innocent pencil drawing which identified a killer.

* * *

Jeremy Fortesque was mesmerised by her voice and that gap-toothed smile, which danced about in front of his eyes. He was being anaesthetised by a circular saw. This was sound in the round and he couldn't get away from it. He knew that he would tell her anything that she wanted to know, not being made of sterner stuff.

Albert Noonday had no alibi. This was the first worrying fact that had become immediately apparent. According to Albert, he had got home from Pauline's house, feeling ill, and gone straight into the bathroom — where he had stayed for a long time. He hadn't seen the whisky bottle and glasses straight away. The front door had been unlocked, but he put that down to his own carelessness. When he had felt strong enough to leave the bathroom, he had gone into his bedroom and tripped over Hangdog's boots. Seeing the mound in his bed, he thought Hangdog to be asleep and retired crossly to the sofa, where he spent an uncomfortable night with many more visits to the bathroom.

When Tom and Pauline arrived, he had been sitting slumped on the bathroom floor where he had collapsed, exhausted and dehydrated. He had neither seen nor heard anything and was as shocked as them to find Hangdog dead in his own bed.

He had not been so forthcoming on the reasons for Hangdog's visit, but Matilda thought that she could dismiss that as unimportant. The killer had wanted to kill Albert: of this she was quite sure. If Hangdog was part of the scheme, why not arrive and do it openly? Kill both of them, if necessary.

The window bothered her, too. Why had it been forced? Had the murderer got in that way and left by unlocking the front door? Had there been a key in the door? She must ask Tom. Or was the damaged window just a blind? And how did anyone know that Hangdog was in Albert's bed? It didn't make sense. Matilda let the unfortunate Jeremy Fortesque go and drove back to Pomery with the intention of making several enquiries of her own.

⋆ ⋆ ⋆

Matilda's deafness, an affliction of her later years, had been a source of annoyance to her from its onset but she was nothing if not resourceful, and more than compensated for this deficiency by a shrewd observation of her fellow man. She had become adept at intercepting a look, a smile, a movement and was fluent in body language. Nothing passed her eagle-eyed gaze, and her short stay in

Pomery had been packed with visual innuendo that it was now the time to recall and rearrange.

Leonora's blistering attack on Matilda's retreating back occasioned by the unlawful borrowing of the Rolls floated away into the fresh March winds. Matilda pretended not to hear and quickened her step. Nothing like a good walk to untangle the ideas. She needed to concentrate on the cameos etched in the corners of her mind. One of those snap shots might hold the key to Hangdog's killer.

She set off in the opposite direction to Edgar Bryan's house. She would sound him out again later when her own mind was clearer. What she wanted to do now was to go through the pictures she had retained of Albert in the company of various residents of Pomery and glean what clues she might.

As soon as she saw him, she knew that he was hiding something and was not all that he seemed. He had a wary look about him, coupled with defiance. He was daring people to challenge him, using the threat of confrontation as his defence and protection. What she had not known was if his secret was ordinary human guilt or something more serious. She had made it her business to watch him at every opportunity.

The woods at the back of the manor

bordered onto Burnt Oak farm, which belonged to the estate, and so in theory she could walk across the farmland whenever the fancy took her. She began to make it a part of her daily walk and saw that he was annoyed by it. Whether out of cussedness or because he had something to hide, she did not know, but she had no intention of stopping.

She noticed the change in him just before Christmas. An assurance of step, a less prickly back turned on her as she strode past him while he was working in the field. She knew that something had happened and didn't think that it could be all to do with Pauline. There could be many innocent explanations and she might have accepted one of them, but for a meeting that she had witnessed in late November and for which she could think of no satisfactory reason.

Leonora had introduced her to Adrian Nonsuch during her first week's stay in Pomery and Matilda had taken an instant dislike to him and his brittle platinum wife. The Babbington-Banburys held an evening drinks party to help Matilda settle in and invited those whom Leonora thought that she ought to know. There was always a jostling of places when an invitation to the manor came up and everyone found that they could come. The Nonsuches arrived last and proceeded to quarter the company like a dog searching for its bone, sniffing out who could be useful to them and for whom they had no use at all. As Matilda was temporary, she came into the latter category.

Matilda rarely actively disliked anyone, but in this case she had been forced to make an exception. It came as no surprise to her that he was engaged upon entering politics. A slightly built man with small features and dark brown hair beginning to recede, he applied his oily charm with a spade and looked people squarely in the eye as if he had nothing to hide. Matilda knew that people who did this invariably had.

His carefully groomed wife had a mouth like a rat trap with white, pointed little teeth guarding a small pink tongue. She chose whom she wanted to charm with care and cold-shouldered the rest — unlike her husband, who at least managed a degree of subtlety. Matilda immediately thought back to this strutting display when she saw Albert and Adrian in conversation outside Albert's house early one morning in late November.

She saw them from a distance and Adrian had his back to her, but she could tell that they were arguing. Not a visit to canvas his vote, then. She stayed among some winter-stark trees and waited, intrigued as to the outcome. As she watched, Adrian stormed off, evidently worsted in the argument, and Albert stood in the doorway, watching his progress across the yard into the woods. When Adrian was out of sight, Albert slowly shut the door. Matilda had gone thoughtfully on her way.

She reached the stump of an oak which had been struck by lightning and sat down, pulling her notebook out of her pocket. *Ask Albert about Adrian Nonsuch*. Her first instruction to Jeremy Fortesque. She was getting under way.

* * *

Inspector Datchett was there in his deductions before Matilda and was able to ask Albert before Fortesque had the chance. It took two days for fear to triumph over a natural disinclination to admit to a crime for which he could be prosecuted, but eventually Albert confessed to blackmailing Adrian Nonsuch and Simon Wintergreen.

By the time that he had been held in custody for three days, Albert knew naked fear for the first time in his life. He was sure that he had been the intended victim all along but was unsure of who it was who wanted him dead so badly. He reasoned that if he admitted to the blackmail, the police would inform his victims and, whether they were innocent or guilty of Hangdog's murder, they would hardly risk murdering him if they didn't press charges and he was released. His big problem was, what if it wasn't them? He had offended enough people in his time for the field to be well populated with contenders for wishing him dead. What if one of them had found out where he lived? There would be nothing to stop them from coming back.

He had toyed with confessing anyway, to avoid being released, but if it was someone from his blagging days, he could be got to inside just as easily. And he had sworn that he was never going back inside. At least freedom meant he didn't have to stay in Pomery. He could choose where he went, once released. All this had been going round his head since his arrest, until Datchett interviewed him again on Wednesday morning.

Wednesday afternoon saw Datchett and the delectable Treeve calling at the home of Adrian Nonsuch to ascertain his whereabouts from Camilla Nonsuch. She looked down her nose at them as far as where their regulation boots would have been, had they worn them, before biting off the name of the firm and spitting it at them. Barbara Treeve suppressed a smirk as they climbed into the car and pointed it toward Chadbury. Datchett hadn't made an impression there, then.

Adrian Nonsuch was a company director for a firm specialising in ceramics. Much of the work was exported, but some ended up in Harrods at vastly inflated prices. His offices were housed in a new complex of office buildings between Chadbury and Silminster. Planning permission had been hard to get and was only granted if the development stayed small and select. Tasteful trees and shrubs masked the building from the road, soft brick-work trying to blend in with nature. Even the sign announcing who could be found at this address was so small and discreet that Datchett missed the turn-in, first time round. This did not improve his temper, already rattled by Camilla Nonsuch, and he applied the brakes with unnecessary force when they eventually came to a stop in the car park. He moved over to park in a space reserved for an executive by the name of George Grafton. Tough luck, George.

A carefully enamelled receptionist doubted if the great man could see anyone before Friday, and was unimpressed by the badge and the official request. Datchett held firm, but it was in her own good time that they followed a pair of good legs into a sanitised lift which purred up to the top floor. Adrian

Nonsuch's office would have housed a family of nine on its half-acre of pale-blue Wilton, and he sat behind a huge desk with nothing on it except a telephone. Busy day he must be having. Datchett felt sour.

Nonsuch rose to greet them, a carefully controlled smile raising the corners of his mouth. Indicating that they could sit, he resumed his own seat and looked at them enquiringly. They sat, as instructed, and Datchett was straight in there, in no mood for preambles.

'Mr Nonsuch, where were you between midnight last Friday and eight o'clock on Saturday morning?'

If Adrian Nonsuch was surprised at the question, he gave no sign of it. Did that indicate guilt or indifference? wondered Treeve. Anyone's guess, at this stage.

He leant back into his chair and she saw the thoughts crowding through his mind and flitting across his face. In this respect, she was in complete agreement with Sadie and Matilda. Men were so transparent. Which explanation would he decide on? she wondered. Or would he demand to know why he was being asked such a question and refuse to answer? It was obvious that he was exercising his freedom to choose, weighing up all the permutations. Datchett sat beside her, tense and impatient, his skeletal body burning off extra fat with each minute that passed.

Adrian Nonsuch moved forward and sighed. He'd obviously made his decision. 'At home and in bed, Inspector.' His tight smile looked like thin lemon peel. 'Why do you want to know?'

'We'll ask the questions, sir, if you don't mind.'

Nonsuch looked amused, now, and Datchett was further rattled. He tried again. Shock tactics. 'Mr Nonsuch, we know you to have been the victim of a blackmailer, and that you have been making regular payments to him since November.'

Nonsuch raised his eyebrows but a wary shadow coloured his face. He made to say something, but hesitated. Datchett saw the chink. 'Any information that you give us will be treated as confidential.'

Nonsuch made up his mind, and took control again. 'I'm sorry, Inspector. I don't know what you are talking about.'

He looked at them with his candid blue eyes and thin smile.

Datchett sighed gently, knowing for certain now that it was going to be one of those days.

* * *

Matilda attended the sewing afternoon as usual. Her travels began again in two weeks and she had almost finished her kneelers. She thought that she would bring them along to the session and pick up any gossip while she was there. It was surprising what was said to her, even though she was a stranger. She was just that kind of person who invited confidences. In emergencies, she was quite good at lip-reading.

Agatha was there and Mary Stringer, struggling with a complicated piece of needlepoint that she had been too proud to refuse when it was allocated to her. Nanette came late, looking pale, not quite her usual self at all, and Becky Franklin arrived with Pat Hunter. Briony came by herself, looking happier than Matilda had ever seen her look before. They always met at the vicarage and were made welcome: although Sally asked for the simplest of jobs, as sewing was not her forte. The children took up much of her time, too, if Nicholas had to go out.

It seemed to Matilda that there was an air of expectancy, as if everyone thought that something else was bound to happen now that there had been a murder. Conversation was sparing, almost apologetic, waiting for the next instalment of sensational news that would eclipse the usual diet of gentle gossip.

Matilda affected to be unconcerned about the sensation, remarking innocently, 'I didn't ever meet this man. Does anyone know what he looked like? I've been to Burnt Oak, of course, so I know where he was found, but I can't put a face to the dead man.'

She was rewarded with the information that everyone there apart from herself and Mary had seen the dead man in the village during the previous few weeks, and that everyone apart from Briony and Mary had been to Burnt Oak at some time or other over the years. Only Nanette had been during the time that Albert had been the tenant, when she had called collecting for charity.

Most people had seen the murdered man when he went to the Post Office to ask for directions to Burnt Oak farm on his first visit, but he had been to the newsagent's two or three times to buy cigarettes, as well. Becky had thought him strange-looking but harmless, while Pat had considered him sinister. Nanette hadn't taken much notice of him, but Agatha had been suspicious of a stranger of that sort and had mentioned it to Quentin Weatherby, who was in charge of Neighbourhood Watch.

Sally had come across him outside the shop, looking up and down the road, and had stopped to ask him if he was lost. She was prevented from saying any more at that moment, due to a small sibling crisis but remembered something else later on that she thought could be useful. Unfortunately, she kept forgetting to mention it to Matilda, who went home in thoughtful mood, to phone Fortesque and learn of Albert's blackmailing activities.

The hours before dinner were spent on compiling a chart in her large, rounded handwriting which matched her figure. At the top, she wrote down the names Hangdog and Albert Noonday and allowed herself the flamboyant addition of 'old lags', a term she rather liked. Underneath, she intended to write the names of the residents of Pomery whom she thought, from her observations, could have known Albert better than anyone else and might have reason to want him dead. She put Adrian Nonsuch and Simon Wintergreen at the top of her list, but could think of no one else and she could think of no one in the village who might want to harm Hangdog, confirming her own view that Albert had been the intended victim. But further than that, she could not get, and had to leave for her pilgrimage with Albert remanded in custody pending more police enquiries and Pauline with a broken heart. Jeremy Fortesque was instructed to report directly to Edgar Bryan during her absence and both were told to report to her, if at all feasible. She felt that she could do no more for the time being and gave herself up to pleasure.

Part Two

In felawshipe wel coulde she laughe and carpe:
Of remedies of love she knew parchaunce,
For she coude of that art the olde daunce.

Geoffrey Chaucer,
The Canterbury Tales

11

April

April had arrived in Pomery with cold fingers to grasp unwary exposed flesh while clouds of icy breath found ways of infiltrating the clothes designed to keep it out. Rehearsals took on a more frenzied air, and temperaments emerged and hardened like the prickles of a newly born hedgehog.

The lighting and sound system, in Harry's care, were causing unforeseen problems. An oversensitive trip meant that if there was sufficient light and sound, the electricity supply cut out altogether, usually taking a fuse or two with it. It took three visits from an electrician, at Agatha's expense, before the problem was solved, only to find that it all went again when Frances put the kettle on. Harry was further unnerved when the enthusiastic wrenching of his doors as the cast swung in and out caused the main entrance door to drop and stick.

There was a point in the play when a loud crash was needed to come from the cupboard where Harriet and Becky were hiding. Not wanting to further tax the electrical circuits, it was Pippa and Sally's job to make a pile of pots and pans offstage and send them crashing down at the right moment. This was not difficult, provided that Frances kept away. She only had to walk within two yards of them to bring the teetering pile down at the wrong time.

April showers brought in the mud and a permanent shroud of dampness enveloped the hall. The newly hung main door began to stick again, this time with the damp, and the costumes hanging in the dressing room felt clammy to the touch. The village hall committee had agreed on one thing at last. They could not afford to keep any background heating on while the building was not in use.

One week before the scheduled dress rehearsal, Frances tripped over her own feet and knocked into the costumes. Several hangers jerked off onto the muddy floor and when Nanette came looking for her, to see why she had missed her entrance, she found Frances trying to rub off the worst of the mud, sticky now with her tears. Nanette swept them all into a sack to take home to wash and sent the unmerry May maiden on her way, late for the festivities but in time for some biting sarcasm from Agatha.

Agatha was now very nervous about her first sortie into the world of amateur dramatics. As the weeks went by, she had slowly come to realise that it was much more difficult than she had thought it would be. In truth, the unpalatable fact was dawning on her that she could be left looking rather a fool, that she might not be demonstrating her superiority but her mediocrity instead. Sourly, she regarded her maidens standing knock-kneed and nervous in front of her scowl, and nodded to Dawn Evans dozing at the piano.

It took a second sharp command before the honky-tonk music started, the introduction played at a different tempo to the main tune as Dawn got into her stride and adjusted her glasses. The maidens were hard put to muster even a hint of dewy-eyed capering as they missed the opening beat and Frances disappeared off stage, being on the end and having faced the wrong way when the line began to move.

Agatha closed her eyes and counted to ten. This was Monday night. Dress rehearsal was Wednesday and the first performance on Friday. They would never be ready in time, and if one more person told her cheerily that it would be 'all right on the night', she would not be responsible for her reply.

* * *

The day of the dress rehearsal began ominously, with a power-cut affecting the whole village and lasting until two; which meant that Nanette could not spend the morning ironing the costumes, which she had washed at home, before going down to the hall to press the remainder. Harry had taken some holiday due to him, in order to spend the day making final adjustments to the lighting, and was frustrated by his enforced inaction. He wandered about the house, getting in the way, while Nanette tried to fill the time dusting and sorting jumble, too wound up to read.

When the power came back on, Harry set off for the hall, promising to come back with the car in a couple of hours to fetch Nanette and the finished costumes. Half an hour later, he was on his way to Silminster, having made an uncharacteristically clumsy grab at a small spotlight, breaking both the fitting and the bulb. A specialist shop in Silminster was the nearest supplier and so it was nearly five when he returned, to find Nanette anxiously waiting with the pile of ironed costumes and twice the amount to do at the hall.

As they hurried to the car together, with Nanette cradling the clean, ironed clothes, they met the only rain that day, which spotted the garments on top before they could get them into the car. Nothing came to any harm, but Nanette was unnerved and not her usual calm self when Frances arrived early and began to wander around nervously, touching things and picking up anything not nailed down. Nanette eyed her over the last garment to be pressed, breathless with the tension and rushed the job, inadvertently creasing the skirt of Harriet's dress and scorching a section of hem. She urged Frances to get into her costume, rammed the maidenly circlet onto her head with a fair degree of firmness and sat her in the front row of seats, put in position to give verisimilitude.

The rest of the cast began to arrive in dribs and drabs, either nonchalantly blasé or affecting a swagger to cover up the nervous embarrassment they suddenly felt, now that the moment of truth was nearly upon them. The air was thick with clichés. They earnestly adjured each other that tonight was the night and oh, well, here we go; donned the unfamiliar costumes; and waited around restlessly for someone to tell them that it was all a ghastly mistake and they could all go home.

It was when they were all ready and waiting that it was discovered that Dawn wasn't there at the piano. Keeping her voice under tight control, Agatha requested sweetly that someone go and fetch her.

Harry was pleased for something straightforward to do, which would get him out of the strained atmosphere. Pomery-upon-Axle looked temptingly peaceful and trouble-free as he drove along the village street. He could have murdered a pint.

Dawn lived in the oldest row of sagging thatched cottages on the far side of the green, opposite the Pieces of Eight. With a single backward glance of longing, Harry knocked tentatively on the dingy green door and soon realised that the urgent requirements of the PADS were no match for the build-up of an imminent crisis in the Wednesday soap. A querulous argument filtered through the thick glass of the tiny windowpanes — his deep and theatrically resentful, hers shrill with indignation. Blue flickering light danced on the glass and Harry knew that Dawn was in there, glued to the set, part of the screen world until the recording was switched off at eight o'clock and the technicians went home. He felt a vestige of sadness that the programme wasn't even live. As if it cheapened her involvement. Shaking off his inappropriate philosophies, he lifted the iron horseshoe knocker and gave a determined fanfare. No room for sentiment tonight.

She had forgotten all about the rehearsal, and made no bones about the fact that she would have preferred it that way. Forgotten. Crossly clicking off the picture, Dawn followed Harry to the car, sitting muttering to herself until they arrived at the hall, where she swept in and spoke to no one. Plumping herself down at the piano, she turned her back on the assembled cast and proceeded to ignore everyone and play when she felt like it, a shrivelled cross fairy, kidnapped from fairyland.

The *frisson* between Henry and Sadie had grown until it was as if there were two extra members of cast. Pique followed each of them wherever they went and made ripples to include everyone else in their argument, leaving the air full of unspoken reproaches. It was an unpromising beginning, but Agatha gave a brave nod to Dawn and the first PADS dress rehearsal was under way.

As she had her back to everyone, Dawn missed the nod, but started anyway at a different tempo to that of the previous practices. The confused May maidens jerked in stiff-leggedly and began their rustic cavorting.

Pippa had arranged that much of the dance centred around Frances. Namely, she kept her feet still and swayed while everyone else moved around her. It had proved to be safer that way. The tricky bits were getting to this position, leaving it afterward and the odd bit in the middle where Frances had to follow someone else.

After the fiasco at the last rehearsal, Frances kept her eyes firmly fixed on Pat Hunter, whom she knew she must follow when she moved to her central position. Unfortunately for Frances, Pat was distracted at the last minute and failed to move, so that the merry line caught up with its own tail and they shunted into each other, squashing up together in a tiny space at the side of the stage.

In the misguided belief that you carry on no matter what, and in the absence of any guidance from Agatha, who was speechless, Pippa and Sally valiantly carried on performing in a quarter of their allotted space until Pat had recovered. Between them, they gradually moved Frances to her proper position, arriving there just as the dance ended. Frances fled to the dressing room in torrents of tears, convinced that it was all her fault, and Pat went to see what was the matter with Robin, whose wild-eyed stare had caused her to stop mid-dance.

Agatha recovered her voice, deciding to

save her barbed comments until later, and demanded Robin's appearance instead as the singers were all in position, especially the condescending one from Rowan Walk who had sung in the chorus at Glyndebourne. Pat caught an anguished, 'Words gone,' as he waved his cuffs despairingly in the air and plunged into the spotlight. Not understanding how, but knowing what it meant, Pat went to find Frances and apologise. She couldn't bear to watch her husband.

It was an uncomfortable five minutes for everyone who could.

Agatha sat down with her hand over her eyes, hardly noticing that the play had started and Henry and Sadie had had their first on-stage encounter and were now alone in the passageway. Robin hadn't remembered any words, not one in the right order, and the chorus had dried up after two attempts to follow him. The supercilious cat with professional experience had enjoyed it. Her exit oozed smugness and gloating.

Peering through her fingers miserably, Agatha silently applauded Hugo's stagecraft as he led Harriet through their first scene, deftly opening the cupboard door and shooing her in as the doorbell rang. Robin's head appeared at the window, as if he was waiting at the door and Hugo went to open it and usher him in, only to find that Henry was standing there glowering and Robin was nowhere to be seen. Hurriedly shutting the door and with a quick glance at Agatha's blank face, he tried again, only to find Sadie, arms folded and defiant, blocking the way for Robin, with Henry behind him clearly visible in the window — when he was supposed to be in Skegness.

Eventually, Robin entered through the door that led from the dining room, having gained entrance to the house by unexplained means, and brought with him snippets of a hissing row, magnified by the acoustics in the passage.

The play degenerated from then on. No one who was supposed to be on the other side of the door or the window was ever there or able to make their entrance at the right time. Henry and Sadie missed all their cues and, when they did appear on the stage, it was often together when the whole sense of the play was that they were apart. The rest of the cast struggled on valiantly, against all odds, but theirs was a lost cause.

Somehow, the play was finished and, after Pippa and Sally's tap-dance, Robin appeared again in front of the curtains for his monologue in mixed dialects. He had chosen a newspaper for a prop and so words were not a problem for this one, but his performance was uninspired while he brooded over who could have erased his words and why.

Agatha did not miss his mediocrity. He would have to do exceptionally well in the future to make up for his amnesiac Major General.

The finale of non-stop popular songs sung by all went smoothly. Lola would not smile and had to be shunted into the back row. Frances looked enchanting because she knew that she need not move. Sadie stood next to Hugo in the front line, smiling fixedly. Henry looked pleased because, while Robin was performing his monologue, he had broached the idea that he and Pippa should take a short holiday together later on in the year — and she had said that she would think about it, not dismissed it out of hand as he'd feared that she might have done. Robin was still preoccupied, but more professional at hiding it.

Agatha wished that she had never started the whole thing and, after icily wiping the floor with the assembled company, went home to a bath and several stiff drinks.

* * *

Datchett and Treeve were getting nowhere. The result of the post mortem and forensic evidence only showed what Hangdog had died of, with no conclusive evidence whatsoever as to who might have done it. It was even possible that he could have done it himself.

The analysis of the stomach contents showed that he had eaten a meal of fish and chips at about half past nine that night, and this was corroborated by the chippie in Chadbury, where they remembered serving him. He had been in three or four times recently, and had frightened the young girl who helped out at the weekend by shouting at her when she was slow. She had seen him come in and called her boss, who served him himself.

The blood sample showed him to be three times over the legal limit to drive and it was thought that he had consumed the whole bottle of whisky during the course of the evening. A key to the front door of the bungalow was found in his pocket, so he could have let himself in and got into Albert's bed before he came home. Albert's story could be true. The only stumbling block was how his wrists had come to be cut with a Stanley knife. And why should anyone force the window, when the door was open?

Broughton was the senior man and he

pottered about his domain like an amiable mole, a small figure with his eyes blinking behind half-moon glasses which glinted in the harsh lights needed for his work. He was nothing if not thorough and he would not be swayed by the opinions of others.

The wrists had been cut while Hangdog was lying in bed and he had been alive when this happened, but Broughton could not say if Hangdog had been unconscious. He could have done it himself. The knife had dropped out of his left hand onto his body after the right wrist had been cut. The left wrist must have been cut first and it could be concluded that he had been a right-handed man and had slashed the left wrist first to ensure a good job, saving his weaker effort for after he had made his strongest cut. Or someone could have done it for him while he was asleep or made comatose by the whisky.

They were talking in Broughton's office, where neat files lined the walls and the shaky April sunshine sporadically lit up his framed qualifications and photographs of smiling family. Eons away from spurting blood and sewn up corpses. Datchett passed some photographs across to him.

'These show his fingerprints on the knife-handle, both sets from both hands, although the second set have smudged the first, as you would expect. Can you tell from these if they are in the right positions for the wounds to be self-inflicted?'

Broughton gave the matter some thought, studying the evidence closely.

'They are not exactly where I would have expected to see them, Inspector, but near enough. I cannot rule out suicide on that evidence alone.' He frowned and hesitated before continuing, 'His prints could have been put on by someone holding his fingers round the handle. That's what you're asking, aren't you? It's not conclusive, though, and I would have to admit to this doubt in court.'

Datchett suppressed a sigh. 'What about the other cuts? Should they be telling us anything?'

'It is surprisingly hard to slash a wrist and quite common to see first attempts that fail to go deep enough. The only thing I would say is that there are attempt marks on both wrists. If he did it himself, he would have been feeling weak after cutting the first one and there would not have been time for him to make many attempts on the other one. The number of attempts and the severity of the wound on the right wrist are surprising, but not conclusive as to whether or not he did it himself.'

'And the blood?'

'It was a very tidy place to do it. Most of the blood stayed in the bedclothes, but there were splashes on the wall beside the bed from the first cut, I would imagine. If he made the second cut himself, his cutting hand would have been much weakened from the first wound and he would have had to do it quickly: that would explain why he could not lift his arms up as high as for the first one. If, on the other hand, he was murdered, his murderer could not have avoided becoming bloodied as he bent over to make the first cut. You found no footprints, I understand?'

Datchett sighed heavily. 'No. Only later ones from the woman and the postman.'

Broughton spread his hands. 'That's all I can do for you, then. You'll have my report in due course.'

They were being dismissed like schoolchildren. And, like schoolchildren, they went unwillingly back to work. It was obvious that they would have to drop all charges against Albert and release him into the cruel world.

12

Matilda had set out for Southampton on the tenth day of the month of April to join her fellow travellers in a voyage of discovery. The *Pride of Hamble* was due to sail on the eleventh and Matilda had booked accommodation for the fifteen other passengers besides herself, who preferred this most leisurely and luxurious form of transport. To travel hopefully was an important ingredient for the success of the venture.

When Matilda left Pomery, the situation regarding Albert Noonday was grave, but she placed her confidence in Edgar Bryan and Jeremy Fortesque and left with a clear conscience. If the worst came to the worst, there would be time for her to save him when she got back. She didn't see why she should miss her journey.

Her immediate companions in the upper state room were Sir Clive Tilling and his son Gregory, wealthy Shropshire landowners; Giles Freebody, a rather pompous defence lawyer; Hugh Wyvern, Harley Street doctor; Grace Treasyre, a lady vicar on whom young Gregory appeared to be sweet; and Fenton

More, estate manager to Sir Cecil Luckly of Stevenage. She watched them covertly, wondering what was going through their minds as she told the story.

Hugh Wyvern, who never let you forget his eminent calling and practice, looked superior when she came to the bit about the cut wrists. No doubt he was thinking that he could have diagnosed it more accurately. He would have charged heavily for his services, she'd be willing to bet. The Chadbury Police Force would be bankrupt in a month.

Matilda drew her narrative to a close and surveyed her audience. 'Well? What do you think of my story? Any ideas?'

Hugh Wyvern lit an expensive cigar drawn from his slim silver case and drew on it, his long nose wrinkling in distaste at the sordid little tale that Matilda had told. 'The usual story of thieves falling out, surely? This Noonday did it because of some squabble and is now trying to get the woman on his side. Seems straightforward to me.'

'Albert had no blood on him at all and, when the police searched, they didn't find any blood anywhere except for in the bed, on the carpet beneath the bed, and a little on the wall,' challenged Matilda. 'How do you explain that?'

Wyvern shrugged. 'He had plenty of time

to get rid of any stained clothing. We only have his word for it that he was ill.'

Giles Freebody, who disliked the doctor and who had barely been able to contain himself while this interchange was going on, managed to speak at last. 'The woman was ill and they both ate the same thing. I find it entirely reasonable that he should have been ill, too.'

Wyvern looked at him in amusement. 'Come, come, Giles. He's not in the dock yet, waiting for you to ride to his rescue.'

Freebody was just replying frostily that when Noonday was, he would be glad to represent him, when Grace intervened. She had a sweet face, innocent of makeup, haloed by soft blonde hair, and possessed the capacity to see good in everyone. Wyvern looked at her tolerantly, although he was contemptuous of her type of woman. He had a string of expensive sophisticates in his own stable.

'It does seem strange that he didn't run away,' she said quietly.

Wyvern made the sort of noise that is commonly written 'Pshaw', then remembered that she was a lady and qualified his comment condescendingly. 'That type don't think things out, Grace. He'd obviously decided on his story and it never occurred to him that it would not be believed.'

She shook her head stubbornly. 'He doesn't strike me as being a fool. What do you think of him, Matilda?'

'He's a clever and efficient blackmailer. Worked out exactly how much to ask for without being too greedy and had a nice little sideline going there. That doesn't strike me as being foolish. Rather the opposite, in fact.'

'What about the criminal connections?' This from Gregory Tilling, who had casually edged himself as near to Grace as he could. If she noticed, she failed to give any sign.

Matilda gave details of Albert's criminal record and that of the victim and of the crime which had involved the two of them: namely, the bank job in Birmingham.

Gregory thought for a moment. 'Do we know of any other members of the gang who might have had a grudge against either of them?'

'Everyone else involved in that job is still in prison,' said Matilda slowly. 'But that doesn't mean that Albert and Hangdog couldn't be got at, of course. It could be to do with the money, which they've got hidden somewhere, but if Albert had touched that, he would have had no need to blackmail. For my money, I'd still say that the blackmail was the key and the intended victim was Albert.'

'In that case,' drawled Wyvern, bored of the whole business, 'your friend Albert had better hope that he's not released before they've decided which of his victims did it.'

Fenton More, who had been watching the exchanges thoughtfully, spoke tentatively. 'Do we know that he has not blackmailed before? It could be that we are looking for a complete stranger from his past who has never before been officially connected with either Albert or Hangdog in Pomery.'

'A needle in a haystack, then?' concluded Wyvern briskly. 'I can't see any point in pursuing it further. Good story, Matilda. Now . . . I have a story, too, which began just after Christmas and is far from over, yet. The first I knew about it was when . . .'

Wyvern began his tale and gradually the party became absorbed as the story unfolded and the little village of Pomery-upon-Axle faded away from sight and thought. Only Matilda let her thoughts wander, surprised and annoyed with herself that she could not shrug them off.

Agatha was in a state of extreme nervous tension by the time half past seven came round on Friday evening. The hall was packed with eager expectancy and, with each second that passed, her stomach wound itself into tighter and tighter knots. She could hear the buzz of conversation and the ripples of laughter as friends met or called out to each other across the rows. She wanted them all to go away, to call it off due to circumstances beyond her control. How could she ever have thought that she could do this? She had no experience and it showed. She would be the laughing stock of the village.

Backstage, everyone looked as if they were in a dreamlike trance, unnaturally quiet and with a greenish tinge around the gills. Even Robin and Hugo looked as if they'd rather be elsewhere. The drum was in her throat, now, threatening to choke her. 'Three minutes to go. Places, everyone.'

Leonora had arrived with Henry in tow during the last five minutes and was seated at the back, scowling because all the front seats were taken. Agatha prayed that the sound system was working properly tonight. This afternoon, when the microphones had been tested, they had been all squeaks and whistles. Harry had fiddled with them for over an hour and they were working perfectly again when it was time to lock up, leaving all in readiness. If only they stayed that way.

Out of the corner of her eye, she saw Frances creeping along the back of the stage and, before Agatha could utter a warning, Frances had tripped over the wires, causing an ominous metallic screech from the microphone suspended above the stage.

At this juncture, Dawn Evans remembered that she had left her glasses on the television and Harry was dispensed to fetch them, with detailed instructions as to the vagaries of her front door key.

Pat had rewritten the words onto Robin's cuffs and dared him to touch them, in case any of it rubbed off. Dawn Evans had been worked on that morning by Harry French, until she rediscovered her Dunkirk spirit and was convinced that she was the vital ingredient needed for the evening's success. Sadie and Henry had called a temporary truce and spoke to each other with icy politeness through thin lips, while their eyes smouldered. Frances had been given a small tot of whisky by her father, which did not make her any the less clumsy, but made her think that she was not. She faced her entanglement with the wires — three minutes before the show had to go on — with equanimity. Harry returned with the glasses and Dawn seated herself unhurriedly at the piano.

The lights were dimmed, the magic hush fell and the show began. Stunning May maidens tripped, blinking, into the spotlight and moved round Frances, who swayed happily in the centre to the Dawn's tinny off-beat. The spot followed Lola across the stage as she danced her solo piece, an angel with attitude in green tulle. There was a small kerfuffle when it was time to join together again for the chorus, when Dawn lost her music and was forced to improvise; but, as the music came wobbling to an end, they were able to gather Frances up and exit to enthusiastic applause. The first hurdle had been cleared by a good margin and they were running down the straight, beyond the point of no return.

Never had a modern major general used such expansive and theatrical gestures: and the audience was visibly impressed, confident that they were watching a real artist. The chorus simpered with relief, and even the cat from Glyndebourne forgot to look superior. The roar of approval buoyed up the cast and the farce was begun at a galloping pace. No one bothered about the odd whistle or two from the microphone. They were having too good a time.

Doors opened and shut on cue like clockwork. The crash of crockery was perfectly timed, and almost all the right wives and husbands were in the right places at the right time. Sadie and Henry began to enjoy themselves. Robin made a slight mistake and started on the last act in the middle of the second: but, after his major general, he was forgiven anything. Anyway, the audience were too taken up with the novelty of spotting their friends to take much notice of mistakes.

Even Lola forgot herself and smiled during the finale of popular songs. The audience were invited to join in and the evening ended in a rush of noisy sentimentality. As the hall emptied, the streets filled with singing and laughter which lasted at least until they got home.

After the three curtain calls and in the aftermath of heightened adrenaline that gave the performers and producer rosy spectacles, everyone looked forward to the following night, and the idea that a similar performance could be recreated in the not too distant future was born. PADS was firmly established as the latest Pomeranian institution.

Briony Brightside was as astonished by her husband's performance as she had been by his recent behaviour. He really was a very good actor and, since the society started, he had been ignoring her in a much more friendly way. She began to wonder if he had found his métier at last. Perhaps she should put off making an appointment with her solicitor in Chadbury for the time being. A couple of weeks, maybe, to see if it lasted. After all, she had been very fond of him, once.

13

Matilda arrived back in England a week before the fete and the second murder. She bade a fond farewell to her fellow travellers with the assurance that they would all meet up again next year, and returned to Pomery, having promised before she went that she would help at the fete. It would be another three weeks before her house was ready, so that would fit in perfectly.

Albert Noonday had been released, and the coroner had recorded an open verdict. That much she knew from her spies, who had kept her informed. Leonora had been reluctant to keep him on as her tenant, and would have been within her rights to evict him, as he had forged his references: but he was a good farmer and she graciously consented to give him another try. He had moved into the second bedroom and slept on an air bed until he could afford another mattress, while Pauline fussed over him, defying the gossips to accuse him of murder.

The idea of a murderer in their midst would not go away, though. It had taken root, even among the least fanciful Pomeranians, and a hush would fall when Albert walked into the room.

The first person Matilda went to see was Edgar Bryan, but he was no further forward in his enquiries. He had not noticed anyone behaving out of character or any strangers roaming about Burnt Oak farm. There was something up with Nanette French, but he didn't see that it could have any connection with the murder. Everyone else was just the same and nothing out of the ordinary had happened.

Matilda couldn't help but voice her disappointment. 'I was sure that you would have come up with a clue. Are you sure that there is nothing that you have overlooked?'

'Nothing. Unless you count your sister being more than usually annoyed with me for using the woodland. I saw young Henry on the farm, by the way. He was doing a water-colour of that old barn and making a proper job of it, too. I didn't know that he could paint.'

'Neither did I. I saw him with his sketch book before I went away, but I didn't know that he was serious about it. That's young Pippa's influence, I suppose.'

'Now that, I have noticed. Always together nowadays and Henry seems to have grown up. He's much more likeable than he used to be.'

'Woman's influence,' said Matilda absent-mindedly. She was trying to remember something that eluded her and she knew that it was important. She shook her head impatiently. It would come back. 'I'm worried about Albert. Things have quietened down, now. It could be just the right time for the murderer to have another go. I'm going to call on Albert and tell him to watch his step. He may be an unlovely specimen of humanity, but Pauline loves him and I promised her that I would help.'

Edgar sniffed. 'Let's hope he takes your advice in the spirit in which it is given.'

To Matilda's surprise, Albert, with Pauline at his side, was willing to listen to her fears and Pauline took them seriously. Albert, who was sure that it was either Nonsuch or Wintergreen who had tried to murder him and killed Hangdog instead, thought that he should be all right, now. Although faces did keep appearing before his eyes: faces of people he had double-crossed and sometimes shopped to save his own skin. There had been no honour in his thievery. And it was just possible that one of those faces from the past had seen him, as Hangdog had done, and decided to come calling. He listened to what

Matilda was saying, in spite of himself.

When she had gone, Pauline did the most daring thing she had ever done in her life and offered to move in with Albert so that she could help him. She had half-expected him to say no, and was rather taken aback when he said yes straight away. Fortunately, she did not know that he was primarily seeking to ease his financial difficulties, and felt a glow of pleasure that she was going to be of use to someone, even if the prospect daunted her.

It was arranged that she should move in during the week, as a temporary measure, and that they would discuss further whether or not she should give up her cottage. Albert was happy to wait a while before enjoying her share of his rent.

Pauline moved a few belongings in on the Wednesday before the fete, and Albert was surprised at how comfortable the house felt with a woman around. They spent all Friday evening and night together, which was just as well. They gave each other an alibi for the second murder.

* * *

It was a tradition of many years' standing that the manorial grounds would be lent for the purposes of accommodating the village fete on the last Saturday in May. When the idea of a fete had first been mooted, back in the late nineteen twenties, the Babbington-Banburys had always gone abroad for the summer and so May had been the month fixed for this important date in the Pomery calendar. Henry's mother had organised it, as had her mother-in-law before her; and, for the last twenty-six years, it had fallen upon Leonora to continue the good work. She had fitted effortlessly into the role. There was a basic committee and then a subcommittee, which did the planning that was then submitted to Leonora, who produced her own plans to which everyone agreed. She did no actual work toward it, but was always there to advise and instruct.

The flat lawns in front of the manor were ideal for the stalls, arranged in a roughly rectangular shape round the edges with the tea-tent in the middle. The lower lawn was devoted to the coconut shy, rifle range, fortune teller's hut and bouncy castle. In front of the house stood a dais with the PA system, connected to the house by long leads. Robin Hunter filled the role of Master of Ceremonies and announced the events and results, drawing the crowds with his jokes and ad-libbing.

As Lord of the Manor, it behove Henry to

say a few words of welcome, written for him by Leonora, and declare the fete open. After that, he usually made himself as scarce as he could. A suggestion had been made one year by the committee that they should get a celebrity to do the opening part, but Leonora deemed herself and Henry celebrity enough and the idea was quietly shelved.

Nicholas firmly refused to judge any of the competitions, explaining that you could make enemies that way and this was not in keeping with his calling. Thus it fell upon Henry to brave the flames and choose the best costume and the most beautiful baby. As most people thought him a tent short of a tent-pole, none of the losers felt particularly hard done by, and there were not many lasting hard feelings.

Saturday morning dawned with indifferent weather, unfairly hiding its plans for the day. Nothing short of a hurricane would stop the fete, but it was helpful to be prepared. This morning, Pomery experienced a prolonged fall of heavy rain, a stiff westerly breeze and a good burst of sunshine that all but dried up the rain: but then the black clouds reconvened to hover over the proceedings like the sword of Damocles. And all of this before eight o'clock.

It had always been agreed that the profits

from the fete would be split equally between all the village organisations, but this did not stop vying for prime places when the stalls were allocated. Agatha Kingsway made sure that she was well placed in the centre of a row with her fancy goods, as far away as possible from Pauline Jones and her white elephant, while Queenie Ryland, a fierce matriarch whose family could be traced back to the wrong side of Charles II's blanket, terrorised anyone who looked as if they might have designs on the position of her bric-a-brac. Nanette and Harriet had taken pot luck with theirs and happily sold dried-flower arrangements alongside Mary Stringer's books. Mary Stringer thought that she should have arranged it better and vowed to improve upon her position next year.

Sally Nesbith, who had originally been earmarked to serve teas, manned the white elephant with Pauline and Matilda Golightly. She was anxious that Pauline should not feel isolated in her difficult situation. A show of solidarity never went amiss. Matilda's reason for helping was rather less altruistic. She wanted to talk to both Sally and Pauline in case she could jog their memory about the day of the murder. A fruitless task, in the light of events.

By half past nine, most of the stall-holders

had arrived, armed with sheets of polythene and bricks, to weight down their wares, and had just completed this task to their satisfaction when the news of the second murder spread from stall to stall like an attack of impetigo.

* * *

To the side of Squires Lane was a paddock ringed by trees, which made it invisible from the road running along the bottom of Squires Lane. There was a footpath from the middle of the lane next to Sadie Strangelove's bungalow, leading through trees into the field that was strictly private, for the use of Squires Lane residents only. Leading out of the field onto the Mole road was a path through the trees, which ended in a locked gate, opened to allow the passage of horse-boxes, or large equipment for maintenance.

Water was dripping off the leaves this morning after the downpour. Datchett and the team walked along the private path, the ground wet and slippery underfoot, the raw, earthy smell of spring filling their nostrils. When they got to the body, they found that the clothes that showed uppermost were dry. The prolonged bout of rain had stopped at half past-seven and so this at least was a positive lead, establishing a reasonable outside limit for the time of death if he had been killed where he was found.

He was sprawled, arched up on his back, at the end of the path, where it left the trees and led into the paddock. Dressed in casual clothes — grey flannels, white open-necked shirt and a navy blazer with grey loafers on his feet — he looked as if some giant bird had picked him up from his natural habitat and dropped him here on this wet, muddy path between the trees. Discarded him as unfitting to adorn her nest. A crimson stain had spread around his heart, from which protruded a wooden handle attached to a long, thin blade. The blade had skewered the body and its protrusion from his back was what was causing the body to arch sideways.

Datchett's face became grim. Murder. No room for doubt about this one. The man had light olive skin, and dark, curly hair, but his features were coarse and doughy and somehow he looked very English, lying here at the entrance of an English meadow.

He had been found by Gerald Kingsway, Agatha's husband, who liked to take a walk every morning and always went where he could be safe from meeting anyone. The private path of Squires Lane suited him down to the ground and he had left home after he was sure that the rain had stopped. He disliked getting wet. He found the body at five to eight and left it unguarded to run home to the phone. He had neither seen nor heard anyone else while he had been out that morning.

Peter Datchett and Barbara Treeve stood on the edge of the hive of activity generated by the dead. The doctor pronounced life to have been extinct at eight fifteen and ventured the opinion that it had been caused by the thin blade that had turned him into a cocktail sausage. Death had been instantaneous and, as far as he could see, the man had died where he had fallen.

Further investigation found a black Audi parked beside the gate on the Mole road side with no sign of the owner. A PNC check revealed the registered keeper to be a jake Morgan of Chadbury, nothing known. No record, no links with anything criminal. Enquiries to his housekeeper revealed that he had left at seven o'clock to go sailing on Renton Water, as he did every Saturday. He usually left at eight, but this morning was different. No, he didn't say why he had left an hour earlier than usual.

Enquiries at Renton Water clubhouse produced no reason either. They usually met at nine, sailed until mid-afternoon and then enjoyed the hospitalities of the club until late evening, sometimes into the night. He had not arrived yet that day and yes, he drove a black Audi. Meeting someone, then. Someone who lived in Squires Lane. Someone he didn't want to be seen with. It should be easy to find out who. There weren't that many residents and secrets are hard to conceal when subjected to the scrutiny of the law.

All things being equal, it should be plain sailing, thought Datchett. The mention of Renton Water had put him in a nautical frame of mind.

The body went to the mortuary and the housekeeper was brought along to identify him, as there seemed to be no next of kin. By ten o'clock, they had confirmed his identity and were beginning the interviews in Squires Lane. Those found not to be in were tracked down later at the fete but, despite an admirable diligence on behalf of the Inspector and his team, no connection could be found between the dead man and anyone in Squires Lane. No one had ever seen him before and Datchett began to feel more than a little irritated that a total stranger should go out of the way to be murdered on his patch on a Saturday morning, when he should have been at home tending Mrs Datchett's geraniums.

Matilda, who had sniffed out the reason for

the activity in the Lane in the morning, made it her business to corner the young, inexperienced constable left guarding the corpse and saw what she needed to see for herself. She recognised the weapon immediately but decided to keep quiet about it until she was ready to tell.

Black storm clouds curtsied over the tea-tent and the faint stirrings of a breeze caused a few shivers among the crowd gathered to hear Henry Babbington-Banbury declare the village occasion open and to invite the fancy dress contestants to parade in front of the dais. Leonora was not interested in the fancy dress and, where there was no interest, she gave Henry the unusual experience of making his own decisions. He discharged his duty with much glancing over the shoulder, as if expecting interference at the last moment.

The under seven section comprised of four fairies, three Thomas the Tank Engines, a Robin Hood and a teddy bear. One other fairy was in the lavatory when the judging took place, and its mother left the fete in a huff with her wailing Titania in tow, vowing never to return. Henry, bemused as usual, chose Robin Hood and the teddy bear because there was only one of each and, under the guise of close examination of the others, executed a secret *eeny meeny miney mo* to choose third place. His last mo fell onto the worst-made Thomas the Tank Engine, which caused waves of annoyance from the waiting parents, before they remembered that it was only Henry and you couldn't expect any different.

The seven to eleven section had only three contestants, which made it marginally easier, although he did award first prize to the White Rabbit that had entered as Bugs Bunny. When it came to he adults, he gave up completely and chose at random. He gave Queenie Ryland's daughter first prize for her Snow White, which brought a further flush to her brick-red cheeks and encouraged her to essay a mock curtsey of thanks, which would have come off if she hadn't got her heel caught in her hem. As it was, her skirt tore in half and she had to receive her prize sitting down, while her mother found a piece of bric-a-brac large enough to hid her predicament. A polite ripple of applause for the winners was quickly stemmed and a frenzy of movement began so that each stall could be visited and a place in the tea-tent assured before the rain came.

Leonora did one regal circuit and then retreated indoors until the whole thing was over. She felt that she had done her duty and that nothing more could be required of her. Had she been more diligent in her motherly responsibilities, however, she would doubtless have advised Emma that it was unwise to let her pet rabbit have the run of the house just as the primped entrants to the most obedient dog competition were encircled outside the open window, awaiting instructions.

* * *

Henry was fluctuating between floating on a cloud of contentment and worrying that it would not last. He and Pippa were going really well together and, for the first time with any of his girlfriends, he knew that if this relationship finished he would have lost something irreplaceable. He didn't want to lose this chance. Henry had always been as dilatory about his love affairs as with everything else in his life, but Pippa was different.

She was a newcomer to the village, moving from Chadbury two years ago last February to live in a rented cottage next to the school. A small legacy gave her the security to give up her job in the Chadbury art gallery and work on her own pieces, while she sold her more commercialised work to earn her bread and butter. A quiet, even-tempered girl, she made friends quickly and was willing to share her talents with the village.

This afternoon, she was face-painting and had a queue of small children waiting to be transformed into cats or clowns or monsters. Children warmed to her quiet calm. Henry passed her and they managed to exchange brief smiles before she became absorbed again in her task, her dark, straight hair forming a curtain across her cheek.

He continued his stroll, thinking it better to avoid the fortune-teller's tent where Sadie was practising her art. She was still annoyed with him for being the one to end it, and had only ceased hostilities for the nights of the shows after the shambles of the dress rehearsal.

A dozen weak drops of rain caused anxious faces to study the clouds but, apart from a quickening breeze, there was no further change in the weather until the end of the afternoon. Henry decided to retreat into the house until later on, when he hoped to persuade Pippa to have a drink with him, as a reward for all her hard work. He ambled across to the side door and drifted in, serenely unconscious of the ungrateful long-eared rabbit that took this opportunity of freedom, unaccountably preferring it to its erstwhile captivity.

14

The police presence was unobtrusive but obvious. By the middle of the afternoon, there wasn't anyone in Pomery, young, old or bedridden who did not know of the second murder. Armed with a faxed picture of the dead man, each stall-holder was approached and asked if they had seen this man, but there was no result until late afternoon when someone was able to ask Pippa.

Pippa had been engrossed in her art, working quickly, as the queue of children did not seem to get any smaller, and so she was left until last. As, at one point, the events of the afternoon seemed to be getting out of hand, no one could really be held to blame for the delay.

At the time that Henry had opened the door into the house, Emma had given up trying to find her rabbit and climbed out of the window to admire the collection of dogs waiting to be put through their paces. The family dogs were labradors and she was involved in looking after them, but she longed for one of her own. She especially coveted a pointer that she thought would be useful in finding her other pets, which had a habit of becoming lost.

Her friend Sophie from North Mole farm had brought hers and was showing Emma its finer points, when Robin's voice crackled over the PA system and announced that the owners should walk their pets round in a circle and then seat them on command. Henry senior was not considered equal to the task of judging such an important competition, and so it was traditional for Cecily Roundtree, dog breeder and owner of Mole Kennels, to perform the task.

Cecily looked like an anaemic specimen of the Borzois which she bred and lovingly tended, never letting a puppy go until she had personally inspected the home to which it was being taken, and reserving the right to visit if the mood took her. Only those in deadly earnest got past her gimlet eye in the first instance, and she seldom had the need to use her follow-up visit. She took her responsibilities as judge very seriously. When ready to begin, she adopted a stance with legs apart, trunk slightly bent forward, her long muzzle quivering as she assessed the candidates.

For most of the contestants, it was a bit of fun and three-quarters of the owners were children putting their adored pet through its paces. Whatever the outcome, they each knew that their own pet was the best. The real earnestness came with the adults, who regarded the success of their animal as a matter of personal pride and for whom the contest was deadly serious.

The chief protagonists were Freda Grant, with her miniature poodle, Trixie — who was no lady and liked to nip from underneath — and Esme Cameron, with her long-suffering bloodhound called Desmond, who was of normally benign nature but hated Trixie to the death.

Contestants and owners awaited instructions. Freda and Esme glowered at each other while simultaneously trying to catch Cecily Roundtree's eye in an effort to establish their superiority. It was at this moment, when the hopes of the canine world were delicately balanced, that Emma's long-eared rabbit, Winston, appeared from the cloakroom and hopped over, nose twitching, to sit framed between the spindly legs of Cecily Roundtree, her over-long tartan skirt draping itself over his head like a rakish tam o'shanter. This was the moment when the dog saw the rabbit.

It must be said that Winston had cotton wool between his ears as well as for his tail. Emma had spotted the problem and was at his side immediately, ready to make a grab, but Winston had other ideas. If he could not stay beneath these legs, then he would find others more sympathetic to his cause. Thus decided, he made a dash for it across the lawn, with twenty assorted tongue-lolling dogs in hot pursuit, totally ignoring their owners' plaintive calls.

On reaching the stalls, Winston stopped abruptly, momentarily nonplussed, while the barking masses came closer and closer. Quick thinking in the tea-tent produced a line of bodies across the opening so that nothing could get past, but it was not so easy for the open stalls. Decision made, Winston dived under the nearest four legs, which were supporting the fancy goods, and twenty dogs of different shapes and sizes attempted to do the same.

Desmond found himself in Trixie's way and was nipped sharply in a place into which no lady should sink her teeth. His cries reached Esme Cameron, who charged forward to rescue her darling, who totally forgot himself and bit her.

It was Matilda who intervened before things got completely out of hand. Stepping out from the white elephant, she strode across the lawn and bellowed at dog, rabbit and owner alike. The stentorian roar had the effect of producing a stunned silence, during which time Emma had the presence of mind to pick up Winston and return him to his cage. Each owner pulled their dog away and St John's ambulance, represented by Bethan Pugh, the ex-Glyndebourne singer, patched up the bite on Esme's arm, while Desmond licked his wounds.

Matilda looked around at the scene now dispersing and let out another shout, only this time it was of laughter. Like the release of a spring, the assembled company began to join in, until the good mood of the gathering was completely restored. By the time Leonora arrived, the dogs had been reassembled, minus Desmond and Trixie, who were carried off to recuperate, and Celia had started judging briskly before anything else should happen.

Emma's friend's pointer won the overall prize, a decision that won unanimous approval. She was taken on a lap of honour by the two little girls and, for a few moments, murder in sleepy Pomery seemed a million miles away.

* * *

Pippa recognised the picture straight away. It was Jake Morgan, her landlord, and she usually saw him about every six months.

Recently, his visits had become more frequent because he had paid for some alterations and was checking up regularly to see if the work had been done properly. She did not know him well and had last seen him at the end of March, when he had inspected another damp patch on the kitchen wall and arranged for someone to come and deal with it. She knew of no other reason why he should be in Pomery, and knew nothing of his work. As far as she knew, hers was the only property that he owned and the only reason for him to come to Pomery. She could not think what he had been doing walking toward Squires Lane and he had not been to see her that morning.

Datchett had no reason to doubt her. He and Treeve went back to Morgan's house to conduct a thorough search and then to the station, to bemoan their unhappy lot.

The black clouds fulfilled their threat at half past four and the fete ended abruptly in a flurry of packing, wrapping and protecting. Leonora sent a message for them to leave the trestles and the litter until morning and, by half past five, all the stall-holders had left and were drying out at home, pleased to be indoors while the rain hurled itself at their windowpanes in frustration. It had been a long day.

Once home, thoughts turned again to the

murder that morning and the unease that had subsided since Hangdog's death returned. Doors were locked and bolted early that night, and sleep did not come easily.

Albert lay awake, staring at the ceiling, long after he thought that Pauline had dropped off. Morgan's death had torn it. He was having no more to do with Fraser, now. He could sort it out himself, once he was out. This game wasn't worth the candle. He, for one, was going to forget it and get on with his life, if he was allowed.

Pauline lay awake with her eyes closed, unable to shake off the feeling of dread that had gripped her stomach this morning when she had heard the news. She imagined the murderer stalking them when they left the house, watching her walk to the village and Albert to the fields. It would be very easy to kill them, too. But why should anyone want to do that? She loved Albert, but hoped that he was telling her the truth when he said that he had no idea why anyone should want to kill him now.

* * *

Sadie was not sleeping. She was waiting for him, sitting curled up on her sofa, purring like a cat. He'd come to her fortune teller's tent this afternoon as part of his political round of being seen but, once inside, had told her to expect him again tonight. He was going to leave his wife: she knew it. Had to keep up appearances for a while, she supposed, but he'd been elected now, so the spotlight was off him for the time being. By the time he was subject to further scrutiny, it could be all over.

She badly needed another boost of cash. Not that she'd done at all badly out of the last settlement, but it was dwindling away fast. Hugo had been a mistake. She'd thought him richer than that. It had turned out that Briony had the money and she wasn't likely to give it to Hugo to spend on her.

Henry would have done nicely, although he was a spoilt child and rather young. Money and land. She'd fancied herself as lady of the manor. Even tried going to church for a while, to show him that she could fit into the mould. Thank God she didn't have to do that any more.

Adrian fitted the bill nicely and it should be easy, living so close to each other. She had found it so with Hugo. Who knows how far he would go in politics? He was young, dynamic, knew all the right people. If she played her cards right, she could be there at his side, sharing his triumphs. Half past eleven. There was a soft knock on the door and she rose to let him in.

In the morning, she woke up to a vague feeling of dissatisfaction. She hadn't expected him to stay until morning, but she'd hoped that he would stay longer — longer than he had on Friday night, anyway. He'd been preoccupied, too. Said it was the murder that had unsettled him, but that was nonsense. He'd better not be having second thoughts about what he'd promised. She was in the position to make life very difficult for him, if he was.

* * *

Sunday morning at the mortuary was not where Datchett wanted to be and certainly not with Hopkins, standing in for Broughton who was on holiday. Hopkins performed every post mortem with the zest of a master chef making an omelette *aux fines herbes*. Built like a dancer, he minced round the still mound on the stainless steel trolley, pulling, pinching, slicing, extracting, talking all the while into a microphone, to record his observations for posterity — or at least his court appearance, to give evidence of his findings. But he was standing in for Broughton this morning and there was nothing to be done about it.

Datchett stood glumly at his side, grunting when an observation was addressed to him, waiting impatiently for the findings, fantasising that he would be told the one fact that would make it a piece of cake to catch this murderer today and still get home to his dinner. In the end, he was disappointed, as he knew he would be. Jake Morgan had been killed by a thin blade, longer than a stiletto, with a wooden handle. A sword-stick, would he like to believe? The blade had pierced his heart and left lung. The weapon had been thrust into his body with such force that it had gone right through him and the tip showed through the other side.

Time of death had been determined by the rain yesterday morning and the condition of the body when it had been found. He had had toast and coffee for breakfast, confirmed by the housekeeper and left at seven o'clock. By five to eight, he had been dead. On a Saturday and at that time in the morning, the journey to Pomery would have taken half an hour. Five minutes to park his car and walk across the field. He had met his murderer then at some time between twenty-five to and five to eight.

Had there been any conversation between them, or had the murderer known just what he was going to do and got on and done it? Forensic examination had been inconclusive. The most useful clue was a footprint made by a wellington boot near to where the body was found, but it was not close enough to form part of a pattern with Morgan's movements: and ten to one it belonged to a regular walker of this path. They might be able to make more of it when everyone who had access to Squires Lane — or had been seen near it — was interviewed and elimination from the enquiry could begin.

Datchett was intrigued by the secrecy of Morgan's approach. He must have climbed over the gate to get into the field, a most undignified method of entry for such a dapper dresser. This would indicate that his meeting was important as well as secret. But how was it secret? Was it that he himself did not want to be seen in Pomery by anyone at all or someone in particular, or was it that he did not want to be seen with the person with whom he had the assignation? Whatever it was, it had worked to the murderer's advantage, so it was up to Datchett to reverse the luck and find out whom he was going to meet and why. And the first thing to do was to interview every resident of Squires Lane and the Manor again, however unpopular he made himself.

15

Viewed from a distance, Pomery stood out from the flat landscape like a nose in profile. The River Axle meandered round its base, and from there the gradient increased sharply, levelling out for the village itself and then continuing gently until it reached the woods behind the manor. From there, it dropped away sharply down into Mole, with Tidworth reached by a road that made a dog's leg at right-angles to Mole village.

It was good arable farming land, the soil enriched by the silt from the River Axle, but further up the hill the land belonged to the sheep. Burnt Oak farm was the exception, being on the summit of the rise where it levelled out before its descent. Burnt Oak could support mixed farming, if any of the tenants ever had the money to get it all going. In recent years, each tenant had just done what he could.

Squires Lane led off uphill from the main village street and stretched for about a quarter of a mile, until it reached the wrought iron gates of the manor house. This geography gave it its sought-after seclusion, a no-through road clearly sign-posted from the village and discouraging unwelcome visitors. It was not the ideal place for a stranger to come if he did not want to be noticed, and the privacy of Squires Lane dwellers was fiercely protected. The right of way through the manor woods, reached by a narrow path at the side of Dawn Evans's cottage, had always provoked controversy and every seen user was subjected to scrutiny. Jake Morgan had been coming to meet someone. Why choose such an unusual way of entry if the person did not live in Squires lane? How many times had he come this way before? These were the issues uppermost in Datchett's mind as he began his house-to-house enquiries in the Lane, that Sunday morning.

He was destined to endure a bumpy ride.

To begin with, he found that two of the residents were in church, and this upset his methodical way of working. He liked to deal with everyone in a house and then tick them off. Now, he was going to have to go back to those houses and start again. The second major irritant was that, when they returned from church, he found that Matilda had beaten him to it. By the time he got to them, they were more than disenchanted with the whole affair.

The Kingsways lived in a solidly built

red-brick house next to the manor. Datchett had been inside, the day before, when he interviewed Gerald about his finding the body and noticed that, although it had a Georgian skin, the inside had been massacred at various different times and was now a mixture of mid-Victorian and early thirties style. No expense had been spared on the furnishings, but the end result was an uncoordinated clutter. Gerald Kingsway stood framed in the doorway to explain that his wife was at church and, as they already had a comprehensive statement from him, Datchett decided to come back later.

The next house on this side belonged to the Nonsuches, who were neither in church nor amenable to being questioned. Camilla Nonsuch looked down her nose at them again but could not shake them off, this time. She invited them in with undisguised annoyance and left them standing in the hall while she fetched her husband.

Their house was Georgian both inside and out, as far as Datchett and Treeve could see. At least, the hall was, and maybe that was all they would see of it, thought Datchett.

Five minutes later, Adrian Nonsuch appeared with a fixed smile and an offer of sherry, which he knew that they would refuse. 'You don't mind if I do?' Without waiting for an answer, he led them into a drawing room with leather furniture and rich, polished woodwork. Camilla Nonsuch would kill to keep her cleaning lady. He opened a drinks cabinet and they caught a glimpse of a selection that would not have disgraced a small pub.

He poured himself a generous measure, then turned to face them, glass in hand. 'What can I do for you, Inspector? Do sit down.'

Nonsuch chose a chair in the corner, shadowed by a shelf with what looked like a collection of Sèvres porcelain inconspicuously displayed. Given his line of business, that would figure, thought Datchett.

Six months ago, he would not have been able to distinguish a piece of Sèvres from Victorian ironstone; but, last November, he had been involved in investigating a series of robberies from country houses, where all that had been taken were good quality ceramics — including a large amount of Sèvres and some good copies, equally valuable, he had been told. Every time he saw some, now, he looked at it with an appreciative eye, knowing the kind of money that it fetched. Suddenly, he realised that Nonsuch was eyeing him, waiting to parry his replies. Treeve seemed vaguely amused at the sight of her governor daydreaming.

Seating himself on the huge leather settee, he began by asking where Mr Nonsuch had been yesterday, between seven and eight o'clock in the morning, and was surprised to see him show signs of discomfiture. Surely Nonsuch had heard about the murder and would realise that he would be likely to be asked, as he lived so near to the scene? He had had plenty of time to concoct an alibi, should he need one. He must know that he and Wintergreen would be under close scrutiny, after their involvement with Albert. Datchett had been prepared to watch closely for the signs of uneasiness associated with a cover-up, and was puzzled by his behaviour. It seemed to be minutes before Nonsuch answered.

'I was here, at home. In my study.' He looked at them closely, defying them to challenge what he had chosen to tell them.

Datchett, always the professional, showed no sign that he had noticed anything wrong. 'And can anyone verify that, Mr Nonsuch?'

Adrian Nonsuch cleared his throat. 'My wife. My wife will be able to confirm that I was there.'

'She saw you?'

'Saw me? Oh. Well, no, but she knew I was there.'

'How did she know?'

'I always go to my study first thing in the morning. I am a man of habit, Inspector; she would have known that I was there.' He was becoming irritated and, with his irritation, his self-assurance returned.

Datchett decided to try one more time, before the shutters came down. 'But she didn't actually see you between those times? Or you her?' he added mildly.

'No. I've told you. She would not disturb me in my study.'

Knowing the weakness that Albert had seized upon in order to blackmail him, Datchett thought it likely that this was true and conceded the point before changing tack. 'Can you think back to yesterday morning and remember if you saw or heard anything out of the ordinary? Anything that struck you as unusual or odd?'

Nonsuch looked thoughtful. 'It was the day of the fete and so there was much coming and going outside. More noise than usual. But that did not start until about nine. Leonora doesn't like anyone to arrive before then. No, I can't say that I heard or saw anything to help you.'

To be expected, really, but Datchett sighed and produced the photograph of Jake Morgan to hand to him. 'Do you recognise this man?'

Nonsuch looked at it and shrugged his shoulders before handing it back casually. 'No. I've never seen him before.'

Datchett could no longer judge if he could believe this or not and decided to talk to Nonsuch's wife instead.

Adrian fetched her and she entered with bad grace. A nasty-tempered woman, vindictive, Datchett wouldn't mind betting. Her husband left them to it — wisely, in Datchett's opinion. Treeve was looking amused again. For two pins, he'd leave the questioning to her, but he'd got the bit between his teeth now and he was nothing if not thorough.

'Mrs Nonsuch. Could you tell me where you were on Saturday morning between seven and eight o'clock?'

She tried to chill him with a look, but he held her gaze, and eventually she snapped, 'In bed, Inspector. I rarely rise before nine.'

'And can anyone confirm this?'

He knew how ridiculous this sounded, the minute the question was out of his mouth, but it was too late to retract.

Her eyes narrowed. 'There was no one in bed with me, if that is what you mean. That being the case, no, no one can confirm that I was in bed at that time.'

'You have children?'

'At boarding school, yes. They were not in bed with me, either, Inspector, if that is what you were asking.' Her rat-trap mouth smirked before it slammed shut.

'Were you awake for long before you got up? Did you hear your husband get out of bed, for example?'

The eyes flared but the answer was ice. 'My husband and I have separate rooms. I haven't the slightest idea when he got up.'

Nor does she care, thought Treeve. The unspoken retort was left hanging unclaimed in the air.

Datchett produced the photograph that she handled as if it were hot. She hadn't seen him, either; nor had she heard anything unusual. She always went out on the day of the fete, not liking the processions of villagers who took the opportunity to visit the manor once a year. She had left the house at eleven and not returned until eight in the evening.

So much for village spirit, thought Datchett.

They took their leave and crunched up the wide gravel path that led to the Brightsides's house. Briony was in church, but Hugo was in and looked no more pleased to see them than the Nonsuches had been.

The Brightside house had been built during the twenties and added to over the years. It was inclined to be dark with fewer windows in proportion to the size of the rooms, but it was decorated cleverly throughout with light colours and small lamps in the alcoves that detracted from the lack of natural light. Hugo took them into the drawing room and they sat down while Datchett repeated the questions that he had asked the Nonsuches.

Hugo had been in bed. He had not woken up until half past eight. Briony had been up when he awoke. He didn't know for how long. He had heard nothing unusual, but they would have to ask Briony herself if she had. He stared at the photograph, as if willing himself to make a positive identification, but failed. He had never seen the man before.

Datchett and Treeve took their leave, feeling like Heracles beginning the Aegean stables. Three possible suspects, none of whom had a confirmed alibi. Probably Mrs Brightside would make it a fourth. Nowhere near to catching a murderer, then.

* * *

Matilda was pleased to see the change in Briony since she went away. She had noticed a new confidence in Briony as soon as she came back and had been quietly congratulating herself on her good advice, but this second murder had thrown everyone and Briony looked as worried as ever. After church, where Matilda had beaten Leonora to the communion rail again, she swept Briony along in order to have a good chat and also to find out some information of her own.

Never one to beat about the bush, she came straight to the point. 'And how are things between you and Hugo?'

Briony flushed. She still couldn't get used to discussing her marital affairs with a virtual stranger, but there was something compelling about Matilda and she couldn't help but tell the older woman. Unconsciously, they slowed down their steps, as if to give them plenty of time to say all they had to say to each other before they reached Briony's house. That way, the discussion would still seem casual, a way to pass the time before reaching home.

'Much better. I . . . er . . . took your advice and it seemed to give him a jolt. I had a long think about our situation, too and realised that my money had made much more of a difference to us than I had realised. Hugo does work very hard, you know. I think he had begun to wonder what he was doing it all for, when I had plenty of money. He'd always called it mine, even though he knows it's in our joint account. Anyway, we had a long talk and decided to spend some of it straight away and he's booked us on a Mediterranean cruise, next month. He knows that I've always wanted to do something like that and that I would hate to go alone, so he thinks he's coming as a favour to me.'

'Clever girl,' encouraged Matilda. She had been listening intently and knew that she hadn't heard it all, yet. They paused for a moment at the bottom of Squires Lane, as if to acknowledge that there was more to be said, before reaching Briony's house. Matilda looked at her seriously.

'So what is worrying you now? Don't deny it. I can see that there is something wrong.'

Briony's lip trembled. It really was absurd the way this woman saw inside your head. How many other people had noticed, she wondered? If it was that obvious, she wouldn't stand a chance with the Inspector.

'Go on, tell me.'

Briony started to walk, looking down at her feet as if she had to watch them in case they strayed from the pavement. 'It's about this second murder.'

'Go on,' repeated Matilda softly.

Briony gave her a quick glance, as if for reassurance, and then began, hurriedly now as her house came into sight. 'I was up and about early that morning, because I had lots to do for the fete. Hugo didn't have to get up, it being the weekend and usually he will lie in until late. That's why . . . '

'That's why what?'

'That's why I noticed, especially when I heard him coming in the side door when I thought that he was in bed. I couldn't think where he had been or why he had been up so early. A few weeks ago, I would have thought I knew, but he was in bed at half past six when I got up, and I heard him at just gone half past seven. Not even Hugo is such a quick worker.' She permitted herself a wry smile.

'And where does Hugo say he was?'

'He denies having been out at all. We had quite a row, but he won't admit it.'

'There's something else, isn't there?'

Briony looked miserable. 'I can't understand why he won't say where he was and he's so jumpy. Only he's not taking it out on me like he used to. He keeps looking at me as if he expects me to help him, but of course I can't, until I know what the trouble is. Everyone says that the murder was committed at about the time he was out and I'm so frightened for him — for both of us. I can't say this to him, though. I can't let him think that I think he could be implicated in murder.'

'Surely he must know that that's what you think?'

Briony shrugged miserably.

Matilda was visited by the overwhelming urge to pick her up and shake her. And then go and do the same to Hugo. Instead, she chose her words carefully. 'Briony. He must tell the police the truth, even if he does not choose to tell it to you. I'll come with you now and make sure that he does.'

They quickened their footsteps and arrived at Briony's house just as Inspector Datchett and Sergeant Treeve were coming out of her drive and making for the bungalow opposite. When they reached the house, Hugo was still standing in the doorway where he had stood to see them out, looking frightened, and Briony hurried to be at his side.

16

Sadie Strangelove welcomed her visitors with a grave face, to show that she recognised the seriousness of the situation, but Treeve doubted if Sadie ever felt any deep emotion — unless it was directly connected to herself and her well-being. Her open-plan bungalow had picture windows on three sides and an indoor swimming pool, where Sadie had evidently been spending her time. She answered the door wearing a loose-fitting bathing robe, her dark hair damp and brushed back starkly from her face, showing off her wide forehead with arched eyebrows over those deep brown eyes. Datchett and Treeve had to concede that she was a striking-looking woman.

Sadie's bungalow was across from the Brightsides, slightly further up the hill. Foxholes, where Quentin Weatherby lived, was next door up from her. There were no other houses on the other side of her until the Needhams and the Frenches at the bottom of the road. Opposite, further down from the Brightsides, were the Wintergreens.

She showed them into the pool room,

explaining that she was too damp to sit down in the lounge. Instead, she reclined on a sun-lounger and indicated that her visitors should avail themselves of similar furniture scattered about the room.

Treeve thought that she detected a secret smile of amusement as she watched Datchett lower himself into a deck chair type of seat, with a garish design of orange sunflowers on a puce background. He gave no sign that he was put out.

'How can I help you, Inspector?' Sadie looked at him enquiringly.

Datchett repeated the question that he had asked of Hugo, and Sadie puckered her brow, as if in an effort of recollection. Her reply, when it came, was trite, and Datchett knew that she had not had to think about it at all.

'In bed, Inspector. As I usually am at that time in the morning. I'm afraid that I cannot bring any witnesses to vouch for me.' It was all play-acting — they could see that — but Treeve thought that she saw a suggestion of pique showing through the charade. As if Sadie had expected someone to be in her bed, early Saturday morning. She wondered who had let Sadie down and thought that she would not like to be in his shoes. Had Datchett noticed? Treeve wondered. He was continuing with his questions, playing the stereotype Plod with no imagination.

'You did not see or hear anything unusual? Think carefully. No unfamiliar sounds: footsteps, perhaps?'

Sadie shook her head. 'No, I'm sorry. I was in bed asleep. I did wake up at about half past seven, but I went back to sleep again.'

Datchett seized on a wispy chance.

'Are you sure that you were not woken by something? Can you think back, please? It's very important.'

She shook her head again. 'No, sorry. If I had been disturbed by a noise, it must have stopped by the time I was fully awake.'

Datchett conceded defeat, but produced the photograph of the victim to show her.

She had been shown it yesterday, in the darkness of the fortune-teller's tent, and you never knew. Sadie looked at it carefully, acting, but then sat up in genuine surprise. 'Perhaps I can be helpful, after all. I've seen this man before and I'm just trying to remember when and where it was. It wasn't recently, though. Before Christmas, I'm sure.'

Datchett held his breath, willing her to remember, momentarily placing all his hopes for solving the case on this chance recognition.

She returned the photograph to him at last, frowning. 'It was in Squires Lane — that much I can recollect — and it was cold. Icy. I was returning by taxi from shopping in Chadbury, and the lane was very slippery, so we were not going fast. I saw this man out of the window and we were going slowly enough for me to notice his face. We've had quite a mild winter, so if you can find out when we had that cold spell, that would pinpoint the time. I'm afraid that's the best I can do.'

'Can you picture if he was going up or down hill?'

She thought for a moment. 'Down. I was sitting on the right-hand side of the taxi and he came past me on that side.'

'You didn't happen to notice where he went, after he had passed you?'

Sadie set her face into a thinking mould, not expecting to be able to help but making sure that she had been noted trying. But she was destined again to surprise both herself and the police. 'Do you know, Inspector, I think that he turned off onto the path. The one that leads to the paddock.' She looked surprised at her own recollection.

Datchett could hardly expect more. He rose to take his leave. 'Thank you, Miss Strangelove. You have been most helpful.'

They left Sadie feeling a little put out, as if she would rather have kept them guessing.

* * *

Matilda was not making any headway with Hugo, and Briony was torn between loyalty to her husband, courtesy toward her friend and fear that Hugo may have involved himself in a murder. He stuck to his story that he had been in bed, and was so convincing that Briony began to imagine that she must have been mistaken, even that someone else had entered her house and crept up the stairs to vanish mysteriously into the woodwork. Matilda saw that if she was going to get any sense out of him, she would have to see him without Briony. As this was impossible, at the moment, Matilda left them to it and went to see if the Wintergreens were in.

The Wintergreens' house was similar in style to that of the Brightsides, but whereas Briony interested herself in the garden, neither Maureen nor Simon bothered beyond mowing the lawns and employing a gardener to keep the shrubs under control. Matilda walked up the path, reflecting on the lack of enthusiasm for their surroundings that seemed to characterise this strangely disaffected couple. The door opened before she could knock and Maureen stood there, looking at Matilda with a face devoid of expression.

Matilda knew that she must have been looking out of the window, in order to see her so quickly, and wondered why. Maureen never involved herself in the concerns of the village and was usually only heard of when mentioned in the same breath as her husband, almost as if she had no existence in her own right. The only person who had ever spoken of her as an individual was Briony, when she had poured her heart out to Matilda as they did the flowers together. Even then, Briony did not seem to think of Maureen as bearing any blame for the affair with Hugo.

From what Matilda could gather, having affairs was *de rigueur* in the Wintergreen household; but while Simon seemed to enjoy them, Maureen looked upon them as a chore. She seemed glad to invite Matilda in and Matilda suddenly saw how lonely the woman was. She was also struck by Maureen's beauty. Her tall, slim figure was further flattered by well-cut dark green trousers, worn with a cream silk blouse. Tendrils of fair curly hair escaped the deceptively casual ponytail caught back by a green velvet ribbon, softening her long face with its serious grey eyes. Matilda followed her into the drawing room and was impressed by Maureen's elegance and grace.

They talked of the murder straight away. After all, it was what everyone wanted to discuss and Maureen had more than a casual interest. Hangdog's murder had not been solved satisfactorily and Simon was one who had had a possible motive. Maureen was saying that if the two deaths could be linked, then Simon would be free from any suspicion.

'There is a connection between them, isn't there?' she asked anxiously. 'I can't believe that two murders could have been committed in the same tiny village, within the space of a few weeks, without there being a link.'

Matilda agreed but could not see why it was an advantage to Simon if they were. 'Why do you want there to be a connection?'

'Because,' said Maureen tiredly, 'he has a secure alibi for this second one. He was out on a call and didn't get back until ten to eight. If the same person committed both murders, then it can't be Simon.'

'Where did he go?' asked Matilda with interest.

She liked to know all the village gossip. 'You wouldn't know him, I don't expect. It was old Bert Winchester who lives in Tidworth. Pneumonia. Simon left just before seven and it would have taken him twenty minutes to get there. Twenty minutes there and back leaves him fifteen minutes with his patient. No time left to kill anyone.' Maureen looked satisfied.

Matilda hesitated before asking, 'Did you know the murdered man, Pippa's landlord?'

'I've never seen him, as far as I know. I suppose he must have visited Pomery, but I don't go out much and wouldn't have seen him.'

'What about Simon? Did he say that he knew him?'

'Not from Adam. He doesn't think that he was registered with the practice, either.'

That seemed to be that and so Matilda took her leave and wandered slowly up to the manor for Sunday lunch, turning things over in her head.

She had toyed with the idea of telling Maureen what she knew, but decided to leave her in happy ignorance for as long as possible. No need to alarm her unnecessarily and it might all be over soon, before she realised the danger.

If Maureen had involved herself in village affairs, she would have known that old Bert had been staying with his daughter in Rose Cottage for the last three weeks while his own cottage was being renovated. And Rose Cottage was next door to that of Dawn Evans on the far side of Pomery Village green.

Simon must have told her the name without mentioning that he wasn't at home. What the police would want to know was why it had taken Simon so long to visit a patient who lived five minutes away and what else he had been doing during those fifty minutes away from home.

* * *

Lunch at the manor was a jerky affair. Leonora alternated between annoyance at the murder by her gate and condemnation of the lack of policing that allowed it to happen. Henry senior was largely unmoved by the death of a stranger, but hoped that it would not provoke Leonora into a fresh onslaught against the thorny right of way problem through their wood. The way Leonora was talking, the next thing would be a body strewn across his path as he took the dogs for their early morning walk.

Charlotte was in love for the first time with a person and not a cause, and was not to be relied upon to tender practical thoughts on such a minor happening as a murder that could almost have been seen from her bedroom window. The twins were goggle-eyed and had to be reprimanded by their mother for showing an unseemly interest in the state of the corpse. They had looked to Matilda for details, but she proved to be a disappointment. Even if she had known anything, she was too immersed in her own thoughts to play ball.

* * *

Henry junior was with Pippa, who was waiting for another visit from the police. She was genuinely sorry that her landlord was dead. He had always been perfectly pleasant in his dealings with her but, if she was honest, she was more than wondering what she was going to do now. She liked her cottage and she liked Pomery. She could not afford to buy a house and rented accommodation came up rarely.

Pauline moving in with Albert gave her a ray of hope, but Pauline's cottage was not big enough to house her studio comfortably, even supposing that her landlord was agreeable. It was a problem and cast a small shadow over their *al fresco* lunch in her tiny garden at back of the house. But not for long. She was getting so very fond of Henry, and being in his company was cheering in itself.

Henry knew that what he wanted to say to her would solve the problem of where she was to live, but did not dare. He thought that she must know how he felt about her, but was still nervous of putting it to the test. Once rebuffed, all would be lost. He preferred to carry on as they were, in blissful ignorance.

Datchett and Treeve arrived at four o'clock to speak to Pippa again, having completed their enquiries in Squires Lane for the time being. Maureen Wintergreen had been helpful only in the pursuit of justice for her husband, and had provided them with an alibi to check but little else. She had heard nothing and did not recognise the picture of the dead man. Quentin Weatherby had been out and the Frenches and the Needhams too far down the hill to be counted as possible witnesses. If Morgan had been visiting either of those households, it would have been less conspicuous to arrive from the village street rather than walk down Squires Lane in full view of its residents. Nevertheless, they had been asked, but Datchett had drawn a blank.

Pippa and Henry were still in the garden when Datchett found them, reluctant to move out of the warm sunshine. Pippa had work to finish and Henry had had plans to work up another of his sketches onto a small canvas, but indolence was easy on this lazy afternoon.

They roused themselves to greet their visitors, not sorry that here was another excuse to delay work.

Pippa was asked again to describe her landlord's visits and to think hard to see if she could remember him mentioning anyone else in the village by name. She applied her mind duly, but could come up with no new information until questioned more closely about anything that could be said to characterise his visits.

It was then that she mentioned that all his visits to her had been after dark. It had never struck her as strange before, because she had assumed that he worked during the day. After Datchett's questioning, it dawned on her that, when the evenings had become lighter, he had arrived correspondingly later. Analysed in this way, it sounded secretive and Pippa could not think of a reason for him to do this — unless he was avoiding someone. Datchett found this interesting, too. It was only the second piece of useful information that he had gained all Sunday, the first being Sadie's recollection of seeing Morgan in Squires Lane.

'Did you notice that direction he took when he left you?'

'He always came from the Chadbury direction, as far as I can remember, so his car would be pointing toward the village. There's no room to turn round, here, so he would go off toward the village. I always assumed that he turned round there and went back to Chadbury, but I never stood and watched what he did.'

'Has he always had the same car since you've known him?'

'I don't know if it's always been the same one. I do know that it's always been a dark colour.'

'Thank you. We can find that out from his housekeeper, I'm sure. I'm sorry to have bothered you on a Sunday afternoon.'

Pippa and Henry made to get up, to see their visitors out, but were waved back into their chairs.

'You enjoy the sunshine! It's only sinners like ourselves who have to work on a day like today!'

Datchett and Treeve let themselves out, leaving Pippa and Henry restless with inactivity but unable to do anything about it.

There was little more that could be done today. Tomorrow, they would have to investigate Morgan's financial position thoroughly and find out if his car had been seen anywhere else in the village, as well as interviewing the Squires Lane people they had missed today. Datchett didn't think that it was looking good and went home a worried man. Two unsolved deaths in one small place were not the stuff of which good reputations were made.

17

Matilda strolled along to see Edgar after lunch. She needed to talk to someone detached, someone who could discuss the murders dispassionately, and Edgar fitted the bill.

There were few people out walking today and little traffic. She spotted some family cars crammed with children off to see Granny on a Sunday afternoon, or out looking for open spaces in that to run free. The smell of barbecues wafted out from behind the small enclave of modern detached houses on the outskirts of Pomery, and mingled with the murmur of adult conversation and children's shrieks as they enjoyed the weather while it lasted. Murder seemed far away from this studied closeness of domesticity.

She came to the small unsignposted cross-roads of narrow lanes and turned right to where Edgar's cottage stood, a hundred yards away, in a lane no bigger than a car's width. He had bought it for its seclusion, its lack of encouragement to those who might want to 'pop in' — and this aim was achieved, for he had few visitors. Those who troubled to seek him out genuinely craved his company and were made truly welcome.

He had told Matilda that ill-health had caused him to retire early, but she had enquired neither what was wrong with his health, nor from what job he had been retired. His was a friendship she valued and she knew that he would tell her in his own good time, if and when he wanted to. She knew that he was gay and that this was why he was unpopular with her sister and others like her.

Leonora was of the opinion that no one of his 'persuasion', as she called it, should attend church or hold any post of responsibility within it, and she had hoped that this new vicar would take a firmer stand than Stoneygate had done. Matilda found it extraordinary that such prejudice should still exist and had chastised Leonora for it, but she knew that nothing would ever change her sister's mind.

Matilda could only guess at his past disappointments and unhappiness and was glad that he had found this retreat where he could indulge his passion for gardening in peace. He gardened with dedication and this occupied most of his time, combining endless patience with artistic flair. Both the front and back gardens of his tiny cottage were riots of blended colours and scents, with every plant placed in the earth with consideration for its size and flowering times, often allowed to self-seed and spread unchecked. So sure was she that he would be in his garden that she came straight round to the back, to find him kneeling down with a tiny trowel, carefully planting out seedlings he had nurtured himself.

He had straightened up at the sound of her footsteps — Matilda was not the lightest of people on her feet, when preoccupied — and smiled kindly when he saw her, choosing not to reveal that he had recognised her tread. Ten minutes later, they were sitting outside in garden chairs with a tray of tea in front of them and Edgar was looking at Matilda enquiringly.

'Well?'

Matilda shrugged, momentarily shy and diffident in front of this self-contained man. 'I wanted to sound you out, I suppose.'

'Sound away. I'm all ears.' He put his head to one side and Matilda thought irrelevantly that he looked like an attentive garden gnome. He had the ears for it.

She took time to arrange her thoughts before beginning briskly, 'I need to go through it from the beginning. Two suspicious deaths in Pomery in just a few weeks.

Could that be a coincidence?'

Edgar frowned, giving the matter serious consideration. 'It could be, of course, but I rather think not. Coincidences do happen, more often than we give credit for, but this one does stretch belief.'

'So you still think that Hangdog's death was murder?'

Edgar poured them both a cup of tea into thin china cups, watching intently as the brown liquid rose up the sides and the steam drifted eastward in the warm breeze. A butterfly hovered over a bed of bright colour and was tempted. After feasting, it closed up its wings and rested in the lazy warmth, before moving on to live its short day.

Edgar answered reluctantly, following the butterfly with sad eyes, as if he were frightened that to admit to his suspicions would be a sin, causing him to be cast out of his cherished Paradise. He breathed deeply. 'Yes, I do. I think he was murdered and that the murderer intended to kill Albert.'

Matilda nodded, as if mentally ticking this question off her list. 'Hangdog had his wrists cut, but Morgan was stabbed through the heart. Why the difference in methods? Don't murderers always stick to what has been successful before?'

Edgar shrugged. 'If we are to believe

everything we read, yes. I can't explain the difference, in this case. But I can't explain the coincidence, either, and I still believe that there is a connection.'

'Well, then. What is the connection? What could it be?'

'Albert and Hangdog were both criminals. It must be something to do with their past. Perhaps this Morgan is a criminal, too, and knew the same thing as Albert or Hangdog.'

'Well, in that case, who killed them both and why in Pomery? It's got to be someone who lives here, hasn't it? Or someone who has access to local knowledge.'

Edgar sipped his tea, allowing his eyes to drift round the garden again so that they should avoid Matilda, who was impatient for her answer. Finally, he put his cup back into the saucer with a gentle clink, before turning his eyes back to his guest, and made up his mind. He regarded her gravely. 'I'm afraid so, Matilda.'

She returned his gaze in puzzlement, at first, and then with a gradual dawning of understanding. 'You know, too, don't you? You know who the murderer is?'

Edgar looked troubled. 'I think I know who murdered Hangdog but I've no proof — just a conclusion I've come to based on very little fact.'

'Yes. That's the one I was almost sure of myself. It was the second one I couldn't make fit.'

They looked at each other bashfully, like inexperienced lovers wondering who was going to make the first move. Matilda made up her mind. She had remembered that morning what it was about Henry's sketch-book that had struck her as significant and had gone on to form her opinions from there.

She was the first to break the silence. 'I'll tell you who I think killed Hangdog.'

When she had told him, Edgar nodded in agreement. 'That was what I thought. But why?'

'Exactly,' echoed Matilda. 'Why? That's what we have got to find out.'

'I can't see any connection with the other one, though, and we have just said that coincidences don't apply, in this case.'

Matilda leant forward pugnaciously. 'Well, then, it's up to us to prove ourselves right, isn't it?'

She sat back and folded her arms over her ample stomach, uncertainly cased in bright red trousers. Edgar had no course left to him but to agree with her as a spoilsport cloud sailed in front of the sun and cast a shadow onto his garden.

* * *

It was dusk when she left him, spurning his offer to walk back with her, as he had known that she would. He stood at the gate, watching her retreating figure and pondering on his own life that had become bound up with hers during the last few weeks. It was such a change for him, that he was not sure how he felt about it. He liked being her confidante and he enjoyed her friendship. But it was all taking a lot of getting used to. Those last few months nursing Gordon had been the most intensely lived of all his fifty-five years, and the happiest. Despite knowing that there was no hope, they had lived serenely within the security of certain death that had come at last in the spring. Death, the great leveller, took Gordon away and Edgar was left alone.

After his breakdown, he moved to Pomery where Stoneygate visited him regularly out of kindness, stirring in him a faint remembrance of cold church childhood, when every Sunday he had held a cross too heavy for his thin, matchstick arms. Stoneygate was a good man and Edgar had begun to attend church to repay his kindness; he continued to go, now that Stoneygate had been replaced, out of unwillingness to break the routine. He had made plenty of Sunday acquaintances, but Matilda was his first friend.

Matilda walked slowly, thinking hard as she went. Why had she become so obsessed with solving these crimes? Pauline had asked for her help when Albert was accused of killing Hangdog, but that was long past, wasn't it? Albert was safe. At least, from the police. So why couldn't she let go? In a few days' time, she would be home and Pomery would be just a memory to her, functioning very well without her help. She walked on, dragging her feet so that she could work this out before returning to the manor, when all the time, she knew the answer. She was stubborn, like her sister and their father before them. None of them liked to be beaten. She was due to go home a week today and she was determined that she would know the whole truth, by then. Angrily brushing aside a cloud of inquisitive insects, she quickened her pace along the darkening lanes.

As she turned into Squires Lane and began the ascent, she thought again about what she knew already. This accumulated knowledge was not pleasing. If it could be proved, it would result in the life imprisonment of someone who must surely have had reason: but then she thought of Hangdog, an unlovely specimen who should have been allowed to bloom in his own area of shady garden until nature took its course. There was no reason, no justification for murder, so she may as well get on with it and bring the murderer to justice.

* * *

Quentin Weatherby was in. She could see that the house lights were on, and as she watched, the security lights spilt out into the pale grey dusk that clothed his garden. Someone must be moving about outside his house, triggering off the light mechanism.

When she drew up alongside, she saw that it was Weatherby himself, standing in his porch smoking. He hailed her awkwardly when he saw that he had been seen, and she decided that this was as good a time as any to quiz him as to his whereabouts, early Saturday morning. She walked up the straight gravel drive and smelt the cigar smoke, heavy in the night air. The face behind the smokescreen looked drawn and tired.

'Lovely evening!' Matilda greeted him, smiling broadly.

It was always difficult to resist one of Matilda's broad smiles and Weatherby was no exception. His frown uncreased itself and he smiled back, stepping into his hall and gesturing that she should follow.

'You've time for a drink, I hope?' He was already opening the cabinet and pouring a generous measure of Scotch into the heavy tumbler. He handed it to her with a smile.

'I'm flattered that you remember my tipple,' responded Matilda archly, causing Weatherby to preen himself smoothly. Remembering what people drank was part of the reason for his success in company. It gave his guests the illusion that he considered their needs to be important and noteworthy. Everyone thought that they had found a friend in Weatherby.

Matilda took a large swallow and allowed herself to shiver pretentiously. 'I'm afraid that I can't get this murder out of my head. Two sudden deaths close to the manor is rather worrying, wouldn't you say?'

'A bit too close for comfort, I agree. Do you know what the official view is?'

'Not yet. I thought I might try to find out tomorrow. I know Datchett's superior, you know,' she lied. Weatherby looked suitably impressed while Matilda ploughed on, 'It's this dreadful 'eliminating from their enquiries'. I feel guilty before they begin to ask me anything. What about you? Doesn't worry you, I expect. It's different for a man.' She essayed to look helpless behind her wide, gap-toothed smile. Matilda's husbands one to five must have been kicking up their heels in hysterical laughter, rolling about in their narrow coffins, to hear her utter such words and in such a manner. Undaunted, she continued. 'They wanted to know where I was between seven and eight, yesterday morning. Is that what they asked you?'

'I haven't seen anyone, yet. I was out for most of the day. I suppose they'll call back when they're ready.'

'Well, at least I've given you time to get your alibi ready!' she tittered, deciding that she was beginning to get the hang of being arch, but hating it.

'I haven't much of an alibi, I'm afraid. I was in bed asleep and I heard nothing at all. No witnesses, either. They'll just have to believe me.'

'Me, too. Just think that while we were asleep, a murderer was prowling around the lane, waiting for his victim. Do you think that he came here on purpose to meet this Jake Morgan? I should prefer it if he did. I don't think I want to contemplate the idea of a random killer. He could still be here, waiting to strike again at any moment, if that is the case.'

Matilda had allowed herself to prattle on inanely while watching Weatherby covertly.

He was pale through lack of sleep and a muscle in the corner of his eye was twitching. He wore a polite smile on his face but it did not reach as far as his eyes. His fingers were moving restlessly round his tumbler and then suddenly he dropped it and the liquid arched out onto the carpet, where it soaked in without a trace. The thick glass rolled away unbroken and there was an awkward silence while Matilda searched his face, before he bent down to retrieve his glass and shrugged off the incident.

She set out for the manor soon afterward with plenty of food for thought. Something had upset Quentin Weatherby, and she thought that it must be to do with the murder; but, whatever it was, he was not going to tell her tonight. And she was not going to tell him what she knew until he was more in control of himself. Was he frightened of being the next victim? she wondered, or did he know full well who the murderer was and had she just been supping with him?

Everyone was in bed when she got in, and she told Wing to lock up, as she would not be going out any more that night. The house was warm and quiet, the sunshine having seeped into the fabric for the first time that year. The oak stairs and landing creaked as she climbed up to her room and opened the door, standing for a moment on the threshold to enjoy the heat. Reluctantly, for she loved to feel warm, she realised that the room would be too stuffy to sleep in and crossed over to the window to push it open.

She leant out to breathe the air and saw the silver of the moonbeams fingering their way through the woodland. A bat fluttered across in front of her line of vision and she wondered briefly where it lived and how many journeys it had to make into the night to feed itself.

She wondered, too, if Edgar would be unable to sleep again tonight and if he were walking his way through another night. He had eyes like a cat and had no trouble finding his way even with no moon to guide him. Funny what he'd seen on the night of Hangdog's death. He was quite right not to say anything, though. There was no proof that it was in any way connected to Hangdog's murder. That reminded her. She must seek out Henry's sketch book for her bit of evidence, if it ever came that far.

But it was the vision of Quentin's pale face that would not leave her as she got ready for bed. She hadn't been able to fathom him yet and it annoyed her for, when it came to men, she was an expert. She had decided that it was time to get to know him better but every time they met, she felt a barrier that she was quite unable to penetrate.

Quentin Weatherby's arrival in Pomery had caused quite a stir. He had bought Foxholes outright for cash, according to the Restaways, who were moving away to be near their married daughter. Foxholes changed hands fairly frequently. Village rumour had it that it harboured a ghost, that of a servant girl murdered by her employer in the late nineteenth century. He was said to have tipped her body into the well — still a feature of the rear garden, although filled in now — and to smile every time he drank from it. He had died in agony a few weeks after the girl, and the story ran that it was her ghost wreaking revenge. Informed opinion now thought it more likely that he died of cholera, but there were still some who believed the story, as some always will.

For the first few weeks after he had bought it, Quentin had stayed at the Royal in Chadbury, while the house was redecorated to his specifications, moving in not long after the Nesbiths and Albert Noonday had come to live in Pomery.

Pomeranians got to know all the details of his move from his daily who had watched in amazement, half-fascinated and half-frightened at the number of antiques that were carried across the threshold. When Quentin had told her what some of them were worth, she had had to sit down on the stairs to recover. She had worked for the Restaways for years and had stayed on at their recommendation, but she was not sure that she was up to this. Even the Nonsuches had only a fraction of the value of some of these.

The most surprising thing, she told Winnie Tomkin, which was the same as telling the world, the most surprising thing was that Mr Weatherby didn't treat his things as anything special and he told her not to, either.

'Just because they're old, doesn't mean that they can't be used, my dear Mrs T,' he'd said. 'I like well-made and beautiful things. To use and to look at. They wouldn't be much use to me if I were afraid of them, would they?'

Winnie had lapped it all up. 'So what did you say to that?'

'I said that I supposed they got dirty like everything else, and he said, 'I can see that you're a realist, Mrs T. We're going to get along, you and me.' '

'And do you — get on, I mean?' asked Winnie, hoping for something more juicy to spread around. Her friend nodded sagely, with a hint of superiority, Winnie thought.

'He leaves me to it. Doesn't interfere. And, I must say, some of the wood comes up a treat. See your face in his dining room table. You don't get furniture like that, nowadays.'

Only if you can afford it, thought Winnie sourly, but she held her tongue. She wouldn't want to discourage any gossip.

It was through Rita that she had learnt about the party, planned for the beginning of December to beat the Christmas round. He had gone about it in a very informal way, inviting people indiscriminately and telling each and everyone to 'bring a friend'. Anyone he saw in the week preceding his party had been invited, resulting in a large sample of the population of Pomery gathering under his roof on a frosty December evening.

Matilda was there with Leonora and Henry. Sadie, Agatha with a reluctant Gerald, both Wintergreens and the Brightsides, the Frenches and the Needhams made a full complement for Squires Lane. Several members of PADS had been invited: Sally and Nicholas; Edgar Bryan and Frank Whittle; Mary Stringer, who had been with Agatha when they were asked together. Even old Enid Brandon had been urged to come, when encountered by Quentin when she was out shopping.

There was no doubt about it. When he wanted to, Quentin had a way with people. Rita had been invited as a guest, while caterers took over the cooking and the serving. She was told that they cleaned up, as well, so there would be no extra work for her to do and she could really enjoy herself.

Knowing a bit about his antiques put her in the position of being able to show off her knowledge, a state of affairs to which she was not averse. She took Enid under her wing and told her what little she knew about the age and origin of the furniture and porcelain, basking in her friend's undisguised admiration. It was through this amateur tuition that the sword-stick was mentioned in front of a group of guests who happened to overhear Quentin gently correct Rita when she told Enid that it was just a Victorian walking stick.

It was an excellent example of its type and Matilda had appreciated the workmanship. Quentin had given way to a burst of theatre, pulling the sword from the sheath and lunging at the buffet table, securing a canapé on the tip, much to the amusement of the by now well-oiled guests.

Matilda thought of this now as she lay in her bed, unable to sleep. Was this why she couldn't erase him from her mind? Closing her eyes, she tried to picture the body lying on the shady path. She had only been able to have a quick look, but she was positive that she recognised the wooden handle that stuck out of Jake Morgan's heart. It was the sword stick. Quentin Weatherby's sword-stick. Did that make him a murderer?

The evening at his house had ended noisily with a visit to the well, to try to summon up a *frisson* of fear at the thought of the sinister secret that surrounded it. They had wrapped themselves up against the cold and anyone would have been able to conceal the sword-stick under their coat. It did not have to be Weatherby himself.

But that would have shown premeditation on someone's part — and who would have known then that they would want to kill Jake Morgan, and why wait so long? And why use a weapon so easily traceable? That argument especially applied to Weatherby.

Matilda heaved herself up into a sitting position, all thought of sleep gone now. She pictured the brick well with its wooden cover on that the Restaways had placed a tubs of flowers, now frosted and ruined. Were the bones of the servant girl buried underneath? And if they were, what had that to do with anything?

It was not possible for subsequent householders to inherit a propensity to murder. If Weatherby had done it, it was because he and no one else had wanted to do it. It wasn't as if this pussy had been dropped in the well. But she did wonder why he had not mentioned that the stick was missing, if it had been taken all that time ago; and if it had been stolen recently, who would have had the opportunity to do so?

It played havoc with the ideas pooled with Edgar Bryan this afternoon. Matilda sat up until dawn, when she slipped into a dreamless sleep. Her brain had been too taken-up with wild imaginings to supply her with more while she slept.

18

Chepstow and Groat were respectable solicitors who would not dream of divulging the private affairs of a client to anyone but, in the face of dour persistence, they succumbed to this break with tradition and told Datchett all he wanted to know.

They had acted for Mr Morgan for a period of fifteen years, overseeing all his legal requirements for the lease and eventual purchase of his antique shop and for his properties, drawing up the tenants' agreements and generally advising him how best to avoid the various pitfalls that existed between landlord and tenant.

Asked for a list of his properties, they were thrown into agonies of legal conscience again, but recovered in no time to provide Datchett with the required information. Morgan had owned his own house, the shop, a small town house in Chadbury, Pippa's cottage and Mary Stringer's bungalow in Pomery.

'Two houses in Pomery,' mused Datchett. 'Now that I call more than coincidence.' He was more than annoyed to find out later that Mary Stringer claimed to send her rent through the post and had only seen her landlord once when he showed her round the bungalow initially. None of her neighbours could remember seeing his car parked in the vicinity, to boot. Another non-starter, he supposed.

* * *

Matilda awoke from a heavy sleep to find that Quentin was her first waking thought. In the half-existence between sleep and waking, she had remembered something else about that party, a previously forgotten conversation of no seeming importance at the time. She must think this through properly. Today was Monday and it had been arranged for her to return home in a week's time. The kneelers were being dedicated next Sunday, during the morning service, and she had made up her mind that she would pray for the murderer then, knowing that he was under lock and key. That meant that she could not afford to waste any time in getting her proof.

It was time to talk to Albert again. It could be that she had been wrong in her first assumption that he had been the intended victim. She needed to find out more about Hangdog and Albert was the person to tell her.

She waited until lunch time before calling on him, wanting to be sure that he was in. The scene that greeted her as Pauline brought her through to the kitchen was domestic and oddly touching.

The table was set with a china teapot, matching plates and cups with a breadboard in the centre sporting a crusty loaf of which two slices lay on the plates. A dish of butter and a hunk of cheese completed the meal. Albert turned as she entered, teacup in hand and the softness went out of his face. Matilda had broken the spell.

Pauline was unfazed by her presence, an unblemished conscience her shield, drawing up another chair to the table for their visitor. Matilda began by apologising for spoiling their meal, but it did not stop her from reminding them of Hangdog and all the trouble he had heaped upon their heads. Albert looked sullen and Pauline worried, but Matilda would not let go.

'What I want to know is if you can tell me anything about Hangdog's past, other than his prison life. Where did he come from, for instance? Where did he live when he was not in prison?'

Albert continued to stare at his plate, and the kitchen clock that Pauline had brought from her own kitchen ticked loudly in the silence. With each quiet minute, the hope that he might co-operate became fainter and, but for Pauline's steady look of encouragement, it would have faded altogether.

Eventually, he met her eyes and, with a sigh, answered reluctantly, 'He was born in Birmingham, like me. His old man got life with a twenty-year recommendation and his old lady dumped him on a friend and ran off. He ended up in the same kids' home as me. Lilac House, just outside Coventry.' Albert fell silent again, as if listening to his own story himself for the first time. Pauline was all concern, moving round to sit close to him while Matilda marvelled anew at the power of love.

Doggedly, Matilda continued, 'Did you leave the home together?'

Albert shook his head.' He was two years older than me. He disappeared, one night when he was nearly sixteen, and no one bothered looking for him. I stayed for another year and then ran away and got a job on a farm near Evesham, where they didn't ask too many questions. Worked for my keep, but they treated me well enough. Learnt a lot; that is how I can manage this place.'

'And Hangdog?'

'Met up by chance. They sold the farm, so there was no place for me, and I went back to

Brum. Got myself fixed up in a squat and, a few weeks later, I saw him in the boozer on the corner. He didn't want to know me, then. He was driving for this bloke, taking him and his women places, running errands — you know the sort of thing.'

Matilda didn't, but she could guess. 'What happened then?'

'To Hangdog? Had his services dispensed with.' Albert put on a refined voice. 'Helping himself to the profits, at a guess, or sampling the goods.' Albert looked at Matilda sideways, wondering if she was following him. She kept her face devoid of any expression except interest, and Albert was reassured.

'He ended up looking for me and moving into my place. We met this bloke called Fraser soon after that, and did a couple of jobs with him. Went down for the third. I didn't want to do any more, after that, but Hangdog had this thing about Fraser and Fraser liked me at the wheel. Hangdog could be very persuasive.' Matilda detected resentment as he remembered the persuasion.

'What about enemies? Do you know of anyone who could bear him a grudge?'

'Only everyone he met. Hangdog didn't exactly have a way with people.' Albert frowned in remembrance.

'Are you sure that there wasn't anyone in particular?'

'Not that I'm aware of.' Albert looked at Matilda boldly, for the first time. 'Are you saying that whoever murdered Hangdog — and I know it was murder, whatever that court said — really meant to kill him and not me?'

'I'm not sure, yet,' mused Matilda slowly, 'but I've got an idea that only makes sense if that is the case. What I need is some information about people he used to know.' She paused thoughtfully. 'Are you sure that you can't remember anything about the person for whom he used to work? Not even a Christian name? He must have called him something. Try to think back.'

'Eddie,' said Albert suddenly. 'He called him Eddie, and he had a girlfriend called Mo. Met him once. Don't expect I'd recognise him now, though. Never met her.'

'And what sort of business was he in?'

Albert looked at her coldly. 'Drugs, of course. And — ' he was warming to his theme ' — and he ran a few high-class girls. Mo was one, before she moved in with him.'

'Your memory has come back rather quickly, hasn't it?'

Albert and Pauline exchanged a glance and Matilda saw the deliverance in their faces.

They had been released from a different sort of prison, one made of fear and Albert was garrulous with relief. 'That's all I do remember, though. I've never touched drugs and I kept well out of it.'

Matilda changed tack. 'What about the others who were on your last job? Are they still all in prison?'

'Hangdog and I were the only ones out. The rest had things to be taken into consideration. Like a jeweller's shop in Aston, a week before the bank. Different M.O. for that one. Fraser trying to go upmarket. They didn't need us, thank God.'

'So if anyone held a grudge against him, it's more likely to be someone from the past?' Matilda stared at the polished kitchen tiles in thought.

'Where did he go when he got out? How was it that he came across you? Rather a coincidence, when you've got the whole country to choose from, isn't it?'

Albert immediately adopted his cagey look and Matilda knew at once why.

'How soon were you picked up after the robbery?'

Albert shrugged and Matilda knew that she had been right. The proceeds from the robbery must be hidden nearby. That was the only thing that made sense. The money must be hidden somewhere where Albert could get his hands on it without the other members of the gang knowing. The police had been on their tails and they needed to pass it to someone to be laundered, if what she read in fiction was true. And they hadn't much time. Ten to one, as nothing had been found when they were arrested, it must have been hidden temporarily with someone they trusted until the heat died down. The question was, where?

Even Matilda could recognise when she was going to elicit no more information. Albert had clammed up and Pauline was looking angry, protective of her loved one. Matilda took her leave and walked slowly in the direction of Banbury Wood, her eyes on the ground as if to raise them would bring in extraneous matters to cloud her vision.

Matilda thought back to Albert's meeting with Hangdog. Hangdog had been in Silminster and seen Albert by chance. What was Hangdog doing there? He didn't know where Albert had gone. And what was Albert doing a few miles away in Chadbury, where he had seen the advertisement for the farm? With all the country to choose from, why should they both end up in this area? There had to be a reason and the most likely one was money. Albert and Hangdog knew where the money was and it was close to here.

So what sort of hiding place were they looking for? The money must have been left with someone and Albert knew who that someone was: had come here, in fact, to approach that person. But who in Pomery could have any connection with a sordid little crime committed in Birmingham three years ago? And why would they be likely to give some of it to Albert when Fraser had left strict instructions not to do so? From what Albert said, it seemed that this Fraser tended to get his own way unless you wanted to lose fingers. Matilda racked her brains and was blowed if she could find an answer. Meanwhile, she couldn't get the idea of the sword-stick out of her mind.

Matilda came to the clearing where the old horse trough lay and stood looking up at the sky, uncluttered by trees. She wished that her mind could see through to the problem as clearly as she could see to the sky. Cottontail clouds chased each other along and the sun shone in their midst, like a benign nanny watching the children'play.

If Jake had been the banker, holding the money for when they all got out, what had been the point of killing him? Unless he had spent it all. Unless, when Albert went to him, there was none left. But would Jake have risked double-crossing Fraser? And, if Albert had been the one to find out, Albert would have to be the one who killed him. Matilda thought hard about what she had seen of Albert today and she didn't believe it.

She spent the rest of the evening in deep thought and, in the morning, announced to Leonora that she was to be away for the night.

'Popping up to town?'

'No. I'm going to Birmingham. Expect me when you see me.'

With that, she borrowed the Rolls and set off, picking up a reluctant Edgar Bryan on the way. Geoffrey's son by his first marriage was a chief superintendent in Birmingham. She was sure that he could be made to pull a few strings.

Strings having been pulled, the kneelers were dedicated on Sunday, as arranged, but Matilda could not pray for the murderer. Despite her stepson's best efforts, she was still not a hundred per cent sure who he was.

Part Three

. . . and on hir heed an hat
As brood as is a bokeler or a targe

Geoffrey Chaucer,
The Canterbury Tales

19

Summer was almost over. A whole year since Matilda had made the final arrangements for the last April pilgrimage and now she was doing exactly the same thing again for next year. But it did not feel the same. This time last year, there had been no fire yet and no murders. She had got over the fire, but the unsolved murders irked her.

Sitting in the study of her restored house, she sniffed at the clinging smell of paint and new furniture. It made her feel uncomfortable, as if she were a visitor to a stately home, able to look but not touch. The whole house was the same and she hoped that, by the time the weather prevented her from flinging all the windows wide open, the smell would have disappeared. She missed her old furniture, its worn comfort and lived-in smells. Even the garden had suffered, trampled on by the firemen in their efforts to save what they could. Possessions mattered little to Matilda, but she liked to feel at home.

This time last year, two people were alive who were now dead, murdered in Pomery by a person or persons unknown. Matilda had done her best to find the culprit and she thought that she had, but as for proof — she may as well have whistled. Datchett and Treeve had done no better.

Edgar had been keeping her in touch with the latest developments. There had been some excitement, the week after she had left, when it was discovered that the wooden covering to Quentin's well could be removed and that the sword-stick sheath had been found in among the rubble. Weatherby had been questioned about it but maintained that anyone could have put it there. He had not noticed that it was missing. It was easy to cross from one garden to another and there was plenty of cover among the trees and bushes. Anyone could have put it there and anyone could have murdered Jake Morgan. There was no more evidence with that to proceed.

Matilda reached for the phone to begin to make her arrangements for next year's art pilgrimage. She wished that she could have the final chapter ready to tell them, by then. It would make a good story and set the tone for their evening entertainment.

As she was setting about her task, a letter plopped onto the newly polished tiles in the hall and skidded to a halt in front of the grandmother clock that had been a wedding present from her third mother-in-law — an oddly appropriate place to land, as the letter was an invitation to a wedding in Pomery. Henry and Pippa were getting married on the fifteenth of October and would love Matilda to be present.

Oddly enough, now that she had the opportunity, Matilda felt reluctant to visit Pomery again, as it had negative associations for her that she would rather not think about. Matilda was not used to failure — and she had failed, this time, despite her best efforts. If she had not been so extraordinarily fond of Henry and Pippa, she would have declined the invitation; but, as it was, she went shopping the next day for a suitable gift and planned her outfit so that she would outdo Leonora. No one would be able to miss her fire-engine red ensemble with matching cartwheel hat. Leonora would probably wear beige, which emphasised her sallow skin, and brogues, to show off her skinny legs to her disadvantage.

* * *

The wedding had thrown Pomery into a state of vicarious excitement. Henry and Pippa were universally popular and everyone wanted to help in some way. Leonora orchestrated this help, as was right that she should, but there was infighting over details at every turn.

The reception was to be held at the Manor with a marquee for the overspill. Leonora had employed outside caterers but was entrusting the flowers — both in the church and at the reception — to the Pomery flower ladies. Normally, this would have run smoothly under the capable management of Nanette French: but in July, everyone who knew her had been delighted to learn that she was pregnant, though anxious to hear at the beginning of October that there were complications, forcing her to have a spell of complete rest in hospital.

Harriet was well suited to take over but Agatha Kingsway decided that the task of overall supervision should fall onto her shoulders. With Mary Stringer in tow, she proceeded to organise all the flower ladies into confusion. Pippa's preference for simple colours and arrangements was largely ignored.

Harriet listened quietly to Agatha's instructions and took the list of flowers to order without a murmur. After talking to Pippa, she made her own list and it was this one that she left at the florist. Nanette appreciated the joke when Harriet visited her in hospital that evening, but was too frightened to laugh.

* * *

Henry and Pippa were to live in Pippa's cottage until told that they could not. No relative of Jake Morgan's had been found and his affairs were in the hands of strangers, who had no plans to convert the cottage to capital yet. This gave them an immediate roof over their heads and time to look around for somewhere bigger. With both of them painting now, they needed the space. Henry had had to store some of his finished canvases up at the manor already.

He had used his sketchbook to work up several of his landscapes and it was these he had moved while he concentrated on a portrait of Pippa, begun one wet afternoon when she had been absorbed in her work and not able to notice what he was doing. It was a major setback — which he refused to let cloud his wedding happiness — when an intruder at the manor slashed every one of his landscapes to ribbons, a week before the wedding.

Datchett suppressed a tut of annoyance on hearing the news. What was it about Pomery that made people murder each other and damage property? As it had happened at the manor, he was obliged to go himself and placate Mrs Babbington-Banbury, who was quivering with rage at the audacity of the villain, but indifferent to the fate of her son's art.

It appeared that they had been stored in a downstairs cloakroom and the vandal had entered by a side-door that had been left unlocked. Wing swore that he had shut it, and offered his resignation. Leonora asked him where he thought he would go, at his age, having spent all his life at the Manor: and he withdrew with dignity, still affirming that he had not left the door open.

When Matilda arrived, two days before the nuptials, she knew that he had been right, but she did not let on to Leonora. Instead, she had a long talk with the twins and elicited some useful information.

As Matilda had realised, the twins had been the ones to leave the door unlocked, on returning from one of their evenings with Edgar. After being admonished for their carelessness, without their mother being any the wiser, they were more than usually keen to think back to that night and name anyone they might have seen while they were out. They were at an advantage on these nights, because they had to move quietly in case they were seen, and consequently were not heard by anyone else who may have reason not to be noticed. After half an hour of patient questioning, Matilda hit the jackpot, but there was still no real proof that would stand up in court.

Nick would not have been nervous about the big wedding if Leonora had left him alone. As it was, she was on the phone at least twice a day, reminding, questioning, cajoling, until even Nick's iron nerve was on the point of collapse. Sally tried to spare him the phone-calls but was usually obliged to fetch him in the end.

He took to wandering round the village, visiting his parishioners, or sitting in the vestry with an unread book open on his table. Since the deaths, Pomery had tended to close its doors more quickly and Nick sensed an unease for which he found it difficult to offer solace.

This unease was changed for another sort that loomed large when he sat in the vestry and heard Dawn Evans practising on the organ for the wedding. The man had been to refurbish the instrument in July and, as Nick listened, it was confirmed in his own mind that the discordant noise issuing from the organ was less to do with sticky stops than with Dawn herself. She really wasn't a very good organist. Indeed her *Arrival of the Queen of Sheba* sounded as if it should be used for 'Exit, pursued by a bear'. Nick broke out into a sweat every time he heard it; he trailed home wretchedly to answer the phone and hear Leonora's voice demanding yet again whether he had arranged for the heating to be turned on, if the day should be chilly.

Sally was a little worried about the children. They had been invited as a family and Joe should be all right, if she remembered to bring a book or two for him. It was Amy who was the handful, being prone to running everywhere full tilt from the moment she got up until her bedtime. She was used to sitting on Sally's lap in church, but the added excitement was sure to wind her up and Sally did not wish to carry the child out, screaming, under Leonora's wrathful eye.

Charlotte, Georgina and Emma had been co-opted as bridesmaids. Thomas refused point-blank to dress up — until bribed by his brother, in order to keep the peace with Leonora. Thomas was to be an usher, along with Pippa's brother and two cousins.

Pippa had opted for white, to please her mother, but had managed to prevail with her choice for the bridesmaids, who were to wear sage-green and dusky-pink crushed velvet. Georgina announced that it was the least puke-making bridesmaid's dress she had ever seen and, with this observation taken from her vast experience of such things, Pippa had to be content.

When Matilda arrived, Henry senior was being schooled as to what he should say on the day, which Leonora had decided would be mercifully little. The main speech would be left to the best man, an old school friend of Henry's, whose nerves were just under control until he met Leonora for the wedding rehearsal on Thursday. By the time this was over, he and Nick were quivering like aspens and in need of a set of restoratives from the Pieces of Eight.

Sally sighed when she saw the state of her husband on his return, but helped him up to bed in the certain knowledge that, after Saturday, she would have the man she had married back and Pomery would settle back down into its usual routine.

For Henry's friend, Oliver, there was no escape, because he was staying at the manor until after the wedding. He went back to his bedroom and lay down for the rest of the evening, trying not to fall asleep. Whenever that happened, he dreamt of huge Leonoras chasing him through fields thick with confetti and he had lost the ring.

Meanwhile, the murderer was thinking about Albert and wondering afresh if there might still be danger. After committing murder without being suspected, it would be foolish to lose it all for the sake of a loose end. On the other hand, murder was always a risk and it was tempting to let sleeping dogs lie. Did Albert know or suspect, that was the question? From past knowledge, he was capable of biding his time. He'd been known in the gang as the one with the slow fuse, able to wait for what he wanted but then striking with deadly accuracy. On the day before the wedding, Albert's fate had yet to be decided, but it was not looking too hopeful.

20

Harriet arranged to have a half-day holiday on the Friday so that she could do the flowers, and Friday afternoon found the church flower-arrangers busily making bows for the posies to be fixed onto the ends of the pews and filling the vases with sprays of pink and white, offset by fern. Agatha arrived in the middle of all the activity to find that the flowers were the wrong colour, but everyone agreed that it was too late to do anything about it now. She spent a little while fiddling about with things that had no need to be fiddled with and then departed for the manor, whence she had sent Mary with instructions to hang out the bunting that Leonora had found for them in the downstairs cloakroom a few days ago.

The marquee was in place and strings of fairy lights had been woven into the branches of the trees nearest to the house. Mary was standing indecisively with the bunting that she had cleverly recovered from the cloak-room, when Matilda espied her and suggested that they fetch the ladder.

They returned to the cloakroom, already

piled high with oddments to do with the wedding, plus Henry's torn canvases, which had to be moved one at a time because he had put them in front of the ladder. As Mary looked reluctant, Matilda did the climbing while Mary held the ladder steady.

Together they arranged the bunting as tastefully as they could, to pass muster for Leonora and Agatha. Some went in the trees and some along the front of the house, looping down from the windows. This had to be done from inside the house and it gave Mary quiet satisfaction to be walking through the bedrooms at the manor as if she were a member of the family.

They had done this job first and, by the time that Agatha arrived, they were tackling the decoration of the trees. Agatha was left feeling lost, now, because there didn't seem to be anything for her to do. Annoyingly, she was asked to help Mary put the stepladder away because Matilda was needed to pacify Leonora over a trifle: one that had been dropped in the middle of the top table when it ought to have been in the fridge.

Putting away stepladders did not please either lady and they both emerged from the cloakroom with bad tempers. Henry senior wandered into view and nodded his head in approval when he saw the red, white and blue flags. His father and grandfather had instilled a sort of blind patriotism into him, which he didn't understand but was convinced was a good thing. He knew that Leonora approved of it, too: that always made his life easier and so he felt justified in smiling amiably at her as she strode past him toward the marquee, with urgent instructions for the caterers.

She totally ignored him.

Henry junior was getting ready for his stag night to be held in The Wheelwright Inn, Chadbury, where he had booked a room at the back. He'd been there before and found the ground floor an assistance when the room started to swim. No steps to negotiate. Oliver, who had managed to avoid Leonora all day, ran out of luck at about teatime and was charged with the responsibility of bringing Henry back in good working order. The very thought of this task made him reach for his hip-flask.

Pippa liked Oliver well enough, but had been worried by the attack of nerves induced in him by Leonora. She had persuaded him to entrust the ring to Wing's care. At least that was one thing less to worry about. Keeping Henry safe on the eve of their wedding was another matter and one to which she could see no solution. She went to see Nanette in hospital and then had an early night, although sleep did not come to unravel her care.

She had been more disturbed by the slashing of Henry's pictures than Henry himself. He had shrugged it off as a piece of mindless vandalism, but she did not see it this way and it upset her to think that there was someone in the village who hated Henry so much as to do such a thing. It had to be a personal attack. Nothing else was damaged. There were more of Henry's paintings here, in their studio, and Henry was sleeping at the manor tonight. Everyone in the village would know that. What was there to stop them from coming and finishing off the job while she was alone in the house?

And suppose that they did not stop at damaging pictures, this time? If they hated him so much, they would surely hate his chance of happiness. She sat up in bed. The luminous hands on her alarm clock said three o'clock and she thought that she heard a noise in the studio. Then minutes later, she was sure and got up to see what it was.

* * *

At half past three, a relieved taxi-driver deposited Henry and Oliver at the gates of the manor and made off, muttering about the young of today. Neither of them could stand up, but they adopted a fairly adequate crawl, which closed the gap between the gates and the front door quite quickly.

The problems began when they tried to put the key in the front door. They did stand a better chance of succeeding when Henry abandoned his finger and used the key instead, but he was still too low on the ground to reach.

After looking at each other owlishly for a while, they decided that one of them should try to climb on top of the other's back to gain height, and they spent a few minutes trying to perfect this technique, with limited success. The one who was being climbed upon collapsed under the weight of the climber, who banged his head on the oaken door — which had withstood Oliver Cromwell and showed every sign of repelling all other boarders. Finally, they abandoned the idea of getting in at all and crawled off to the barn, where the hay and Emma's pony kept them warm while the barn ebbed and flowed comfortingly all night.

* * *

Henry was always saying that they should get a mobile phone or an extension for upstairs and now Pippa wished that she had listened to him. There was definitely someone in the studio. She could hear them moving about and the thought of damage to their paintings gave her more courage than she had thought she possessed. All the same, she wished that she could phone for help.

She crept down the stairs, pausing on each step to listen. She had no weapon — nor did she want one — but it would have been comfortable to have something in her hand. Her eyes lit upon an old walking stick in the corner of the hall. If she made for that, it would give her more confidence: but, before she could begin her stealthy creeping, the door of the studio opened and light flooded all around her. A figure stood in the doorway, looking up at Pippa who waited, white-faced, feeling more than foolish in her night gown with nothing at all with which to defend herself.

* * *

It was quiet on the ward now. The nurses had had their tea and the patients were able to settle down for the night. Nanette tried to sleep, tried to push her fears away from her. She couldn't lose the baby now, after all the years of waiting, could she? Life couldn't be so cruel. Miserably, she turned onto her side.

The pain in her back was getting worse and it was spreading. Should she tell someone? It was very bad now and the stabbing pains in her stomach felt too severe to be normal. It couldn't be, could it? She had another three weeks to go. She willed herself to believe that it was a false alarm. The baby must be lying awkwardly. Mustn't say anything. They would tell her things she did not want to hear.

She closed her eyes and tried to ignore it all. But, just as Henry and Oliver were crawling to the barn and Pippa was facing her intruder, Nanette's finger found the bell and pressed firmly as another pain left her screaming and gasping for breath.

* * *

Matilda's deafness and her absorption in what she had found prevented her from hearing Pippa coming down the stairs. She had opened the door to let the revealing light escape in a moment of aberration, intent upon getting back to the manor with her find. Gaining entry had not been difficult. She had let herself in with Henry's key and, but for Pippa's vigilance, would have shut and locked the door without Pippa being any the wiser. They stared at each other in mutual amazement and relief, mingled with suspicion on Pippa's part.

Pippa ran down the last few steps and faced the intruder. 'What are you doing with Henry's sketchbook?' she asked, not altogether agreeably.

Matilda had the grace to look abashed, but answered with great sadness. 'Looking for a murderer,' she said.

A car sped past the cottage — Harry French, on the way to Chadbury hospital, did they but know — breaking the silence between the two women, who had both been overcome with a weariness that came not solely from a night of no sleep.

Pippa's shoulders sagged. 'Come back into the studio. We keep some coffee things in here.'

Matilda followed, torn between insisting that Pippa return to bed so that she would be fresh for the next day, and the need to talk to someone about what she thought she had found.

Pippa put the kettle on and answered Matilda's thoughts. 'You may as well tell me. I'm quite awake now and dying of curiosity. I'm sure that you had a good reason for doing what you did.'

Matilda sat down heavily in one of the old armchairs, where Pippa and Henry would sit sometimes when they took a break, sipping coffee and looking out into the garden. 'I've been worried about the pictures that were ruined. I looked through them this afternoon and found that they were ones that I'd seen in his sketchbook when he started painting again. It occurred to me that there were two probable reasons for the attack. Either someone has taken a serious dislike to Henry, or there was something in one of the pictures that was dangerous if seen by someone who could put the right connotation on it. I vaguely remembered being struck by something odd when I looked at the book when I was here last, and it made me think of the murder. Not of Jake Morgan. The first one. Hangdog.'

Pippa looked surprised. 'I thought that that was suicide.'

'That's the official view,' said Matilda slowly, 'but I don't agree with it.'

'And you think that Henry saw the murderer?'

'I think it's likely.'

'But what's it got to do with his painting? Unless he actually painted someone murdering Hangdog, I don't see that a painting would be any proof of anything. Which one is it, anyway? I saw them all, don't forget, and there was nothing in any of them to make me think that I was looking at a murderer. Hardly any of them had figures in, and those that did were small. Lightning sketches, really.'

'Would you say that Henry was good at getting a likeness from one of his lightning sketches?' said Matilda abruptly.

'It's one of his talents,' admitted Pippa. 'He's a really good caricaturist.'

Matilda nodded furiously. 'Did you recognise anyone from one of them?'

Pippa frowned. 'I must confess that, as he was showing and asking my opinion about his landscape technique, I didn't study the little figures in detail. He was anxious for my opinion on his style and brushwork, and that is what I concentrated on.'

Matilda passed the sketchbook across the low table between them. 'Can you bear to look again? I would welcome your opinion.'

Pippa took the book and opened it at the first page. She was halfway through when she stopped suddenly and peered more closely. 'I remember him doing this one. He asked me about the composition and made a water-colour in situ. Two, in fact, from a different angle. It was March and he caught a cold. The water-colour didn't have the figures in, but he must have looked at his sketchbook again and added them to give focus when he made the oil painting. Now that I look at it again, I can see who they are. There's the man you call Hangdog — and isn't the other one . . . ?' Pippa tailed off and lifted her head to look at Matilda. 'Surely that's . . . ?'

Matilda stretched out her hand for the book. 'That's what I thought, the first time I saw it. I hoped that it would prove to be a stranger.'

'But is it proof of murder?'

'No. Not in itself. But it's proof of an unnecessary lie: and that always makes me wonder.' Matilda stood up determinedly. 'Enough of this, now. Have you got anything to help you sleep?'

'No. I never take anything. I'm sure I couldn't sleep now, whatever I took.'

'I'll stay here while you go and try to get some rest. I've found out what I wanted to know and I won't do anything else about it at the moment, not until after your big day.'

Matilda was feeling guilty now at involving Pippa and wished that she hadn't been so hasty in coming here tonight. Pippa looked at Matilda, big and comfortable-looking in her armchair, and suddenly thought that she might sleep if she tried hard, with Matilda here as her bastion. Stifling a yawn, she went back to bed and slept the sleep of the just.

The murderer slept badly, still in two

minds about Albert. Did he know or did he not? Tossing and turning was no help. The concern should have been for the little book that Matilda was, at that moment, planning to place beneath her mattress when she returned to the manor. That and what Matilda had found out on her visit to Birmingham. She might have lacked proof, still, but she knew where to point the finger. She might not like it, but she knew where her duty lay.

21

Matilda arrived at the manor in time to see Henry and Oliver standing in the hall, pungent with smell of horse, and hay protuding from every visible orifice. They were being soundly carpeted by an outraged Leonora. As Matilda walked through the door, Emma arrived on the scene and threatened Henry with the direst of consequences if they had upset the pony, before flouncing past her aunt with a face set for thunder. True Lancet-Brickway, mused Matilda admiringly, as the door slammed behind her niece.

Henry's head was in an invisible metal box that was being hammered on from the outside, each blow echoing around his skull and bouncing off the bones only to return, like radar. Someone had lit fires in his eye-sockets and a cauldron bubbled in his stomach. He didn't feel very well. When he tried to turn his creaking head to look at Oliver, he thought that there was something the matter with his friend, too.

Gradually, the shrill noises ceased, to be replaced by a steady booming like a foghorn sounding through the mist. Things were moving past him now. Stairs and pictures. Leonora's angry face was left behind. Something hard was pushing into the small of his back. Oliver was beside him, thinking the same thoughts with a similar hand in the small of his back. Aunt Matilda was pushing them both upstairs.

Niagara. Deafening. Cold water splashed over his head and under his collar, wriggling down inside his shirt. He gasped with shock. Not a good idea. Matilda took no notice of choking. Nor of shivering. Funny. She wasn't usually like this. He'd always rather liked her. What was she saying? Couldn't hear her properly, under this tidal wave. It was ten minutes before he understood that he was getting married in two hour's time, and his best man was propped up against the bathroom wall, dead to the world.

* * *

The wedding was to be a village affair, with all those people and organisations over whom Leonora felt that she had patronage invited. There was plenty of room at the manor. Pippa did not have many relations of her own and was pleased to join this extended village family. Consequently, there were few households in Pomery who were not preparing themselves for the wedding on this bright October day.

Nicholas was outside, checking the temperature, worrying if the small amount of background heating that he had put on at seven o'clock would be enough. The church looked lovely with the colours and the scent of the flowers.

But then, Nicholas thought that the church was always a beautiful place, and was humbled by the history that the mellow stones had seen over the years. It was peaceful in the frank early morning light. Behind the altar, bright sunshine streamed through the stained glass window that depicted the Annunciation and he wished for once that time would stand still.

Ashamed of this selfish thought on the wedding day of two charming people, he shook himself briskly and went back to the vicarage, where Amy had spilt her corn flakes all over the floor and Joe was having a tantrum about eating anything at all. Guiltily, he waded in to help and was not able to think about the wedding again until three-quarters of an hour beforehand when Hubert Fright, chief bell-ringer, knocked sheepishly at the door to tell him that the key to the belfry had broken off in the lock and they couldn't get in to ring the bells.

Harry French was their man but he was out — visiting Nanette, they supposed — and so it was decided to remove the whole lock and worry about shutting the door later. It was only kept locked as a precaution against anyone getting up there and having an accident, anyway. They could put a notice on the door.

Two minutes after the bells should have started, Leonora rang the vicarage to ask why she could not hear them yet and tutted loudly at the explanation. Before she could muster a more cutting rebuke, the ringing-up process began and she replaced the phone firmly, as if her phone-call had made all the difference.

Nicholas wiped his brow before occupying the children, while Sally finished getting ready. Ten minutes later, the vicarage party were on their way to the wedding.

Matilda turned Henry over to Charlotte and took charge of Oliver herself. Pelham, her fourth husband, had been an habitual drunkard and she was well used to dealing with the after-effects. There had been some criticism at his inquest when she explained that she had been treating him for drunkenness and that was how she came to miss the unmistakable signs of heart failure.

'How could they be unmistakable if she

had mistaken them?' she had demanded of the coroner. He always looked like that when she slapped his face to waken him, she had said. Indeed, she thought that death by misadventure was taking things altogether too far, when it was implied that she was the misadventure.

She administered the slap round the face and was pleased to see it have the desired effect. The cold water treatment completed the cure and Oliver's hurt blue eyes widened in surprise as he struggled to sit up. From then on, it was plain sailing. She brushed aside his modesty as she poured him into the wedding suit and left him propped up against the front door, while she made her own toilet.

Her one mistake was to overlook the drinks tray that waited in readiness beside the door. By the time that the fire-engine red costume and huge cartwheel hat hove in sight, Oliver was looking almost perky. He willingly submitted to a firm arm under the elbow that swept him along until he and Henry stood together beside the open car that had come to take them to church. No turning back now.

Leonora and Thomas — who was fidgeting in his new suit — appeared and settled themselves in the car with Matilda, whereupon it was indicated that Henry and Oliver should do the same. Henry senior was to come with Georgina, Charlotte and Emma. The car pulled away slowly and made for the sound of the bells.

It was then that Henry realised that Oliver had been indulging in the hair of the dog. He could smell it on his breath and the blue eyes had a distinctly far away look. With Oliver, it meant that he could be very unpredictable. Very unpredictable indeed.

* * *

Pippa had woken up to the sound of hammering on the door and was amazed to see that it was ten o'clock already. Matilda had left a note wishing her good luck and saying that the rest of the night had passed uneventfully. Despite her fractured night's sleep, Pippa felt refreshed and ran lightly down the stairs to let her mother, father and brother in. Of all the households preparing for the wedding, that of the bride was the calmest of all.

* * *

Nanette had never known such pain. She would have borne it gladly, if she had thought that everything was normal, but this was too early and she could not accept it when the doctor told her that all was well. There were too many nurses. Too many machines. Too many lies.

Harry sat miserably by her side, unable to say anything to help. She didn't want him. She had shut him out. After all these years of waiting, now, when it mattered the most, she had ceased to believe.

He was aware of more movement, now. Someone else had been sent for. Another opinion. Nanette lay with her face contorted with pain and misery. People crowded round her: looking, talking, urging. How much longer could this go on? When would they pluck up the courage to tell her that her precious little baby was dead and that motherhood was to be denied to her for ever?

* * *

Dawn was playing a little gentle organ music, filling in before the bride arrived. Nicholas had had no time to think about the Queen of Sheba, this morning, and was just thankful that she was not playing in her wedding hat, which looked like a halfmade strawberry pavlova. The congregation would have found it terribly distracting, wondering if the strawberries would stay on every time she nodded fiercely at the keys, as she was wont to do. Nicholas thought that perhaps she was cajoling them into making the right sound.

The church was packed. Henry looked nervous, but his best man seemed on the ball. Nice to see one who gave real support. Nicholas was waiting to greet the bride when she arrived, and there was the familiar stir ruffling through the pews when those at the back espied her in the porch. The Queen of Sheba attempted her arrival and Pippa walked slowly toward her future husband, on her father's arm. The groom and best man turned to look at her and Henry thought that it was all worthwhile. Oliver pulled himself together when he realised that he was leering and it was at this point that Oliver remembered that Wing still had the ring.

For some reason, the little rhyme amused him no end and, for a minute or two, he savoured his amusement, singing to himself inside his head,

'Wing's got the ring, hey, ding-a-ding-ding,' quite a few times to a bluesy beat, until he realised that Nicholas was looking at him in a puzzled way.

It was then that the cold truth hit him.

Wing did indeed have the ring, and Oliver did not. And he needed it right now, or there could be no wedding. The wedding that had filled the church with three-quarters of the village. The wedding of his best friend, whose mother was called Leonora.

He swayed and Nicholas telegraphed a look of enquiry.

As the first hymn began, Oliver leant toward the vicar unsteadily. 'No ring,' he muttered out of the corner of his mouth. 'Wing's got it.'

Nicholas felt the cold clutch on his heart. Everyone would soon be waiting for him to begin the ceremony and he would have to think fast. But before he had time to make plans, he noticed that something very strange was happening to the congregation. If he didn't know better, he would say that they were doing an unusual form of a Mexican wave.

This wave only affected the people standing on the outer edge of the groom's side and consisted of a turn of the head, a raising of the hand to the left shoulder and a leaning forward to tap the left shoulder of the person in front, whereupon the procedure was repeated.

The sweat that had broken out on Nicholas's forehead began to cool. It was the ring, making its way toward him. All was well. When it reached the capable hands of Matilda Golightly, he began the solemnisation with a light heart.

Dawn trilled some wandering notes during the signing of the register and then it was time for her second *pièce de resistance*, *Toccata and Fugue*, as Henry and Pippa walked down the aisle as man and wife. Everyone was murmuring now, anxious to be outside with their confetti and good wishes. Nicholas thought that Dawn's final piece should rightly be renamed *Toccata and Fudge*, but what did it matter? She had given her gifts freely and it was a day to remember.

Bells pealed, confetti flew, kisses smacked. The air was packed with greetings and laughter. The children had cottoned on that the festivities were only just beginning and had become excited, tired of the photographer — who was taking too long for small patiences. Grown-ups nodded sagely. Plenty of room to run about, up at the manor.

At last, everyone was ready. Henry and Pippa left in a carriage pulled by two plaited greys, the family climbed back into the cars that had brought them, and then everyone else made their way up to the manor in whichever way suited them the best. The skies stayed bright, the air warm and the breeze gentle. Someone was smiling on Henry and Pippa.

On the way back, Matilda was thinking about her own marriages, remembering the hopeful way they had all started, and hoping that this couple would find the happiness they deserved.

This sentimentality did not last for long. Once the guests had arrived, she was busy helping Leonora with the greeting, and then the rest of the day was spent pondering about the murders and if she should pursue what had now become close to an obsession.

With her second glass of wine in her hand, she thought, let sleeping dogs lie. The victims did not seem to be mourned and there may have been good reasons for their deaths. Who was she to play the avenging angel? If the police couldn't find out, why should she take it upon herself to persist in her quest for the truth?

Nodding to herself, she went in search of Edgar, who had been invited along with the other churchwardens: not warmly, but with tolerance for this special day.

Albert was there with Pauline, who had been invited as a flower lady. They were in among the ladies' darts team, looking as happy as the bride and groom. Matilda caught Pauline's eye and smiled. It would be a tragedy if something happened to spoil their happiness, found late in life when both had given up hope.

And something could.

Matilda had never been convinced that the murders had stopped and the next person on the list had to be Albert.

She was turning away when she saw the other pair of eyes looking calmly in the same direction. Meditatively, coldly. Someone had Albert in their sights and it was no surprise to Matilda to see who it was. Not over, then: just as she had feared, the last time she was in Pomery. She had no choice. She could not let this go. She had to get proof before Albert lay dead and Pauline nursed a broken heart.

It was time for the speeches. Henry senior managed commendably well and Oliver, fortified with Dutch courage, spoke entertainingly, his anecdotes well sprinkled with spoonerisms that the guests thought were intentional. He ran out of steam just in time to avoid becoming repetitious and escaped Leonora's wrath by the skin of his teeth. His duty discharged, he waded into the champagne like an innocent and was discovered sleeping it off under the coats in the downstairs cloakroom, when the last of the guests chose to leave.

* * *

Eight o'clock. Henry and Pippa were on the seven o'clock flight to Rome for a honeymoon of art galleries and antiquities in Italy. The caterers and resident staff had cleared all signs of the wedding away. The family resumed their usual pastimes. It was almost as if the wedding had never been.

Matilda, all memories bar one of today firmly relegated to the back of her mind, was walking back through the velvet night, returning from Edgar's cottage, where they had been discussing how to trap a murderer. As she walked into the hall, Wing was answering the phone. He passed the receiver over to Matilda, a solemn expression on his face.

'Mrs Needham for you, madam.'

Nanette! Matilda had forgotten all about her today. She put the phone to her ear, hoping that Harriet would remember to speak up.

'Matilda?' It was all right. She could hear Harriet.

'Speaking.'

'I'm phoning about Nanette. She's had the baby. A little girl. Four o'clock this afternoon.'

There was something she was not saying. Matilda asked the question that always lurks. 'Is everything all right?'

Harriet sounded worried. 'Nanette's fine, but the baby's in an incubator. Nothing serious, they say. Just a precaution. Will you be visiting?'

'Tomorrow. I'll come tomorrow.'

'OK.' She hesitated. 'I'm sure it's nothing to worry about.'

Matilda put the phone down, her mind made up. Life was precious. No one should be allowed to take it away. She would put her plan in motion immediately.

22

It was decided that Pauline would spend a few days with Matilda at her house on the outskirts of Bath. Albert was agreeable. He couldn't leave the farm now, but didn't begrudge Pauline a few days' holiday. Leonora and Henry took them to the station on Monday morning, but did not wait to wave them off. Leonora had always thought waiting until the last minute a bourgeois habit and Henry never knew what to do when he was away from open countryside. Town streets and municipal buildings only served to make him more vague and unpredictable, and he had never got the hang of department stores. Better all round to bid a brisk farewell and head back home.

Matilda had counted on this. It would have been tiresome to have to get out at the next stop. She waited five minutes after her sister and brother-in-law had gone, to give them time to get through the traffic, and then she and Pauline went straight to the garage, where she had arranged early that morning to hire a car. By eleven o'clock, they were slinking back into Pomery by the back road, entering the farm by means of the rough track where Albert had found the doctor and his unknown lady friend. Albert was ready and waiting, which was as well, because a trying time followed when all they did was wait.

* * *

The shop bell jangled loudly, and Winnie Tomkin's eyes lit up at the chance of another gossip. She could keep going for weeks on the subject of the wedding, but she was always on the lookout for whatever crumbs her customers dropped for her. When she saw that it was Edgar Bryan, she wilted a little. He was not one to gossip but, with careful handling, he might tell her something about the wedding that she did not already know. He was very thick with that Matilda.

Winnie fixed him with her most confidential smile. 'Good afternoon. Pretty wedding, wasn't it? I expect you heard all about the ring. Still, all's well that ends well is what I say!'

To her surprise, Edgar looked interested and not as if he were trying to back away, like he usually did.

He cleared his throat. 'Yes. It was fortunate that Wing remembered in time and had the foresight to send it down with someone.'

Winnie said encouragingly, 'Oh? Sent it down with someone, did he? Who was that?'

'One of the caterers took it in the van. It wouldn't have got there in time, otherwise. All the family had gone, by then.'

'Everyone had a good time, then?' she asked hopefully — not exactly hoping that someone had not, but that something gossip-worthy had happened.

Edgar was not very good at this. 'Er — yes. I think so. As far as I could see, that is.'

'And Mrs Golightly? She always seems such a jolly lady! Fancy her house burning down that time — and her as cool as you like. Did she enjoy herself? Gone back now, I suppose?'

Not sure which question to answer first, Edgar answered the one he had been primed to impart. 'Yes. As a matter of fact, she's taken Pauline with her for a few days. Things between Pauline and Albert have been a bit . . . Well, anyway, Pauline hasn't had a holiday for years and Matilda thought it would be nice for the two of them to do some sight-seeing.'

Winnie was in heaven. 'What about Albert? Is it all over, then? I wondered how long it would last. Not exactly compatible, were they? And him a jailbird, too. The Joneses have always been respectable. Her mother would turn in her grave if she knew what her daughter's been up to. Come to her senses at last. I am glad. Will he stay on here, do you think? Doesn't look the farming type to me, I must say.'

She paused for breath and Edgar saw his chance. 'Well . . . '

Winnie leant forward, sensing that the best bit was coming. 'Well, what?'

Edgar sighed, as if it pained him to speak. 'Well. I've just come from Burnt Oak and . . . '

'And what?'

'He's taken her going very badly, I'm afraid.' He broke off and looked at her significantly, moving his right hand up to his mouth as if it had a glass in it.

She raised her eyebrows at him.

Edgar looked away and spoke into the body of the shop. 'When I left him, he was three-quarters of the way down the bottle. There won't be any farming done at Burnt Oak today.'

It was a good performance, in his opinion. Just the right amount of reluctance, but everything said that had to be said, ready to be passed on to the next customer. And in case Winnie Tomkin missed anyone — which was unlikely, he had been instructed to give a repeat performance at the PCC meeting, that night. Matilda thought that that should do it. And Matilda was usually right.

* * *

Edgar had a bit of trouble with Nicholas at the PCC meeting. He let them wring the news about Albert from him and found that he was getting rather good at it. Winnie had done her job well, because almost everyone knew, but Nicholas did not and was filled with compassion for this member of his flock. Nothing would do but he had to visit him that night. Agatha tutted and tried to move the meeting on, but Nicholas would not abandon his stray sheep.

Thankfully, Edgar was able to persuade him that his words would be wasted on Albert tonight and it would be better to wait until the morning. Edgar would go round after the meeting and make sure that he was comfortable and the vicar could call the next day. Nicholas agreed to this suggestion, eventually, but it was going to be difficult for them all to hide when he called round. Matilda didn't know it, yet, but Edgar was going to stay as well. What she was proposing was very dangerous.

Half an hour after the meeting had

finished, everyone in Pomery knew the situation at Burnt Oak Farm. Agatha and Dawn had picked up their phones the minute they returned home and put them down again only when they were satisfied that there was no one left to tell.

Edgar arrived at the farm, out of breath, to apprise them of the latest developments, and announced his intention of staying the night. Matilda said that it wasn't necessary, but he could if he really wanted to, and they began their preparations.

First of all, the door was to be left unlocked. They wanted the house to be as inviting as possible. Albert would have to sleep in his bed, or it might look suspicious, but now that Pauline had moved in, they slept in a different room on a new bed, which Pauline was buying from her catalogue.

They had to decide whether or not to let him sleep where he usually did or whether he should go back to his old room. They didn't want to put the murderer off — but he might get cold feet if things looked too different.

In the end, it was decided that it would be more natural for Albert to sleep in his new bed as it was all prepared. That raised the problem of where the three of them should wait. The murderer could well take a look round, first, and there was nowhere in the house to hide.

The closest hiding place was the copse, about a hundred yards from the door. Matilda judged it too far to pre-empt any sudden quick action, but near enough to get in there in time to help Albert. Anyway, they had no choice. The trap was set and now it was up to them to catch the killer.

Pauline and Matilda paid some attention to the living room, leaving an artistic tangle of cushions, dirty clothes and glasses. They left an empty whisky bottle on its side on the table and a few coins, as if he had been searching for enough money to buy some more. Then Albert was packed off to bed with strict instructions not to fall asleep and Matilda, Pauline and Edgar wrapped up warmly and hid themselves in the copse.

'You two do the listening,' adjured Matilda, 'and I'll be first lookout. If we all stare for too long, we'll start to imagine things.'

Pauline and Edgar nodded and the long hours of waiting began. None of them really expected anything to happen on the first day of setting their trap. They had left the lights on in the living room and the curtains open, to encourage their murderer to look in. It had the added advantage that light split onto the path and they could see any figure which approached the door.

Matilda squinted into the night and wished that she could hear properly. Silence was a lonely companion.

Pauline and Edgar could hear the rustling of night creatures in the crunchy dead leaves under the trees behind them, and the hoot of an owl. Sometimes they heard the squeak of its prey as well, and in the distance the barking of a dog fox or the annoyed squawk of a disturbed pheasant.

Albert could hear the beat of his own heart and imagined that it was death coming for him, beating a drum.

It was Pauline's turn to watch and then Edgar's. Matilda looked covertly at the luminous hands of her watch. Two o'clock. No one would come tonight. She might be wrong altogether. Too clever by half. This sort of thing only worked in detective stories and now she had involved three other people and cast doubts on Albert and Pauline's relationship. She would have to own up and be prepared to look foolish — and perhaps she deserved to be. The Greeks had a word for it, no doubt.

Edgar held up his hand and Matilda dragged herself out of her reverie. They stood either side of him and watched. Someone was trying the handle of the door and, as the three witnesses held their breath, the door was pushed open and the grey figure went inside.

They moved with one accord, Matilda and Pauline mouthing, 'Please, God, don't let Albert be asleep.'

The problem was not knowing where the figure had gone. If the stranger had gone straight to the bedrooms, they needed to be in there without delay. If their careful stage set-up was being viewed first, they would have to wait.

Matilda signalled to Pauline to look through the window, keeping down until the last minute, while she and Edgar waited by the door.

Pauline returned, out of breath. 'No one there,' she whispered, miming for Matilda's sake. For an agonising moment of indecision, they stood in the doorway, until a shout from the bedroom sent Pauline and Edgar hurtling into the house with Matilda following closely behind. They must catch the murderer in the act or it was no good.

They gained the hall in time to see a figure running out of the bedroom and along the passage to Albert's old room, slamming the door after it. Pauline went to see if Albert was all right, while Matilda ran after the wraith, throwing the door open in time to see her quarry slip out of the window and drop to the ground.

Edgar turned and ran out of the house, keeping his eye on the target. He was just in time to see a grey silhouette sprint into the trees and vanish into Banbury woods. Edgar gave chase, with Matilda close behind him. This was a bad idea, as she was twice as heavy as he was and ten times as noisy. By the time he had stopped to explain this to her, the figure was lost to the night. After all their plans, they had been too late.

Sitting drinking steaming mugs of coffee while Pauline fussed over Albert's slashed fingers, they were all feeling let down. It had been such a good plan and then they had bungled it. Albert's wounds were not bad enough to need stitches but nasty enough to hurt and incapacitate him. They were waiting for the police to arrive and Matilda was feeling very cross with herself for crashing through the woods and giving their position away, although Edgar assured her that he was unlikely to have caught the assassin anyway, given his head start.

Albert had seen nothing. The footsteps had been stealthy and he had been slashed as he shot out his hand to switch on the light. In the rush to rescue him, no one had thought to put the passage light on and all anyone had seen was an anonymous figure who could run fast.

Inspector Datchett was going to love this, thought Matilda. She hoped that it wouldn't be him who came. She would like to feel more in control of the situation before she faced him.

They all turned their heads at the sound of a car and Pauline went to answer the knock at the door. Inspector Datchett wished her a good morning and strode into the living room, unsuccessfully keeping his temper under control.

23

Datchett took the attack seriously. He didn't want to think that Hangdog's death might have been murder, after all, but he knew when he was beaten. That Golightly woman had made a complete mess of it, but if she had come to him with the story — as he had told her primly last night that she should have done — he would not have gone along with it, whatever he had led her to believe. He wasn't going to tell her that, though. What a foursome. He asked himself again. What was happening in Pomery to provoke two murders and an attempted murder, plus wanton vandalism to Henry's canvases? It had started with Hangdog. That had been the beginning, but what had he to do with the other one? Despite numerous enquiries, no connection had been found.

He left a guard at Burnt Oak Farm and went straight to the station in Chadbury. Ten minutes later, all the files pertaining to the murders were on his desk and when Treeve arrived, fresh as a daisy from her untroubled sleep, she was given her pile to sift through, with instructions to find something or lunch was on her.

For an hour or two, the only sound was of pages being turned and the occasional sigh. By half past eleven, there were no more pages and the time had come to use the information they had read to make head or tail, of the two killings. Hopefully, SOCO were going to be useful in this latest attempt.

By the time that Datchett left, early this morning, they had already found a footprint underneath the window where the escape had been made. Datchett was sure that the Golightly woman knew more than she was saying, but he didn't fancy forcing her to divulge it. For the moment, he would concentrate on tangible evidence.

No weapon had been found, but the wounds looked similar to those found on Hangdog. Same MO, then. Who on earth had got it in for these two? It must go back quite a few years. They'd been inside for most of the last ten. Could that be it? Was this whole shooting match being organised from inside? Fraser, perhaps? He was mad enough for anything. But Morgan? Where did he fit in?

Datchett shook his head to clear the cobwebs. He had enough reliance on his instinct to know without doubt that they were dealing with someone dangerous and to risk another murder using village gossip as the intelligence meant that not only were they dangerous, but desperate, too.

Treeve put down her last piece of paper and looked across at Datchett, who was looking back at her. 'Well?'

Barbara Treeve pushed her shoulder-length golden hair away from her face and leant back in her chair, her slender fingers clasped behind her neck. 'I thought at the time that the two were connected and I still think so. I think that the murderer lives in Pomery and Albert and Hangdog and Jake were all in Pomery because of the murderer. I think we're looking for a link between all four — those three and the murderer himself.'

Datchett yawned. 'Sorry. Had an early start this morning. We drew a blank, before, when we enquired along those lines.'

'Yes, but we didn't enquire very seriously about Hangdog, did we? Not after the inquest brought in its verdict.'

Datchett had to agree. Reluctantly, he added, 'The Golightly woman ties in the vandalism at the manor, too. What do you think about that?'

'I think it's strange that someone should damage pictures in such a way: and using a knife could be significant.'

'What else would you slash pictures with?' demanded Datchett tersely.

'They must have had a knife with them. Couldn't rely on finding one handy — and why would anyone carry a knife?' continued Treeve patiently. They must have known that the pictures were there and gone to slash them deliberately. If you ask me, I'd say that was unhinged sort of behaviour. Like slashing someone's wrists, or stabbing them through the heart.'

Datchett nodded slowly. He didn't want to say this. 'The Golightly woman. We'll interview her together. You can lead.'

It was lunchtime, but neither of them noticed.

* * *

Matilda was tired of doing nothing. At her insistence, Edgar had gone home to sleep. Pauline was fussing over Albert, and the constable guarding the stable after the horse had gone was not inclined to talk. He liked Matilda, but he had his instructions. The forensic team were still busy and it was difficult to find somewhere to go where she could think undisturbed. Matilda did what she always did on these occasions and went for a walk. Datchett and Treeve arrived ten minutes too late to interview her, which was unfortunate for Matilda.

Avoiding the manor, which would have involved her in explanations she did not want to give, she walked across the farmland and into the village from the western end, nearest the church. It was very quiet. The children were in school and those who stayed at home were having or preparing their lunch. The air was crisp but the sunshine still clung on, unwilling to give way to the ageing year.

Matilda wandered along to the church, kept locked during the week nowadays. She had not expected to be able to get in, thinking instead that she would walk in its quiet hallowed ground and find her solution. Indeed, she had begun to walk round the churchyard — widdershins, to be perverse — when she noticed that the door was ajar and, on venturing in, found Briony dusting the pews. The smile that greeted her reaffirmed that all was well. The cruise had been a success — a second honeymoon, in fact — and now things couldn't be better between Briony and Hugo.

Briony gathered her cleaning things together and they sat in the back pew to talk. Matilda reflected that it seemed to be her destiny to have meaningful conversations with Briony in St Wilfrid's. It was here that Briony had poured out her heart over the flowers and Matilda had given her advice, all those months ago. It didn't seem possible that they were here again together, talking about her marriage and rejoicing in its success.

All the same, there was something she had to ask and now was as good a time as any. Briony would give a truthful answer in church. She was that sort of person.

'Briony? You remember the morning of Jake Morgan's murder?' Matilda regretted the loss of easy companionship that she knew her words would bring as soon as they left her lips, but she had to know.

'Of course. What about it?' Briony had tensed — as Matilda had known that she would — and refused to meet her eye.

'You said that you had heard Hugo coming through the side door and he denied it?'

'Yes.' A tight little sound. Giving everything away, saying nothing.

'Where had he been?'

Briony answered with a question of her own. 'Do you believe in sanctuary?'

'In what way?' answered Matilda cautiously.

'That if you are inside a church, you are safe and no one can touch you?'

Matilda shook her head. 'I'd like to think that it's true, but the modern world doesn't work that way, more's the pity.'

'I'll only tell you where he was if you

promise to keep the secret safe.'

Matilda was silent while she thought. Sighing, she said what she knew that she must. 'I can't be a party to covering up a murder.'

Their eyes met and the silence between them grew thick. Suddenly, Briony spun round. 'What's that?'

'What? I didn't hear anything.' But then, I wouldn't, thought Matilda crossly.

'Over there, by the steps up to the tower. I'm sure I heard a footstep.'

Both women went across and looked up at the worn stone stairs that led to the belfry and the tower. Emptiness. They turned to face the body of the church, but nothing moved. Whatever or whoever it had been had vanished. Uneasily, they walked slowly toward the altar and searched every shadow behind the squat pillars, but found nothing. Eventually, they returned to the foot of the steps leading up to the tower. Matilda looked up and noticed a large piece of monumental stone outside the belfry door. 'What's that doing there?'

Briony explained about the lock breaking on the morning of the wedding. 'They put that there, in case any children should climb up during the times when the church is open. They could get right up to the tower, which would be very dangerous. Nicholas said that he'd feel happier if the door was wedged shut.'

Matilda took a last look round. 'There's no sign of anyone, anyway,' she said briskly. 'Perhaps it was the wind.' Even to her own ears, this did not sound convincing.

'Perhaps.' Briony did not look as if she had been fooled. She edged toward the door. 'I think that I'd like to go now. I'd almost finished when you came in. Shall we lock up together? I need to drop the keys into the vicarage.'

She was anxious to be gone, but Matilda was not ready. She was thinking about something else. 'You go ahead. Give me the keys and I'll drop them in.'

Briony didn't argue. She put the keys into Matilda's hand and walked briskly through the Norman arch into the sunshine, turning once to ask if her friend was sure that she wanted to stay on. Matilda nodded, impatient for her to be gone. Her hearing was poor and let her down. But there was nothing wrong with her eyes, and her sense of smell was superb.

She had lied to Briony.

There had been someone there, she knew it. Someone with a distinctive perfume. Matilda had smelt it at the foot of the stairs.

Smelt it and recognised it. Resolutely, she began to climb the stairs and was not surprised to see that someone had moved the stone away from the door, just enough to squeeze through into the belfry. Aptly biblical, thought Matilda as she too squeezed through the gap. Who had moved the stone? A knotty theological problem.

Matilda was not of the size or build to squeeze happily through small gaps and she made a good deal of noise in doing so. It was grossly unfair that, at the very zenith of her success, all that she saw were paltry stars before a moonless night descended upon her.

* * *

Nicholas thought that Sally had the keys and Sally thought that Briony had given them to Nicholas, so neither of them gave the locking up of the church a second thought. Frank Whittle spent the afternoon digging a grave in a plot beside the door that had been in the family for several hundred years.

This was inconvenient for the murderer.

Datchett and Treeve wasted much of the day waiting for Matilda to appear and, when she did not arrive, cursed her roundly before going home for their teas, which were to be denied them. As soon as they sat down, the message came through that Matilda had been found in the belfry in a damaged condition and in the worst of tempers. The first that Nicholas knew about it was a violent and unexpected tolling of the bell, in what he had every reason to believe was an empty church.

Matilda had come to in the darkness and wondered if she were dead. Having always thought that she deserved a heaven and, being convinced that heaven was full of light and happiness, she was more than put out to find that she had been sent somewhere cold and dark. Her sins had been no worse than the next man's or woman's. She had emphatically not caused the deaths of any of her husbands — especially not that of Malcolm, whose demise had occasioned some most unpleasant gossip. She had distinctly told him that she was about to reverse. He should have known that she might make a mistake and select the wrong gear. After all, he had criticised her driving often enough. It was all most unfair.

She had evidently been thrown into this place of correction, because her limbs were crumpled up and she was on the floor. Very solid for the afterlife, and she had been left her body. Would that her hearing were restored, but that was probably asking too much of purgatory — or was it hell, after all?

She tried to sit up, hoping that the solidity of the floor was not an illusion and she would not find herself flying through time and space. There seemed to be a wall joined onto the floor and she aimed to put her back against this. Nausea overcame her, at first. She would have thought that the dead could be excused nausea. This was not what she had attended church all her life for.

Gradually, she eased her back up to the wall and rested her head on the cold stone. The sickness faded when she stopped moving and she risked opening her eyes again. She had been wrong. The darkness was not complete. She could make out eerie shapes in a grey gloom. Familiar shapes. A superhuman effort led her to raise her head a little higher and she was sure. She knew where she was and she was not dead. And it seemed obvious what to do about it.

The bell disturbed more than the vicarage. The murderer heard it too and took immediate evasive action. Flight.

24

Datchett viewed the patient with exasperation. Silly, interfering old woman. The infuriating thing was that she had found out more than him, and she was an amateur. Grudgingly, he had to admit that she wasn't boasting about it, but it went against the grain to ask an amateur for answers, in order to improve his crime figures. Especially when she had just provided him with another pile of paperwork pertaining to her assault.

It was Wednesday afternoon and he was at the manor. Mrs.Golightly was sitting up in bed with a bandage swathed around her head and a brightly coloured shawl around her shoulders. Leonora's doctor from Chadbury had just left with strict instructions that his patient should not be tired by visitors, and Leonora was hovering in the background, to make sure that he did not intimidate her sister. At times like this, blood was infinitely thicker than water, but *noblesse oblige* and Datchett was being treated with icy courtesy until he stepped out of line.

She had spent Tuesday night in hospital, but had demanded to be taken to the manor, as soon as she had awoken from her drugged sleep. She had something to say about that, too. In all her life, even after her frequent bereavements, she had never resorted to sleeping tablets and was outraged that she should be thought in need of them. It was only a crack on the head. Not even very hard, at that. It had caught her on the right place, that was all. Or the wrong place, she supposed.

Once ensconced at the manor, she fell to wondering why she had not been finished off. Something must have prevented the murderer returning. Caught off-guard, the obvious thing to do would be to knock her out and then . . . What? The knife from Monday night? What else? Another kind of knife from home? Or a polythene bag over the head? That might be the simplest of all.

Then why had Matilda been left? She would like to know the reason.

Thinking made her head ache, but she had the bit between her teeth now. So near. But Datchett must take over. She was in no state to chase murderers, any more, and involving the other three had been foolhardy and dangerous. She would state her case and leave the rest to him.

When he arrived, she bade him come in, not oblivious to the expression of annoyance on his face. Treeve looked more sympathetic, but that was not what she needed. She needed to tell them where to find a murderer and she wanted no sympathy to do that — because she had let the murderer escape once too often. It was rare for Matilda to eat humble pie, and she wanted to get it over and done with.

Datchett eyed her severely, devoid of sympathy. 'I think that you'd better start at the beginning.'

He seated himself — at her invitation — in a comfortable armchair, close to the bed. Treeve sat on a straight-backed chair to the side of him and retained an air of respectful attention, while her boss looked thundery.

Matilda was equal to the storm. 'I would not normally have become involved, Inspector.' She paused to allow for his acquiescence of this and saw disbelief. Unperturbed, she continued, 'But Pauline Jones had taken a liking to Albert and I thought that she would be good for him. All he needs is some feminine guidance and he will not be troubling you again, I assure you. There's many a man who would benefit from the sense of a good woman.'

She glanced at him sharply, as if to assess his suitability for inclusion in this scheme, but was evidently satisfied that Mrs Datchett did her job properly, because she continued immediately, 'First of all, I never believed that Hangdog killed himself. Simply not the type and no reason to, that I could see. So I looked at who might have killed him. And as soon as I began my enquiries, I found that I did not believe in Albert's guilt. He has been foolish, in the past, but not stupid. If he had intended to kill Hangdog, he would have done it somewhere totally unconnected with the farm.'

'Could be a bluff,' ventured Datchett.

Matilda considered it. 'Still too risky, for a man with a record. Look at the trouble you had in believing him. I'm not sure that you believe him, even now.' She looked at Datchett shrewdly and saw that her point had gone home.

'I thought that you were of the opinion that the intended victim was Albert himself?'

'Until I visited Birmingham, where they both grew up,' said Matilda mysteriously. 'But, first of all, I looked at his blackmailing habits and thought that one of them was to blame. Simon Wintergreen or Adrian Non-such.'

'So did we,' interjected Datchett defensively.

Matilda ignored him. 'Until I found out how much Albert had been asking. A pittance, Inspector. They could easily afford it. And if they were worried that he would expose them — why should he? They were his source of income. It was in his best interests to keep them sweet. Take away that motive, and what have you got?'

'An unknown?' ventured Treeve, making Matilda and Datchett jump. They had forgotten that she was there.

'Yes. Albert told me that he had made enemies, but it would have to be someone who knew how to find where he lived. That's different from knowing the actual address, when you're talking about the countryside. And it would have to be someone who knew a little bit about his habits. Albert had come to live in Pomery to be near the money he thinks he is owed. You may have other ideas about that. The only people who have any connection with both Pomery and Albert are those involved in the Birmingham bank raid and, as far as Albert knows, they're all in prison still, apart from Hangdog and Albert himself. How would any other enemy know where he was?'

'So you think they were after Hangdog, after all?'

'I'm sure of it.'

'But doesn't the same argument apply to him?' Datchett was getting rattled.

'It applies to old enemies, but supposing that he made a new one?'

'Blackmailing, too?'

'In a way. On account, you might say. And I think that he would have enjoyed playing with his victim.'

'And so he was silenced before he could begin to enjoy it too much?'

'That's about the size of it.'

'He only came here three or four times. How could he find a victim in such a short time?'

'I think that they already knew each other, but that no one else in Pomery knew the past she was desperate to hide. Of all people to turn up, it would be the one person who could expose her.'

'She?'

'She.'

'And she killed Jake Morgan?'

'Possibly.' For the first time, Matilda faltered.

Datchett looked at her sharply but decided to leave it for now and get to the point quickly. 'And she attacked Albert on Monday and yourself yesterday?'

'Yes. And slashed Henry's paintings.'

'Why do that? What reason could she have?'

'I'm afraid that Henry is an excellent artist,

Inspector.' Datchett looked baffled, but before Matilda could tell him about the sketchbook underneath her mattress, she was suddenly filled with weariness and found that her eyelids were beginning to droop.

Leonora, who had been tapping her feet over by the window, took charge. 'That's enough for now, Inspector. My sister has had a severe shock.' For once, her sister did not argue. Matilda yawned, leant her head back into her pillows and went to sleep.

⋆ ⋆ ⋆

Treeve knew that she should not laugh but, having suppressed it on the way out of the manor, she could not control the peal as they settled themselves into the car.

Datchett did not see the joke.

'I'm sorry, sir,' said Treeve, abashed. 'It reminded me of those old westerns where they get to the 'old timer' just as he's dying, and he dies before he can say who shot him. My Dad likes to watch them. It's always happening,' she finished lamely — having seen Datchett's face, which was not amused.

'You'd have thought that she'd say who it was straight away. She's probably getting away at this moment and we still don't know who it is!'

'Connections,' said Treeve emphatically, trying to make amends for her mirth.

Datchett scowled at her. 'What?'

'Connections. That's what we've always known that it's been about. I think that we should concentrate on the victims again and search for whatever it is that binds them together. Our murderer will be in there somewhere.' She paused. 'Or we could just wait for Mrs Golightly to wake up.' She glanced mischievously at Datchett, morose and unbending beside her.

He started at her words. 'Back to the station, Miss Treeve.'

Barbara Treeve smirked. Datchett in determined mood was an experience in itself.

* * *

Who would have thought that she'd be back in Birmingham, after all these years? On the run and looking for favours, too. She should have left the country last night, but she didn't know if that woman was alive or dead and, if alive, what she might have said. For all she knew, they could be watching the ports. Why hadn't she made sure of that woman when she'd had the chance?

She swirled the last of her drink round and gulped it down, ordering another so that she could continue to put off her decisions. No more panics. Panicking had forced her to flee when she had seen the crumpled figure on the belfry floor. That bit of stone had been handy. Must have tried shutting the door with it first, before they found a bigger bit.

It was only when she got home that she regretted leaving in such a hurry and she had only paused for a minute to pick up a plastic bag to tie over Matilda's head. Nice and small, to fit into her pocket. No one would notice anything. Too squeamish to use the stone again. How stupid can you get?

But when she'd returned, Frank Whittle had been there by the door, whistling to himself as he dug the grave, and she could not risk passing him. She'd hung about for a while but her movements could look suspicious and she didn't want to attract attention.

She'd gone home eventually and packed hastily, before making for the city that night. In her heart of hearts, she knew that it was all over, but she was not ready to tell herself so, yet.

The night was cold and unfriendly, full of eyes watching her, sizing her up. She turned into a side street to escape, but saw too late that she had taken them with her. Found by a passing patrol car in the early hours of the morning, she had been mugged and beaten, left for dead in an alleyway near the casino where she had worked as a croupier before Eddie had picked her out of all the others. He'd taken her off to live a life of luxury, or so he'd said. Well, even Eddie could get it wrong, sometimes.

Squinting between her swollen eyes in the blinding whiteness of hospital sheets, she saw that there was someone waiting silently at the end of her bed. She had seen him before, but a lifetime away, in Pomery — where she'd thought that her chance had finally come knocking on her door. Lady Luck! What would she know about it?

25

By the time that the phone call from Birmingham came, Datchett and Treeve had covered two boards with names and arrows pointing in every direction. Miraculously, they were beginning to make some sense of it all.

They began with Jake Morgan, as they both agreed that he was the surprise figure. In their original enquiries, they had found no hint of anything irregular in his private or business life. Paperwork in order, taxes paid, no complaints from his tenants, receipts for all the goods in his shop, VAT up to date. His housekeeper had been genuinely distressed at his death and his yachting colleagues not heartbroken exactly, but sorry that he was gone. They had not been able to find anything to explain his murder, but had come away with the uneasy feeling that he had been too good to be true. Got to be proved that he'd been up to something, though. No good documenting feelings for the judge and jury.

As with all other unsolved cases, the file had been left open and any new information noted and collated. There had been a tip-off, a couple of days ago — no more than an unsubstantiated rumour — that the antique shop, now closed, had been a front for stolen goods. Not just any stolen goods, either. Information suggested that Jake Morgan had been the fence for a series of robberies from big houses where only small, expensive items had been taken, especially eighteenth-century porcelain.

Datchett knew all about those robberies. He had been assigned to the case and one of the robberies had taken place in Pomery itself. Adrian Nonsuch had had several pieces stolen, about a year ago. Datchett had been reminded of it, when they had interviewed Nonsuch after Morgan's death.

This made him look at the story twice. If it hadn't have been for the Pomery robbery, Datchett would have dismissed the information, as it came from a dubious source from someone out to do a deal; but, in the circumstances, he decided to do a little digging. He had been digging on the day that he was called out to Burnt Oak Farm, but had failed to come up with anything else and had almost decided to put it down as misinformation. Now, he picked up the thread again, frustrated at the lack of progress.

'Let's assume, for the sake of argument that

Jake Morgan was a fence. Where does that take us?'

Treeve wrote 'Fence?' against his name and stood back from the board, biting her lower lip — as she always did, when deep in thought. 'What sort of jobs did Fraser's gang do?'

'Banks, usually. A jeweller's once. Not specialist jobs from big houses, if that's what you're thinking. This lot didn't have that type of finesse.'

'Adrian Nonsuch had some porcelain taken, didn't he?'

'Ye-es,' admitted Datchett. 'I've been thinking about that.'

'And Morgan knew Pomery well. He was meeting someone in the lane where Nonsuch lives, when he was killed.'

'That's what we have been assuming.'

'And Sadie Strangelove saw him there before Christmas, don't forget.'

Treeve turned away from the board.

'How well did we enquire into the properties owned by Morgan?'

Datchett shrugged. 'Checked the list we had from his solicitors. No complaints from his tenants. We didn't search the properties because we had no reason to, at the time. There was nothing to indicate that he owned anything else.'

'What about renting? Did we check to see if his name cropped up as a tenant rather than a lessor?'

Datchett stared at his colleague. 'No. I hadn't thought of that. Get onto it straight away, will you? And then get back here.'

Barbara Treeve went off to delegate while Datchett thought through the possibilities. If he had been a fence, he would need a secure place to store the goods, while he waited until it was safe to offload them. Close enough to be able to reach in a hurry. The goods would probably be brought into the shop and then transferred. The shop must always be squeaky clean, to avert suspicion. He could have rented somewhere, but it seemed unnecessarily complicated, when he had so much property of his own. On the other hand, it had to go somewhere.

The man had been murdered in Pomery. Datchett kept coming back to that. A germ of an idea was growing. The two houses Morgan had owned were at the other end of the village. They hadn't been searched. It had not been thought necessary, as he hadn't lived there. Supposing that he'd kept the goods in one of these houses? He wouldn't have needed much room. But that would mean that the tenant — whichever one it was — would have to know. He couldn't keep a thing like that a secret.

Wait, wait, wait. They didn't even know if it was true about him, yet. Softly, softly. After all this time, Datchett wanted to be sure. He went back to the reports and cursed when he realised that he had missed the obvious. The robberies from big houses had started after Fraser and company had begun their last sentence. Morgan would have been left without his secondary source of income and the time just might have been ripe for ventures in another field A different partner. Higher class. Someone who lived in Pomery?

Treeve came back, having organised a trawl through rented properties within a radius of five miles to begin with. 'That should keep a few people busy for a few hours. And that's only if he's using his own name!'

Datchett told her the way that his thinking was going.

'So we're looking for an unknown partner with information on private houses, and the possible use of his leased houses to store the goods?'

'I could be wrong . . . ' Datchett let the unspoken retort hang in the air.

'Are we going to search the houses first?'

'That would tell us if I'm on the right lines, although a willing accomplice would have moved it straight away, unless they planned to take over from him. Then we'll need to look again at the residents of Squires Lane. The other man — or woman — has to be living there. Why else was he there, otherwise?'

Treeve looked brisk, as she always did when they were on the scent. Bright-eyed and bushy-tailed, as Datchett put it when he wanted to annoy her. 'Pippa or Mary first? This could mean a very short honeymoon.'

It was then that the phone rang, with a request for information on a Mary Stringer, resident of Pomery, who had been found unconscious and taken to St Roland's in the centre of Birmingham. She had no identification on her, but she had been found outside the casino where she used to work. The owner recognised her earlier in the evening, as he arrived, but had no wish to renew their association. Even her mother would find it difficult to recognise her, now.

* * *

The keys to Mary's house were still with Jake Morgan's effects at the station. No one had come forward to claim the body or the estate, and so he rested in limbo, while the wheels of justice idled away, waiting. Datchett signed for them, and then he and Treeve the eager set out for Pomery into the blustery night, which promised rain before dawn.

Pomeranians in quiet closes are all abed before midnight, and the only light came from the street lamps at the end and the centre of the small curve of respectability, snug behind net curtains, with neat borders in the front garden. If Morgan had visited her here, he must have parked elsewhere and walked. Any strange car would have been noticed straight away. No wonder he'd saved his visits for darkness.

* * *

This had been Mary's first step toward her new life. A far cry from the high rise of her childhood, with graffiti on the stairway walls and urine in the lift. When Jake had offered her the chance to live there rent free, she had assumed that he would take his payment in the usual way, but was willing to put up with it until she had moved up to where she really wanted to be. When she discovered that all he wanted from her was to store a few things in the loft, she'd thought that she had got off lightly. He would arrive after dark with a small box and was gone before anyone was the wiser. She began to mould herself to her new lifestyle, willing to learn from tutors such as Agatha, all the time watching for her chance.

Datchett and Treeve found what they were looking for in no time. He must have felt confident enough not to bother with anything elaborate. The proceeds from two of the unsolved robberies on the Chadbury patch were stored, wrapped in soft dusters, in a variety of dusty cardboard boxes wedged in the loft space. That would improve, the look of the crime sheet, but where did it leave them on the murder front?

Datchett gritted his teeth, knowing that in the morning he would have to pay another visit to Mrs Matilda Golightly and hoped that she was awake this time. But first, they'd wait to see what forensic could tell them. As well as the stolen goods, forensic had removed all her shoes and clothing. If they didn't find a fibre to match from those taken after Hangdog's murder in that lot, he would retire and grow hollyhocks.

26

Datchett looked at the sketch and then at Matilda, baffled. 'This is Mary Stringer talking to Hangdog?'

Matilda nodded and then winced at the pain that nodding produced.

'I'm sorry, but I don't see what you're getting at. What's the crime?'

'None, Inspector. It is not a crime to tell an untruth, but I have been asking myself why.'

'Untruth?' Datchett was lost and showed it.

Matilda fixed him with her look most severe and enunciated carefully, 'Mary Stringer told me that she had never been to Burnt Oak Farm and had never seen Hangdog.'

'And here she is, talking to him at the farm,' said Datchett slowly. 'So she lied: but that does not mean she murdered him.'

Matilda sighed. 'Why should she lie, Inspector?'

Datchett looked as exasperated as he felt. 'I don't know! Perhaps she was frightened of being implicated. People often tell unnecessary untruths when they panic. Much of our time is spent sifting through them all, and very irritating it is, too, I might add.'

Matilda took no notice and continued, 'She slashed Henry's canvases.'

'You have proof of this?'

'No. But I know that she knew they were there. I've found out that Leonora showed her where to find the bunting and they had to move Henry's pictures to get to it. She would have seen them then and realised the danger. And I know two people who saw her in Squires Lane, very late, on the night they were slashed.'

This was more like it. Actual witnesses. Treeve reached for her notebook.

'Who?' Datchett waited expectantly.

'My niece and nephew. But I do not want them questioned about it. You'll have to take my word for it.'

'What were they doing out so late?' Treeve was interested rather than censorious.

'Nothing that need concern you,' answered Matilda briskly, with some of her old spirit back.

Datchett rearranged his legs, too long to sit for any length of time without sprawling. 'Mrs Golightly, was it Mary Stringer who attacked you in the church?'

'Certainly.'

'How can you be so sure?'

'I smelt her perfume. She always puts too much on.'

Datchett couldn't help himself. 'And did you smell her on Monday night, when Mr Noonday was attacked?'

Matilda gave him a cold look. 'Naturally not. I set a trap for her and she fell into it. Who else would it have been?'

Datchett counted under his breath. It seemed like he'd got to a thousand. 'Did you see Mary Stringer attack Mr Noonday or yourself?'

'No.'

'Did you see or smell her slashing the pictures?'

'No.'

'Forensic have found a footprint, but no shoes at Miss Stringer's house to match. They haven't finished with her clothes, yet, but the knife used to kill Hangdog has no traceable prints and at the moment cannot be said to belong to her.'

'She'll have destroyed the clothes and shoes that she wore. You'll find them dumped in the river, I expect. Or on the Silminster tip. She has a car, you know.' Matilda looked at him as if he were a halfwit. 'What does she say about all this? Surely you've questioned her?'

Datchett didn't care if she was up to knowing what had happened to Mary

Stringer or not. He told her and left, Treeve running to catch up with him. He could only take small doses of Matilda Golightly at any one time, and he wanted to relish the picture of her over-large face looking nonplussed, even if it was only for a short time. He'd a good mind to get her to tell them what on earth those children had been doing wandering about, seeing vandals, when they ought to have been home in bed.

* * *

The newspapers had got hold of the story. There was no escape, now. It had all been in vain. A chance encounter had put paid to her dreams and she had acted before thinking. The story of her life.

Her looks had been her downfall. Growing up where she did, she had been encouraged to use them to get what she wanted. The trouble was, she wanted different things from those that her looks bought her. Money, yes: but, most of all, she wanted to belong. To be respected. She wanted to be like her cousin Davina.

Her Mum's sister had cleaned for a vicar over in Aston, whose wife had been killed in a car accident. He and Auntie Sue had got married, a year later, and had had two girls,

Davina and Sylvia. Sylvia had been trouble from the day she was born, but Davina had been the exact opposite. Almost too good to be true. Everyone loved her and Mary wanted to be loved, too. And she didn't want to have a man hanging round her neck in order to achieve her aim.

Mum had been worn out by having six kids in as many years. They'd taken away her hope and most of her reason. Dad had been worse than useless and had cluttered off when the youngest was three months old, leaving Mary, as the oldest, to cope as Mum couldn't. No wonder Davina could afford to be nice to people. She'd never had to change a nappy or cook or take the young ones to school. She'd never had to steal enough food each day to feed the family.

Davina had spoilt it all, marrying so young. She had two kids of her own, now. Her boring husband worked in an office and they were always doing things to their tiny bungalow and the immaculate garden. Davina helped out at the school and was active in church matters, while her husband played cricket at the weekend. All very cosy and unexciting, when she could have had so much more if she'd held out.

Mary did not envy Davina's life, now, but she still had the need to belong somewhere.

She wanted what Davina had, but on a larger scale. She wanted respectability — with power. This was why she put up with Agatha Kingsway. She'd thought that she could learn at Agatha's feet and then use her looks to overtake her. Her aim had been to be the biggest fish in a small pool and then to move on and do it all over again, only somewhere bigger. She'd had it all planned.

The first need was money, to dress the part, and it was Sylvia who had introduced her to Marco at the casino. He'd liked what he saw and employed her as a croupier. After a few weeks, he'd made it plain that there were other things she could do for him and, for a while, she'd complied, although he'd disgusted her. His breath had smelt of rancid butter. She'd made sure that he paid her well over the odds.

Then, one night, Eddie had walked in and made her a proposition she could not refuse. She'd joined his 'stable', as one of a select few, performing services for rich clients. Her chauffeur and bodyguard when she began had been Hangdog and, just when she thought that the past was about to be buried forever, he'd arrived in Pomery and threatened to expose her. Not for money, but for fun.

She hadn't even worked for Eddie for long.

He had tired of her aloofness and, for a while, she'd hung about with Fraser, who was generous but beginning to suffer headaches and bouts of depression when she first knew him. Soon he could think of nothing but fulfilling his fantasy of the ultimate bank job that would go down in history as the biggest, or the best, or the cleverest. He was into superlatives in a big way. Or the biggest way. He didn't need or want her, any more, and then through him she'd met Jake, who'd looked after her for a while. They'd pulled off a few scams together and she'd been able to put some more money away.

They'd parted amicably but kept in touch and, when Fraser and the others went down for the bank job, Jake had offered her the bungalow in Pomery, in return for the loft space. She'd thought that it would give her time to look around while she thought what to do. Jake had been talking about making her a partner in his business, which would have meant that she'd have enough money to buy one of those big houses in Squires Lane or somewhere similar.

If she had known that Jake had laundered the money for Fraser's gang and that, the minute they were out, they would all be coming to find him for their share, she might have thought twice. But then again, probably not. There was no need for any of them to come to Pomery and she couldn't know that Hangdog would turn out to be such a bastard. If only Albert Noonday hadn't chosen to live here, Hangdog would never have come, and she would not be lying here with a broken nose, her looks gone, and the prospect of a murder trial waiting for her when she was allowed to leave hospital.

If only.

There was a line in a poem about that, wasn't there? She'd heard it at school a million years ago.

She turned her head at the sound of footsteps in the doorway. A tall, thin man and a slim blonde woman who reminded her of herself as she used to be were walking toward her. No need to ask who they were. They had 'pig' stamped all over them.

* * *

The news of Mary Stringer's arrest spread like a snowstorm, touching the Pomeranians with a tingle of cold alarm at the thought of a murderer living in their midst; it soon melted to relief as they realised that, for them, the ordeal was over. Harriet stopped off at the hospital after work to tell Nanette, but her news was eclipsed by the news that Nanette was waiting to tell her.

Harriet was directed to the main ward and the first thing she saw was Harry sitting at Nanette's bedside with tears streaming down his face. Nanette had been crying, too, and Harriet's heart shook with sorrow. She felt a surge of anger that they were not able to grieve in private and was about to find someone to whom she could protest when she noticed something else.

Harry was holding a small white bundle and tiny white-clad arms were waving about in the air. Slowly, with a sense of wonder, Harriet moved towards them.

A cot stood beside the bed and there was not a machine in sight. She heard the little creaky, newborn baby noises and understood the reason for the tears. Harry and Nanette's baby was alive, well and coping on her own. The tears had been for joy.

Harriet did not stay long and, when she got into her car to drive home, she realised that she had not told them the news from Pomery. Smiling to herself, she dismissed her lapse as unimportant. They would not have listened to her if she had.

27

November

Nicholas's gaze took in all the congregation on this first Sunday in November and he reflected that, in a year, little had really changed despite the murders. In the main, people liked to get on with their own lives, and non-family murders were turned into a nine days' wonder, with no discernible lasting effect on individuals and their families.

Harvest festival and supper had come and gone, with the same amount of manoeuvring and argument among the organisers. It was ever thus and would ever be so.

At least Enid Brandon had been well under control and there had been no distractions during his harvest sermon. He was sorry for Mary Stringer, and would be visiting her as soon as he was allowed to. Agatha Kingsway had been very subdued in the first few days after Mary's arrest, but she was busy with the new PADS production now and he doubted if she gave more than a passing thought to the fate of her erstwhile companion. She looked as if her mind was on the production now, her lips moving to the words of the hymn but her mind out of step.

Leonora and Henry were in their usual pew with the twins and Emma. He wondered how much longer the children would continue coming to church. As long as Leonora could wield her influence, he supposed. He hoped that Matilda would be well again soon. It had been a nasty crack on the head, and he was glad that she had consented to stay at the manor until pronounced quite fit again. Leonora was not the most restful of people, but she did have servants who could look after the invalid.

They had reached last verse of the offertory hymn and Edgar and Frank were making their way toward him, carrying the wooden platters with the offerings of the people for the upkeep of St. Wilfred's crumbling masonry. Funny that Edgar and Matilda should be such friends. He would never have thought that they could have anything in common. They'd taken quite a risk that night, waiting in the darkness to catch a murderer. Albert had been brave, too. It was amazing the difference that Pauline had made to him.

He would have to tread carefully with Leonora, but he thought that Edgar's board game — which he had been devising over the last year and a half — had distinct commercial possibilities. Fancy he and the twins keeping it a secret all that time! How many times had they crept through the village to visit him at night, knowing that their mother would disapprove? Not very tactful of Edgar, but Nicholas could understand how the secrecy had come about. Properly marketed, the game could make quite a little nest egg for him, money that he had sworn to share with the children. One way or another, Pomery was really putting its name on the map.

He received the offerings and knelt in prayer. A baby started to cry. An annoyance for some. A source of wonder for Nanette and Harry. Briony looked across kindly. If any couple deserved some luck, it was those two. God willing, she would have some luck of her own, soon. She closed her eyes and prayed.

Pippa and Henry weren't in church, that morning. They had intended to be, but somehow the time had reached eleven o'clock without them noticing. Souvenirs of their honeymoon were strewn all over the cottage, and every time one of them said that it was time to get back to earth, the other would pick up a piece of pottery or a postcard and they would be lost in reminiscences. They were due to be floating for some time yet.

Sadie never spent time reminiscing. She

was busy planning her new campaign. Adrian was proving to be a dead loss, never willing to commit himself: and when she hinted that she would tell his wife, he called her bluff. She considered her options and, in the end, decided that the satisfaction she would get from denting his image was less important to her than her need for money, and she would be better occupied in finding someone else. And who better and more convenient than Quentin Weatherby?

* * *

Datchett had thought that it would be the same old story when he came to interview Mary Stringer; but, as soon as they began he was reminded that although every story may have similar components, each story is unique and he felt compassion for this disfigured woman. That's not to say that he regretted her capture. She had taken two lives and attempted a third, not to mention the assault. She had to be punished for her disregard for human life, and stopped before she did further damage. All the same, he felt sorry for her.

Rich purple bruises had spread across her nose and round her eyes, but the swellings had gone down on her face. Part of her ear had been torn when they took her earrings and her wrist had been broken where one youth had stamped upon it while the other pulled off her gold bracelet. She was covered in scratches. Her eyes were dull and lifeless and her body hunched in on itself. She made no sign that she had heard while Datchett cautioned her, but the interview began. She had chosen not to be represented.

Datchett said, 'Mary, do you realise why you are here?'

She made no sign that she had heard, until Datchett had repeated the question. He had to make do with a slight inclination of her head that Treeve asked her to verbalize for the tape.

'Did you kill the man known as Hangdog?'

'Yes.' The answer was no more audible than a soft sigh. 'I killed him.'

'Let's deal with that first, then. Would you like to tell us what happened?'

She raised her pale eyes to his face. 'He recognised me,' she said simply.

Datchett waited while she struggled with her next words. They came in a low voice, peculiarly detached — as if from an instrument unconnected with her mind or body.

'I have done things in my past that I do not want remembered by anyone. Not even me.

He recognised me and threatened to tell everyone I knew.' She shrugged. 'Even if they did not believe him, mud sticks.'

'Did you try to dissuade him?'

'Yes.' The memory of her pleas made her tighten her lips in anger. 'He wouldn't listen. He laughed at me.'

'Did you speak to him at Burnt Oak Farm?'

'He phoned me at home, boasting about what he was going to do. I went round to the farm the back way and pleaded with him, but he would not listen. He thought it was all a big joke.' For a moment, the old spirit blazed. 'My whole life a joke!' Subsiding, she added, 'Well, maybe he knew more than me, after all.'

'When did you decide to kill him?' Treeve asked softly, trying to turn away the wrath, which was unproductive.

'Not then. Despite what he said, I still thought that I'd have one more try at talking to him. When he phoned up again that night, to taunt me, I took my chance.'

'But you took the knife in case you did not succeed?' Datchett wanted to prove premeditation. Easier, that way. No grey areas.

Mary replied as if she had not heard. 'I knew that Albert would be with Pauline in the Pieces of Eight. I'd seen the posters for ladies' darts night.'

'And he wouldn't listen?'

'He was drunk. Invited me in for a drink. Even got a glass out for me! I thought that I might be able to take advantage of him in that state and get him to forget it, but he got more and more abusive. He was really enjoying it. I knew then that I would kill him.' She stopped and moistened her lips, scared of her own words.

'And?' It was Treeve again, gently encouraging.

'I went outside to cool down, walked round the house and peered in to see where the bedrooms were. Judging by the state of him, I didn't think it would be long before he passed out. Then I had my bit of luck. At least, I thought that it was luck, at the time. Not so sure, now. I saw the light go on in the passage and then in the bedroom. All I had to do then was wait a little longer, and he would be a sitting target. He hadn't locked any doors.'

'What about the window which was forced?' This from Datchett. Crossing and dotting.

'I did that afterward. Read about doing that somewhere. It's supposed to put you lot off the scent.'

'What did you force it with?'

'Found a spade leaning up against the

door. Albert had been using it to clear up, I suppose. There was a wheelbarrow as well. Forced it underneath the window frame and then pulled. The frame was rotten and it just came away. Easy.'

Datchett spoke quietly now, looking straight into her eyes. 'But before that, you killed him?'

'Yes. I killed him.' Mary frowned with distaste at the memory. 'Slashed his wrists. Didn't like doing it.'

'No.' Datchett scratched his head.

Mary fixed him with her hunted gaze. 'He didn't know anything about it. He was asleep Snoring like a pig. It's me who bears the scars, now.'

Her present state made it seem as if she could be speaking literally, but they knew that her scars had gone deeper than those on Hangdog's wrists. They called a halt to the interview to enable her to rest. Even such a short time had tired her and they needed to get it right. She wasn't going anywhere.

* * *

Matilda was allowed to potter about in the morning, as long as she agreed to an afternoon rest. She was as yet rather unsteady on her feet and so, after being guided down the stairs, confined her pottering to one floor of the manor, where she could do the least damage to herself.

Never a vindictive woman, she was satisfied that Mary had been caught and that was all. She held with dues being paid but had no wish to gloat. The puzzle had been enjoyable, no more than that; and although she had had her fair share of clues, she had started off on the wrong tack — thinking that the victim was meant to be Albert — and wasted a lot of time that way. She had no reason to feel pleased with herself.

It was bad luck for Mary that she had chosen a village to start her new life. She might have guessed that nothing is secret in a village and that someone will always see you, if you are doing something that you want no one to see. The twins had seen her on the night she'd slashed the pictures and Edgar had seen her on the night she murdered Hangdog. Henry had sketched her talking to him in the doorway of the farm, but the deciding factor for Matilda had been when Sally finally remembered what it was that she had seen on the day that Hangdog had visited the Post Office to enquire about the whereabouts of Burnt Oak Farm.

Mary had denied ever seeing him at all in Pomery, which could have been true, but he had seen her. Sally had asked him if she could help, when they had been standing outside the Post Office, and then her attention had been distracted by Amy in the pushchair. When she'd looked up again, he had been staring down the road, where Sally could see Mary Stringer walking home with her shopping. When she'd stopped to cross the road into the Close, they had been able to see her profile and she thought that he'd made a small exclamation, but she could not be sure. He had moved away, directly afterward, and Sally had not remembered until after the second murder.

Not that any of this was proof. Matilda would have to leave that to the Inspector. At half past two, she went upstairs to her blameless rest while Datchett was congratulating himself on not having to find the proof that he knew he did not have. Mary had confessed to the murder of Hangdog. All he had to do was to extract a similar statement on the murder of Jake Morgan and he was home and dry. The gods let him enjoy his Sunday afternoon.

28

Pomery had almost forgotten Mary Stringer. On Monday, Sadie invited Quentin to a dinner party planned for the following Saturday. She also invited the Kingsways, the Wintergreens and that funny old woman from the manor, if she was well enough, with Edgar Bryan. She hoped that Simon would not be called out at the last minute. She did not want the three men's attention to be divided between four women. She knew that she could sparkle, put beside Agatha and Maureen — not to mention the old bat — and that was the idea, to arrange herself in a setting designed to show herself off to the best advantage. Maureen had class, but Sadie was aiming to appear warmer and more approachable. She had no doubt that she would succeed. She was an old hand at this game.

* * *

Matilda was feeling stronger with every day and, on Wednesday, she announced that she was well enough to venture outside. No one argued with her. It was always best not to.

She had a particular visit in mind, long overdue. Something had been niggling at the back of her brusied brain, ever since her ignominious dispatch in the belfry.

Briony.

Matilda had just been asking her about Hugo's movements when Briony had turned round at the sound on the stairs, and she had never had the answer. Where had Hugo been, on the morning of Jake Morgan's murder? It was a loose end and she was curious. She was also curious as to what Datchett had found out about Simon, who had the time of the murder unaccounted for — like most of Squires Lane, it seemed. It was her bet that he'd been visiting that platinum blonde whose husband was away. She lived on the Mole road, well out of sight. He would not have been able to resist it. Facile man.

But Briony would not have mentioned to Datchett that she'd heard Hugo creep up the stairs, despite Matilda's advice. That was still between the two of them. Unfinished business. And Matilda was beginning to be obsessed by it. When Briony told her, she saw what must have happened and, with a heavy heart, walked slowly back to the manor and lifted up the phone.

'Chadbury Police Sation? This is Matilda

Golightly. I wish to speak to Inspector Datchett. I have some information for him regarding a murder.'

* * *

At the time of Matilda's phone call, Datchett and Treeve had been going round and round in circles all morning. Mary had confessed to the murder of Hangdog and furnished them with enough details to satisfy the Spanish Inquisition. She had confessed to the slashing of the paintings and the attack on Matilda Golightly, but she flatly denied having anything to do with the murder of Jake Morgan.

'Why should I kill him?' she had demanded wearily. He had provided her with a home and money to live on. Promised her a partnership.

No, he wasn't getting rid of her. She was as useful to him on the day of his death as she had been on the first day they had met. Nothing had changed. She freely admitted to killing Hangdog, which would get her into trouble when she went to prison. Fraser had friends everywhere. Why should she lie about Morgan? Without him, she had nothing. No home. No prospects.

On and on they went, getting nowhere and

then setting off again in the same direction. Datchett was beginning to lose his cool, when they were interrupted by Matilda's offer of information. Knowledge is not proof and the information was more annoying than useful. They still couldn't prove a thing.

April again

The last searing flames of the sun were doused on the tropical horizon, and the blue black night sky filled with stars. Most of the party were on deck, watching the lights of Bombay growing smsaller and smaller, like the last dying sparks of a bonfire. Out on the ocean, they were fanned by a breeze, chilly in the bright starlight and the moon's pale sheen. Matilda took a last look, wrapping her silk shawl round her large bare shoulders before turning away and entering the lounge bar, where the rest of her immediate party soon joined her. She had promised them the final instalment of her Pomery story, although it was with an uncharacteristic reluctance that she began the final chapter.

When they were all settled, she still took her time before she spoke. What had started out as a jolly adventure had become grown-up and serious, full of portent and consequences. Most of her wished that she had left well alone but, looking around at her audience, she knew that she must begin and end it now, for the last time.

The clock struck midnight. A new day. It was time to begin.

'I had never been happy about the two different weapons for the murders. It didn't fit. The Stanley knife was such an amateur weapon, taken by Mary more in self-defence than with the idea of murder. It was only when she saw the inebriated state of him that the idea really came to her that she could use it to kill her enemy. The sword-stick was a different matter altogether. Whoever went out with a sword-stick meant to kill. We don't know how long it went missing before the murder, but someone took it with murder in mind. Jake Morgan had been lured there. Given the sword-stick element, he must have been lured there for the purpose of being killed. This was premeditated murder.'

A silent steward replenished their drinks. They were the only party in the lounge. When Matilda paused for breath, the only noises were the whispers of night. The young had gone to the disco and the elderly to their beds.

Hugh Wyvern stirred, as if to proffer his

views on the need for medical knowledge to administer the fatal blow, but thought better of it. It was Matilda's story and his turn would come. He contented himself with a look he had spent years carefully cultivating when in company. It intimated that he was interested but that nothing was new to him. He was still the cleverest person there. He would never have admitted that he was as fascinated as everyone else.

'I would have got there sooner, if I hadn't mismanaged my talk with Briony. Mary knew that I knew, you see. I wasn't very subtle with my enquiries and it was easy for her to put two and two together. She's an intelligent girl. Would have done well, given the right circumstances.'

Grace put her drink down quietly and moved imperceptibly closer to Matilda, as if subconsciously underlining that women are particularly vulnerable to the whims of chance and she had every sympathy. But they were not talking about Mary, now. Someone else had gone along the same road, but for what reason? There was always an urgent reason — sometimes incomprehensible to most other people, but overwhelming for the murderer. She found the thought of it almost too hard to bear.

'Mary had followed me. Perhaps she had

been going to accost me, find out what I knew — but then she was discovered and acted without thinking. The trouble was that she interrupted Briony and me when Briony was going to tell me where Hugo had been on the morning of Morgan's murder. The bang on the head put it out of my mind. As soon as I got the answer to my question, it all fell into place.'

'And so the murderer was apprehended as a result of your endeavours?' asked Sir Clive, with false bonhomie. He habitually regarded the prosecution with distaste, but could not bring himself to regard Matilda in this light.

Matilda looked at him with a troubled face. 'No. There has been no arrest for the murder of Jake Morgan.'

'Even though you know who it is?' objected Gregory, cushioned by money and position and still innocent of the ways of the real world.

'Knowing isn't proving.' said Matilda grimly: and her grimness stemmed not just from knowing that the murderer was free.

She had known, as Datchett had deduced, that Morgan's murderer must live in Squires Lane. There could be no other explanation for him arriving across the meadow. All she had to find out was who he had been supposed to be meeting and who could have had access to the sword-stick.

Her first surmises were not helpful. All of Squires Lane had been at Quentin's party and, as far as she could see, any one of them could have had a reason of which she was unaware for wanting to kill Morgan. She had further been led astray by the memory of Mary Stringer's face at Quentin's party when the sword-stick had been demonstrated. There had been a look of heightened perception as he'd fooled about with the deadly blade. She had seemed to be fascinated and thoughtful at the same time.

But the fact remained that, if the sword-stick was stolen on the night of the party, the thought of killing someone must have been uppermost in a mind then, so the reason could go back several months. Someone had waited their chance or taken advantage of Hangdog's murder. A useful smoke-screen.

No one had a proper alibi. She had discounted the Frenches and the Needhams as being too far-fetched; their houses were far more accessible from the village. That left the residents of the upper part of the lane, and she did not forget the manor.

She looked objectively at her own family. On the morning of the murder, all the family — apart from Henry junior, who had stayed in Chadbury with a friend — had slept at home. Did Henry senior have hidden depths? she wondered. She tried hard to imagine him plunging a sword-stick which he had had the foresight to steal several months earlier into the heart of a man, and failed.

Leonora was a different matter. She was quite capable of the planning and the execution of her plan, but she would never allow herself to be put in such a position. The sisters weren't related to Wellington but, with their temperament, they should have been. Leonora would have said, 'Publish and be damned' to any suggestion of blackmail and she had no need to kill to get her own way.

Matilda couldn't contemplate that it could be one of the children. They hadn't been at Quentin's party, but she supposed that there were ways in that they could have acquired the weapon, if they'd been determined to do it. The twins were deft at entering and exiting without attracting attention. But then they would have to have known that it was there, and who might have mentioned it? There was no suggestion that they had known Morgan and why would they need to kill him if they had? Matilda was as sure as she could be that none of her own family was involved.

Adrian or Camilla Nonsuch? She had to remind herself that unpleasantness in itself is not a prerequisite for the act of committing murder. The Nonsuches had had a burglary, six months previously. Could it have been an insurance fraud and Jake Morgan their fence? It was a possibility. He could have threatened to expose them and, unlike Albert, asked too much. He could have been killed to gag his greed.

Briony and Hugo? Briony would have to be a very good actress to fool Matilda into thinking that she was worried about Hugo, when she had done it herself. And why should she? Briony's life seemed like an open book. Still . . . It was a possibility that she had used Matilda her confidante in order to get Matilda's sympathy and to lull her into thinking that Briony was innocent. And then there was Hugo, whom she was trying so valiantly to protect. Where had he been at the time of the murder and why had he lied about it?

Matilda didn't want to think about how she would feel if it were Hugo. Although she found Briony exasperating, she was very fond of the girl, despite her lingering suspicions. Hurriedly, she moved on to the Kingsways.

Could it be the Kingsways? Only if they were in it together, or if Gerald had done it alone and only discovered the body when he himself had killed it. There would have been too much coming and going if Agatha had done it without Gerald's knowledge. She knew that he was an early riser and where he would walk. Why do it then, when she would have to skirt round her husband? That didn't make sense.

But Gerald on his own? Why? He didn't strike her as a man who cared much about his wife. He wouldn't let himself be blackmailed about an affair, because he wouldn't care if she knew or not. Anyway, if Matilda were any judge of men — and she prided herself that she was — he was not the type to stray. He thought more of his stamps than he did of any company, male or female. He could have done a dubious deal over some rare stamps, though. Or could it be money? Either the lack of it or an unexplained windfall.

Her own enquiries had proved negative. Gerald earnt an adequate wage and Agatha had private money of her own. His only interest was in stamps and walking. She knew that these could be costly, but how did it involve Jake Morgan? Somehow, she couldn't see Gerald Kingsway as being on the wrong side of the law, but she had not dismissed him. She knew enough about human nature to know that, the more she knew, the less her capacity for surprise at its quirks.

The Wintergreens? If Datchett had investigated Simon properly, he would have found out where he was in his missing forty minutes. Matilda stuck to her opinion that he was dallying. Otherwise, Datchett would have chased him harder. Maureen, though, worried Matilda until she realised that there was a significant stumbling block. Maureen had been alone plenty long enough to commit the murder, but Morgan had been lured there to meet someone and Maureen could not have known that Simon was going to be called out. Given the state of their marriage, he might not have noticed that she was missing, but she couldn't suddenly have taken advantage of his long absence. Matilda couldn't visualise anything serious enough to make Maureen commit murder, but you never knew. Matilda would have to bracket her with Gerald Kingsway, for the time being.

She thought Sadie Stringer quite capable of murder, if it suited her purpose. She lived in an expensive house and dressed to match it: but, although capable, would she really resort to murder? Matilda recognised in Sadie a woman who got what she wanted but who was also a realist. She was also a woman who liked her comfort. Would she risk it all in a bold venture? Possibly. But the stakes would have to be very high. All the same, she put

Sadie second in the list — after Adrian Nonsuch, whom she was determined would remain her prime suspect.

Quentin Weatherby was an enigma. A friend of the Nonsuches, which Matilda found disappointing, for she would have thought him a man of better taste. It was while he was visiting them that he had seen the house opposite for sale and was moving in within a few months. Judging by the furnishings, he was not short of a penny or two. He must have had the cash to buy, or a property that sold at a very fast rate.

She supposed that it was antiques that had brought him and Nonsuch together, and this was a connection with Morgan. Quentin could have known him. So could Nonsuch, for that matter. And if Quentin had killed Morgan, there would have been no need to take the sword stick in advance Matilda resolutely moved him up to equal first with Nonsuch, when she went to have her talk with Briony.

* * *

No one so much as moved a wrinkle. It seemed as if they were all holding their breath and the liner rested on the crest of a wave. The stewards were motionless, frozen in the tableau of teller and tale. Matilda related the outcome of her visit to Briony.

On the morning of Morgan's murder, Hugo had woken up, ashamed of what he had done. He had treated Briony badly and he wanted to make it up to her, but he wasn't ready yet to shoulder all the blame. The need to pass his burden of guilt onto someone else was burning inside him when he looked out of the window on the morning of Morgan's murder and saw Adrian Nonsuch walking across Sadie's garden from the back of the house toward the road. Hugo knew that he had let himself out of the pool room after staying the night. He was certain of this, because he had done the same thing many times himself during their brief affair.

Afterward, Hugo couldn't imagine conjuring up again the feeling of black anger that the sight had wrought in him of another person doing what he himself had done. It was all a game to her. He wanted to shout at them both, and especially at Sadie, for tempting him and making him as miserable as he felt this morning. No guiding voice warned him of his irrationality, and he was acting purely on instinct when he ran down the back stairs and out onto the wet grass.

Adrian had stopped to light a cigarette under the magnolia, not caring whether or not he was seen. He had the cigarette in his mouth and then turned sharply on his heels after patting his pocket. Must have left his lighter behind. Hugo waited a moment and then went across into the garden and marched off after him. He was out of sight already, but Hugo knew where he would be.

It was quiet in Squires Lane. Gerald Kingsway had not yet set off for his walk and Jake Morgan was already dead. When Hugo heard the sound, he did not recognise it, and why should he have done? The well was shallow, rubble-lined, and the sheath of a sword-stick thin. It didn't sound like anything much louder than two falling twigs. But he turned his head at the noise, noticeable in the morning stillness, and he saw an expression on the face of a man who thought himself unobserved. Hugo didn't know what it meant, but his anger faded as quickly as it had flared, to be replaced by guilt and — inexplicably — fear. He went home to Briony, ashamed of his maelstrom.

'He had seen the murderer,' concluded Matilda quietly. 'But he didn't know it and neither does anyone officially. He had seen the man who had entry into the houses that had later been burgled and who supplied the information to someone else for a share in the proceeds. I think that he wanted to stop, but

Jake Morgan wanted to continue the partnership and, when Jake threatened to turn nasty, he was killed.'

'What about the sword-stick sheath?' asked Fenton More, intrigued.

'It was discovered, of course, but anyone could have put it there. Hugo only heard a sound and saw a face that was not out of place there.'

'Out of place?' expostulated Wyvern. 'Surely you told us that the well was in Quentin Weatherby's garden? The Nonsuch chap was trespassing.'

'I think,' said Matilda patiently, 'that you have misunderstood.'

She explained. Shooting stars entertained unobserved as Matilda's voice gave up her secret.

Epilogue

She was a worthy womman al hir live:
Housbandes at chirche dore she hadde five,

Geoffrey Chaucer,
The Canterbury Tales

Matilda wore a brick-red turban for the christening. Since her blow to the head, her hair grew at a strange angle and she was training it to lie flat. The baby seemed to like it. She gurgled happily in Matilda's arms when Nanette passed her over to her soon-to-be godmothers.

Matilda stood with Harriet at the back of the church, each taking turns to hold Harry and Nanette's child. They made their promises and then it was time for the baby to receive her names and the warmed water on her forehead to welcome her into this cold English church, where the all-embracing presence of past lives waited and kept their counsel.

Matilda Nanette French, cradled in Nicholas's arms, watched the vicar's wet finger with serious round eyes. A new life for Pomery. A new beginning for Harry and Nanette.

* * *

Quentin Weatherby had offered Matilda a new beginning, last night. He asked for her hand over dinner and she was tempted to take up his offer, but regretfully declined. She did not think that this sixth union would be wise. All her previous husbands had had their faults, but not one of them had been a murderer.

Other titles in the
Ulverscroft Large Print Series:

THE UNSETTLED ACCOUNT

Eugenia Huntingdon

As the wife of a Polish officer, Eugenia Huntingdon's life was filled with the luxuries of silks, perfumes and jewels. It was also filled with love and happiness. Nothing could have prepared her for the hardships of transportation across Soviet Russia — crammed into a cattle wagon with fifty or so other people in bitterly cold conditions — to the barren isolation of Kazakhstan. Many did not survive the journey; many did not live to see their homeland again. In this moving documentary, Eugenia Huntingdon recalls the harrowing years of her wartime exile.

FIREBALL

Bob Langley

Twenty-seven years ago: the rogue shoot-down of a Soviet spacecraft on a supersecret mission. Now: the SUCHKO 17 suddenly comes back to life three thousand feet beneath the Antarctic ice cap — with terrifying implications for the entire world. The discovery triggers a dark conspiracy that reaches from the depths of the sea to the edge of space — on a satellite with nuclear capabilities. One man and one woman must find the elusive mastermind of a plot with sinister roots in the American military elite, and bring the world back from the edge . . .

STANDING IN THE SHADOWS

Michelle Spring

Laura Principal is repelled but fascinated as she investigates the case of an eleven-year-old boy who has murdered his foster mother. It is not the sort of crime one would expect in Cambridge. The child, Daryll, has confessed to the brutal killing; now his elder brother wants to find out what has turned him into a ruthless killer. Laura confronts an investigation which is increasingly tainted with violence. And that's not all. Someone with an interest in the foster mother's murder is standing in the shadows, watching her every move . . .